"Okay." Marc n...............................be-
have, because the killer has to be someone in
these pictures, which means there must be something . . . a hint, a clue, as to what is about to take
place. And we need to keep looking until we find
it. The longer a murderer goes free the more
likely they are to get away with it or—"

"Kill again?"

"Exactly, and since we don't have a motive and a
sweet old lady is dead, we don't know what we're
dealing with." He sat back; his unblinking eyes
gazed past Addie at the sidewall. "Of course, it
could mean the poison must have been in the cup
before she drank from it."

"But look at all these pictures. It appears as
though she used the same teacup all afternoon
and as far as all these photos and videos show, no
one but her, Laurel, or Catherine refilled it."

Marc regarded Addie and he slightly shifted on
the sofa beside her. "There is one other possibility
that we haven't considered yet."

"Which is?"

"She took the poison herself . . ."

Books by Lauren Elliott

Beyond the Page Bookstore Mysteries
MURDER BY THE BOOK

PROLOGUE TO MURDER

MURDER IN THE FIRST EDITION

PROOF OF MURDER

A PAGE MARKED FOR MURDER

UNDER THE COVER OF MURDER

TO THE TOME OF MURDER

A MARGIN FOR MURDER

DEDICATION TO MURDER

Crystals & CuriosiTEAS Mysteries
STEEPED IN SECRETS

Published by Kensington Publishing Corp.

DEDICATION to MURDER

Lauren Elliott

Kensington Publishing Corp.
www.kensingtonbooks.com

KENSINGTON BOOKS are published by

Kensington Publishing Corp.
119 West 40th Street
New York, NY 10018

All Kensington titles, imprints, and distributed lines are available at special quantity discounts for bulk purchases for sales promotion, premiums, fund-raising, educational, or institutional use.

Special book excerpts or customized printings can also be created to fit specific needs. For details, write or phone the office of the Kensington Sales Manager: Attn.: Sales Department. Kensington Publishing Corp., 119 West 40th Street, New York, NY 10018. Phone: 1-800-221-2647.

The K and Teapot logo is a trademark of Kensington Publishing Corp.

First Printing: May 2023
ISBN: 978-1-4967-3514-0

ISBN: 978-1-4967-3518-8 (ebook)

10 9 8 7 6 5 4 3 2 1

Printed in the United States of America

DEDICATION
to MURDER

Chapter 1

Addie Greyborne turned the key and jiggled the front door of Beyond the Page Books and Curios to double-check it was secured tightly. She stared in disbelief at the CLOSED sign she'd hung in the door window before leaving. Never in all her years as the owner, did she think her bookshop would be closed on a Saturday, one of Greyborne Harbor, Massachusetts', busiest shopping days of the week.

"Did you find it?" called her best friend and local tea merchant, Serena Ludlow.

Addie waved the small brown stuffed bear in the air and grinned.

"Good, now pick up that dress, and don't you dare get the train or the hem grimy! You're already late for your own wedding, so let's get a move on," Serena hollered through the open back door of the awaiting white limousine.

"Sorry," panted Addie, maneuvering herself and the floaty tulle skirt of her ball gown styled wedding dress into the back seat. "I just couldn't let Catherine go through her first night of dog sitting, with Pippi not having her little buddy Baxter with her. Been there, done that—Pippi would cry all night and Catherine would hate me forever."

"I know, I know, you don't want to take the chance that Miss Catherine will never speak to you again, because you know as well as I do that you couldn't run your bookstore without her and Paige's help, but really, was all *this* necessary right now, on our way to the church?" Serena said, finally getting Addie and her ivory wedding gown into the back seat.

"Yes it was, and not just for Catherine but for poor little Pippi. She's going to be so confused by me disappearing for three weeks as it is," Addie puffed, sorting out the sparkly beaded border at the hemline of her dress. "And since you made a point of calling her *Miss* Catherine, if my hunch is right, I don't think she'll be Miss Catherine Lewis much longer. I have a feeling the next wedding invitations we receive will be announcing the marriage of her and Felix Vanguard, and we can go through all this again." Addie grinned. "Fun, hey?"

"Yeah, so much fun," Serena said, shaking her head with disbelief. "But after all these years of being single, I really can't see her getting married at this stage in her life."

"I can, and she deserves to find happiness too. I mean, you've seen them together. They're like two love struck teenagers."

"Well," Serena huffed, smoothing out Addie's

skirt. "We'll worry about *their* wedding if it happens. Right now I'm only worried about yours, so let's get a move on."

"Okay, okay." Addie laughed and reached over to pull the door closed.

"Whatever you do, don't catch the hem in the door," screeched Serena. "It's bad enough that Simon's probably standing at the altar right now thinking you're a runaway bride, let alone having to have your cousin Kalea re-sew the skirt and delaying the service even longer."

"We're not late."

"Pretty close, and I wish you'd have let me go to the bookstore to look for that stuffed bear this morning like I wanted. You know, before we got you dressed in your gown."

Addie struggled to draw in a deep breath. As much as she loved the fitted bodice when she was standing, sitting was a different matter as it confined her ribs and her ability to breathe.

Serena took one look at her face and pinned her fingers under Addie's arms. "You're lucky you picked June to get married in and not December, or you'd freeze in this sweetheart neckline." She gave a tug up. "There, that should keep the girls in place now," she said as she fluffed out the full skirt that cascaded around Addie's lace appliqué ivory shoes. "Perfect."

It would be perfect if the placement of the girls were the issue. Addie fidgeted in her seat, leaned her elbow on the armrest, extended her corset encased upper body as far up as her spine would allow, and sucked in a much-needed breath. "I would have let you go in," she managed to wheeze, "and look for it, except I couldn't remember where Baxter was."

"I've got eyes too. I could have looked around just as well as you, and not taken a chance of ruining the most perfect gown in the world," Serena added, her tone clearly showing her disapproval over Addie's actions. "Now let me see your hair." Serena pulled back, scanning Addie's appearance, grinned, and sighed. "You are the most beautiful bride I've ever seen. Now here, let me fasten the veil so when we get to the church you just have to march through the door and straight up the aisle."

Addie fidgeted with the veil Serena pinned to her hair. "This knotted braid at the back doesn't look too old-fashioned, does it?" Addie asked, trying to glimpse her reflection in the side window.

"No, my friend." Serena approvingly gazed at her. "The knotted braid, along with the golden highlights you had put into your natural honey-brown hair, make you look so regal with that veil. It's all perfect." She sniffed.

"Now don't you start crying, you'll make me cry too and ruin my makeup. Simon will think he's marrying a raccoon instead."

"I can't help it." Serena dabbed a tissue at her damp eyes. "You're beautiful and Simon is a lucky man, raccoon eyes and all."

When they finally arrived at the church and managed to get inside without mishap, Serena peeked through the door from the foyer into the sanctuary. "Oh no!" she exclaimed.

"What's wrong?" A wave of panic coursed through Addie.

"My brother brought Ryley Brookes as his plus-one and she's holding my little Oliver!"

"Is that all?" Addie patted her chest as she peeked out into the sanctuary. "Oh, he looks so cute in his little tuxedo, and just look at little Addison. She's such a doll. Well, she will be when your mother can get her hair barrette to stay in place," Addie said with a soft laugh.

"Geez, look at the expression on Ollie's little face. He knows a witch when he sees one. I give it about ten seconds until Ryley hands him to Marc, because I don't think kids are really her thing. One, two, three . . ."

In that moment, little Ollie grabbed a handful of Ryley's dark, short-bobbed hair and gave a yank. "Ouch." Addie winced and said, laughing, "That wasn't even ten seconds."

"I know, and I hope Marc figures her out pretty fast. Knowing how much his life has changed since becoming the doting uncle, I wonder why she even agreed to be his date today."

"Perhaps now that she's the police chief in Salem, they've found they are on a more equal footing and have decided to give their relationship another try?" Addie steadied her voice, noting the difference in how Marc responded to the wiggling one-year-old in his arms and how Ryley's face told her she wanted to get as far away from the scene as she could. "I don't think you have much to worry about," said Addie, stepping back and smoothing her veil. "Judging by what I see, I doubt Marc could ever truly be happy with the likes of Ryley Brookes."

"It doesn't appear that way to me. I think that

now that you're getting married to someone else, he knows this is ultimately the end of any fantasies he's had about you and him getting back together. She feels free to dig her claws into him again without worrying he'll want to, or *be able to* go running back to you," Serena said smugly.

"That was never on the table and you know it, and as far as him being with Ryley—well . . . you know what Emily Dickinson wrote, 'The heart wants what it wants,' even if little sisters don't get it."

"I don't remember that last part in the quote."

"I added it because clearly Marc sees something in her to make giving it another try worthwhile, even if you don't agree with him."

A piano and cello rendition of the Perri and David Hodges song "A Thousand Years" began playing and Serena's dad, Wade Chandler, stepped in beside Addie. "Are you ready?"

She looked up into his reassuring eyes and nodded.

"You're beautiful," he whispered, linking his left arm through her right one. "And thank you for allowing me the honor of walking you down the aisle today."

A smiling Catherine slid up to them and took her place on Addie's left. "Me too," Catherine whispered, leaning into her. "You have no idea how much this means to me." She gave Addie's arm a slight squeeze.

Addie could see through her own tear-blurred eyes that Catherine and Wade's weren't any drier than hers as they all sniffled. These two people meant the world to her. Since her own father had passed, Wade had taken her under his wing without reservation, and treated Addie like another daughter since she and Serena had become friends. And Catherine—well, if it hadn't been for Addie's grandmother's interference after Addie's mother died when she wasn't much more than a toddler, Catherine would have ended up as Addie's step-mother back then. In Addie's mind, there were no two people she would rather have had walk her down the aisle toward her new future.

Serena pulled three tissues out of the hidden pocket in her Caribbean-green, floor-length bridesmaid dress. "Now stop it or we'll all end up bawling our eyes out as we walk up the aisle." She sniffed and tugged another tissue out and wiped her nose, and glanced at Paige Stringer, Addie's assistant bookstore manager, and Addie's cousin Kalea Hudson as they took their places in the front of the procession line. "Do you guys need one too?"

Paige shook her head of blond free-flowing curls and gestured to the tissue she already had clutched in her hand that held her bridesmaid bouquet, and Kalea just shook her upswept, auburn head of hair, and smiled stoically.

"Ready?" asked Wade again.

Addie nodded at Serena, who had moved to the front of the procession and she gave a soft tap on the closed doors. In perfect unison, the ushers, two of Simon's coworkers from the hospital, opened the double doors into the sanctuary. When all the guests turned toward the entering wedding party, it struck Addie that *this* was really about to happen.

Her knees wobbled. Her heart raced, and she struggled to fill her lungs when Paige, Kalea, and

Serena, her maid of honor, started down the aisle. Wade placed his right hand on their linked arms and urged Addie to follow. Catherine gave her hand a light squeeze, as they stepped into the sanctuary behind her bridesmaids.

It occurred to Addie in that moment why it had become common practice for both parents to escort the bride down the aisle: It was to keep her from running away—because that's exactly what her initial reaction was. Then she remembered what Serena said she did at her wedding. How the only way she had managed to make it through the aisle walk to the altar on her big day, was to block out every other face and focus on Zach, and him only, because this was *their* day; no one else mattered but the two of them.

Addie clung to her friend's words as her eyes darted from one face to the other while she frantically searched for Simon by the altar. When she caught sight of him, she fixed her gaze and took the next step. Her only thought now, was of the man who made her believe the world could be a better place. When she was with him, he made her believe in Camelot and other fairy tales; and at the end of her long walk down the aisle, she'd be met by her Arthur. Or, was Simon her Lancelot? She really didn't care. Addie only knew that the dream she had shared long ago with her dearly departed David was about to become a reality with the only other man she'd truly loved since him, and this was her fairy-tale princess bride moment at long last.

Through her tears she took her place at the front of the church. Her head was spinning; her heart ready to leap out of her chest. This was finally happening, and in a few minutes the man she loved like no other was about to become her husband. The minister's words faded in and out in Addie's mind, and as Simon smiled and took her hands in his, she wasn't even certain if the vows she recited were the ones she'd written, or some semblance of incoherent rambling, but since no one snickered or laughed, she figured she had pulled it off as written and rehearsed.

When they kneeled on the plush bench to each light a candle that represented them being separate, which the minister would then use the flames of each to light a third candle, representing the marriage union, she let out a soft gasp as a wave of panic surged through her. Simon gave her a curious side glance. She forced a smile, but her mind reeled. The soles of her shoes were now in clear view of everyone. Had she remembered to take the price sticker off the bottom?

The rest of the ceremony went by in a blur because all she could think about was the bright red SALE sticker flashing like a neon sign to her guests. When the minister looked out at the congregation and asked, "If anyone has an objection to this union, speak now or forever hold your peace," she knew it was nearly time for him to say—*I now pronounce you husband and wife*—and bubbles of excitement raced through her. It was almost over. Simon and she would be married, and she could finally check her shoes and put her mind at ease . . . but her sense of relief didn't last long. A crashing sound came from the back of the church, and the double-wide doors flew open.

"Stop, stop the wedding," yelled a petite, gray-haired woman as she hustled down the aisle waving a file folder; an attractive, younger, dark-haired woman was close on her heels.

"Laurel? Laurel Hill, is that you?" Simon gasped staring wide-eyed at the younger woman as he took a step down from the raised altar platform.

Addie looked at Simon. "What's going on? What're Pippi's veterinarian, Doctor Hill, and her aunt Valerie doing?"

"You mean *this* Laurel Hill is your new veterinarian?" He looked questioningly at Addie. "And Valerie Price, the woman you met in Pen Hollow last year, is her aunt?"

"Yes, and I don't understand. They were invited to the wedding, but they said they couldn't come. So what are they doing interrupting it?" Addie stared in bewilderment as the two red-faced women continued to race toward them.

"Laurel," said Simon, clearly shaken, "what's the meaning of this? This is our wedding, what are you doing?"

"We know it's your wedding," Valerie snapped, shaking the papers. "We're trying to stop you from committing bigamy."

Addie stepped down and grabbed Simon's arm. "What does she mean by bigamy?"

"Yes." Simon stared at Laurel. "What is she talking about?"

"You and Laurel are still married," blurted Valerie.

"What does she mean," Simon looked pointedly at Laurel, "we're still married?"

"She means," said Laurel, "that when we signed the annulment papers and gave them to my uncle George—remember, he was a lawyer?"

Simon blankly nodded.

"He said he would file them with the court on our behalf, but they—"

"They got crushed up in the back of his desk drawer," cried Valerie, waving the crumpled folder. "I only found them this morning when I finally got around to cleaning out my dear departed husband's old desk and files."

Simon raked his hand through his black hair and shook his head. "No, that's impossible. We filed those papers sixteen years ago."

"Look." Valerie shoved an accordion file folder into Simon's hand. "They were never filed with the courts."

"But this is impossible," repeated Simon, reading over the crumpled papers.

"They must have gotten snagged in the drawer and when he didn't see them, he assumed he had filed them as planned. I found another file, just like this, also jammed in the back of the drawer." Valerie glanced at Addie; her eyes filled with tears. "I really am sorry, my dear, but you can't possibly marry Simon today. He's still married to Laurel."

The only sound that could be heard in the church was Addie's breaths coming short and fast. Simon locked his apologetic gaze on her.

"I . . . I . . ." He glanced at the two women, then back at Addie. "I don't know how this . . ."

Addie looked over at an open-mouthed Serena, shook her head in disbelief at what was happening; grabbed her skirt, fighting back the tears burning in her eyes; raced down the aisle and out through the doors into the church foyer. She sucked in a deep breath, and then another, and another, staggering back against the wall beside the doors. Her knees gave way, and she slid into an ivory tulle heap on the floor.

Chapter 2

Addie sat hunched over on the window seat in her bedroom and stared out the window. The faint glow from the streetlight made the drops of rain shimmer like threads of a jeweled web on the glass. Her fingertip traced their path as the wind swirled and tossed them gently in a synchronized dance from one edge of the windowpane to the other. She thought how like those droplets of rain she was, no longer in control of her own destiny.

She recalled that when she and Simon picked the early spring date for their wedding, a year away, June rains could be a strong possibility. So, being the practical person she was, Addie selected the perfect venue for their reception, The Grey Gull Inn. Between the main floor harbor-view dining room and the rooftop terrace, they'd be covered no matter what Mother Nature threw their way.

It also got her to thinking about what it might mean if it rained on her wedding day, so she'd put her research skills to use and was relieved somewhat when she discovered that Hindus believe it symbolizes unity and that rain on the day of a marriage is good because it means the marriage will last. Other sites relieved brides' worries and claimed that if it rained on the wedding day it was good luck, because it symbolized the last tears the bride would shed for the rest of her life.

She choked back a sob. Little did she know then that the unity and the marriage lasting would be for Simon and Laurel's marriage of sixteen years, not hers. She could no longer fight back the tears that burned behind her eyes and they spilled freely down her cheeks. The part about the last tears a bride would shed clearly didn't apply to *almost* brides like her. She wiped the back of her hand across her cheeks and sniffled.

"Come in," she croaked, responding to a soft knock on the door.

Paige peeked around the door frame. "Sorry to bother you, but Simon's downstairs *again*."

"I don't want to see him right now."

"This time he says he's not leaving until you talk to him."

"Then hand him a blanket and tell him to make himself comfortable on the sofa for the night," Addie snapped, and refocused on the droplets of rain skirting across her window.

"You should talk to him . . . let him explain."

Addie's head sharply pivoted toward the young woman. "Let him explain? Like how he was married sixteen years ago and not once, in all the time I've known him, did he ever tell me? Even after Laurel moved here last month, he never said a word about knowing her and certainly never mentioned they had been married," she hissed with indignation. "I think all the explaining was done today in the church, don't you?" Her eyes flashed with all the pent-up hurt and anger raging inside her.

Paige twisted her hands in front of her and dropped her gaze. "I know, but in all fairness, he really did believe the marriage had been annulled years ago, and she doesn't mean anything to him now, so it wasn't important," she whispered.

"Pfft," sputtered Addie, considering how the news today had smashed her soul to the outer edges of the universe, just like the wind was doing now to the raindrops on the windowpane. "It sounds like he's been downstairs working his Doctor *Dreamy* charms on you." Addie shook her head in scorn and glared past the raindrops into the blackness outside her window. "Tell him that when I'm ready, *I* will phone *him*, and to stay away until then."

"Okay," said Paige meekly, backing out of the door.

The door flew open with such force that it banged against the doorstop with a *thwack.*

Addie jerked but continued to stare into the comforting blackness of the storm outside. "You can also tell him—"

"Catherine and Kalea made up this tray for you," said Simon, closing the door behind him with a kick of his shoe heel. "And Kalea told me to tell you she had to get to Boston to catch her flight to London in the morning, but she'll call you after her business meeting on Monday and let you know how it went and when she'll be back. Catherine also told me you haven't eaten a bite all day, and, as your local, friendly doctor, I really must insist you eat something," he added, setting the tray on a small table beside Addie.

She looked up at him in disbelief. "Get out!" she snapped. "I told you I didn't want to talk to you today!" She drew her knees up and wrapped her slender arms around them, hugging them close to her heaving chest. "Please go, now."

"No, I won't. I've been trying to tell you all day that I'm sorry." He took a seat on the bench, reached for her hand, and flinched when she promptly pulled it away. "I tried at the church, but you and Serena raced out of there so fast you didn't give me a chance to explain."

She turned her head and glared at him. "You're sorry? Sorry for what, the fact that you never told me in all the time I've known you that you were married before? Or are you sorry because all the hopes and dreams we pinned on today, have been shattered by the fact that you're *still* married?"

"It's not the end of the world. We'll just reschedule the wedding and everything will be as we planned."

"Tell me, Simon, Laurel moved to Greyborne Harbor just over a month ago when she took over Doctor Timmons's veterinary practice, and you didn't think to tell me about this then?"

"No, I had no idea she was the new vet."

"But I told you last week I took Pippi in for her annual shots. I distinctly remember telling you how happy I was that Laurel, the woman I met last year in Pen Hollow when Paige and I got stuck there, had finally worked out a deal with Doctor Timmons to take over his practice when he decided to retire."

"Yes, but how was I supposed to know it was my Laurel?"

"*Your* Laurel?"

"You know what I mean."

"No, I don't, because I can't believe you had no idea she'd moved to town."

"How would I? I haven't spoken to her in nearly sixteen years. Combined with my hospital schedule and how busy we've been with last-minute wedding preparations, I didn't have time to keep up with the latest town news." Simon shifted uncomfortably on the bench and faced Addie.

"*Really?*" Addie shook her head in disbelief and refocused on the raindrops splattering across the window. "She didn't contact you after I dropped off their wedding invitations when I took Pippi to her appointment last week?"

"No, why would she? As I said, she and I were through a long time ago."

"But we found out today you're not, are you?" She turned her cold gaze directly on Simon. "When I think about meeting them last year, how none of us knew then that we had you as a connection. It must have come as a real shock to them to see the name Doctor Simon Emerson as the groom on the wedding invitations. At least now I know why Laurel said they couldn't come . . . too much history, or maybe too heartbreaking for Laurel to see you marry another woman."

"There was no heartbreak; she wanted the annulment as much as I did."

"Yeah maybe, but it must have come as a shock to them because today sure the heck came as a shock to me." She shook her head in disgust and turned to look out the window. "I feel like such a fool, finding out that you were married . . . *are* married to her, a woman I've known for a year, and I never knew about it."

"You're not a fool. It's me who was foolish because I didn't—"

"But they knew, as soon as they saw your name on the invitation." She huffed out a deep breath. "And here I was feeling hurt when they said they couldn't come and I couldn't figure out why, because I thought we were friends."

"Look, I don't blame you for being upset with me and for what happened with our wedding, but Laurel and I will get this all sorted out, and then you can be friends again. I've already spoken to an old friend of mine who's a lawyer in New York City, and he said the best thing to do is file the papers there, since that's where we were married. He told me also to file the original annulment papers Laurel's uncle had, along with the new annulment petition, and that should speed up the process. Don't you see, it's not the end of us, it's just a slight delay in our plans?" He looked at her. A weak smile graced his lips. "I don't blame you for being upset, it was as shocking to me as it was to you," he whispered and reached over to her.

She recoiled. Her head snapped up, and she glared at him. "You don't blame *me* for being upset?" Her voice reflected her disbelief in his words. "Simon, I'm not so much *upset* because you were married before, I'm angry." His brows rose questioningly. "Yes, I'm *angry*, because in all the time we've been together, you didn't trust me enough to tell me that you *had* been married before."

"It wasn't a big deal. It only lasted a few weeks and was so long ago, I didn't think it was important."

"Not important?" She stared at him in astonishment. "No, no." She struggled to find words. "You know what. I can't do this right now." She shook her head, locked her arms around her knees, and stared out the window again. "I have no idea how to move forward from this."

"I told you. We're going to get it annulled, and we'll make sure it is this time. Please, Addie, don't throw away everything we have now. We'll get it worked out. You and I love each other and our union is meant to be, we both know that. Laurel and I are going to file again and in a few months the annulment should be finalized. Trust me, it will all work out and then we'll move forward as planned."

"Trust you? I did trust you. I told you everything about my past, but it seems you're the one that didn't trust me with yours. So, excuse me if I'm a little short on trust right now." She shook her head. "I can't even . . . not right now. Don't you see, what matters to me is what our love was built on, and that was trust. We both might have had a second shot at love when we found each other, but . . ." She shook her head. "Trust . . . how can I ever trust you again? No, you can't get a second shot at that. Now please leave until I can figure out all this in my mind."

Chapter 3

For the next few days, Addie couldn't shake the surreal brain fog that blanketed her mind. She'd managed to go through some of the motions of taking care of basic daily hygiene, like brushing her teeth, and she vaguely recalled Serena steering her into the shower at one point. She'd even managed to swallow bites of the food Catherine, Paige, or Serena put in front of her, and occasionally mustered the energy to scratch her little furry companion Pippi, who hadn't left her side since Addie had raced through the door, stripped off her wedding dress, and threw it in a heap behind her bedroom door.

The light finally penetrated Addie's dejection the day Martha Stringer, Paige's mother and the owner of the bakery next door to her bookshop, took over *babysitting* duties. When Martha hovered over her as she served Addie breakfast, then encouraged her to eat with an *attagirl* look in her faded blue eyes, and smiled a saccharine smile when Addie complied by eating a forkful of scrambled eggs, it became clear to Addie that the woman had been told her charge for the day was no more than a wilting, delicate flower that required constant mothering and nurturing. Well, that was the last thing Addie was or wanted today—or any day, for that matter.

Addie brought her hand down with a thud on the tabletop. "That's it. I'm going to finish cleaning out the attic," she exclaimed.

"You're going to do what?" a befuddled Martha asked, staring at her.

"Don't you see? This is the perfect time for me to finish what I started when I moved in. I already arranged with Paige and Catherine to cover all the shifts at the bookstore for the next three weeks while I was supposed to be on my honeymoon. The bookshop always needs new inventory, and I have half an attic to still clear out." Addie rose to her feet from the kitchen table, feeling victorious in her decision.

"So you see, this will free you up for the rest of the day and you can go back to the bakery. I know Tuesday is scone day, plus it's the day the cruise ship docks. I'm sure Bill is run off his feet being there on his own today, and he'll be thrilled you're back."

Martha tutted and shook her white-haired head. "No, missy, Bill Unger will be just fine." She thrust her creased hands on her rounded hips. "I told Serena, Paige, and Catherine I was available for the day when they said they were all busy, and that's just what I'm going to do. Besides, I already hired that Nicole Harrison, Serena and Marc's cousin from Chicago, to work part-time, and I'm sure she wouldn't like being let off early. You know, with the nasty divorce she's going through and all. She really needs any money she can make right now." Martha glanced around the kitchen, snatched the kitchen towel from where it hung on the oven door handle, wrapped it around her head of tight-knit curls and tied it neatly in the front. "There, point me to the mop and bucket. You sort. I'll clean."

Addie forced her lungs to expand and drew in a shaky breath. *That* clearly hadn't gone as planned. Who knew that at Martha's advanced years, she'd be so willing to take on the monumental task of helping Addie clear up the third-floor attic, and by way of insisting on staying, snatch away Addie's last hope of finding the solitude she craved.

Addie directed her to the broom closet, and once Martha had acquired all the cleaning implements she thought she'd need for the day, she stood back and allowed Addie to lead the way to their destination.

Addie surveyed the stacks of books surrounding her and gave a nod of approval for a morning well spent as she pulled over boxes to start filling with the treasures she'd unearthed. Like in the past, she'd made three piles: one to sell in the bookstore, one to donate to the Boston Library—her old employer and stomping grounds—and another for books and memorabilia she couldn't bear to part with, reminders of her great-aunt Anita Greyborne, her benefactor.

She glanced over at the headway Martha had made with cleaning and dusting the bookshelves and cubbies as Addie emptied them and marveled at the energy this late-sixty-something woman had exhibited. Even the wide, wooden-planked flooring gleamed under her efforts, as she washed and polished the spaces that Addie revealed with her sorting and shuffling of bookcases and crates.

While it hadn't been an easy morning by a long shot, Addie remained very much aware that even though she and Martha had come to the point of treating each other amicably—after getting off to a rather rocky start when Addie first moved to Greyborne Harbor—she still found it trying to come up with conversation topics that might appeal to both of them, which had made for some rather uncomfortable bouts of silence during the past four hours.

However, as Addie's brain fog lifted like the dust motes floating in the air—thanks to Martha's meticulous cleaning—she did vaguely remember one thing Martha had said earlier that might give them fuel around a conversation they could explore as they continued to work.

"You mentioned that you'd hired Serena's cousin to work part-time. How's that working out?" asked Addie.

Martha paused, leaned on her mop handle, and puffed out a deep breath. "It's okay for now, I guess. She's a lovely woman, so much like her aunt Janis, you can certainly tell she's Janis's sister's child." Martha began urging the mop across the floor again.

Not quite the conversation starter Addie was hoping for. She swallowed hard as she dropped an armful of books into the store box. "I know Serena mentioned a few weeks ago that her cousin Nikki had moved here, but with the ... wedding ... I was so busy I didn't pay much attention. How on earth did she end up working for you?"

Martha paused again and rinsed the mop in the bucket. "She's staying with Serena and Marc's parents while she figures out what to do after her divorce. Janis brought her in the bakery one day and pulled me aside and asked if I had any work for the poor girl. Well, she reminds me so much of my own Mellissa, you know, and what her husband has put her through, my heart went out to the girl and I took her on, but . . ."

"But what?" Addie paused and studied Martha. "Isn't she working out?"

"Oh no, she's great with the customers. I just don't have enough work for her. It's nice to have the extra set of hands on Tuesdays now that it's spring and the cruise ships come in again, like today, but other than that"—Martha shrugged— "Bill and I do just fine. The two of us have a rhythm, you know."

Addie was dying to ask what rhythm Martha meant between herself and Old Bill, as he was known when he lived on the streets. Now that Martha had taken him under her wing and her roof, they had rekindled their childhood friendship, and he was now known as just plain Bill Unger. *Is what they have now more than a friendship rekindled?* Addie was itching to know; however, she knew that personal topics could easily set Martha's "prickly cactus spikes" on edge, and she thought better of any further inquiries and decided to stick with the safer topic of Nikki Harrison.

"You said she was great with the customers. What's her background?"

"My, my, aren't you a Miss Snoopy today." Martha glowered over the mop handle. "I would have thought Serena had told you all about her since Nikki's living here in town now and all."

And there it was! Would Addie never learn how to best deal with the cactus woman? "I'm sure she mentioned it at some point, but I was focused on . . . other things and well . . ." Addie shrugged, setting another stack of books into a box.

"Yes, yes, I suppose you were." Martha turned her blue eyes on Addie, and if Addie wasn't mistaken, they even held a glimmer of sympathy in them.

"Nikki went to college to be a librarian, you know, but after she married that monster of a man, he moved her away from all her family and friends to Chicago and put her to work in his sporting goods store. He was an ex–football player or something and couldn't let go of his glory days. Morning till night, seven days a week, she did that man's bidding and took the brunt of his anger over his failed career. And then one day, she couldn't take it anymore and . . . well, let's just say, she's here now and she's safe. Marc will make sure of that," Martha declared matter-of-factly, energetically rewashing the same spot she'd just finished on the floor.

Addie's mind replayed her own feelings on her wedding day, before it all went sideways, and how she felt like it was her fairy-tale moment. It made her wonder if Nikki had had the same feelings on her wedding day, one that certainly hadn't ended in a happily-ever-after. Her chest constricted because neither had Addie's, but obviously for different reasons. An idea struck her, and the last load of books slid from her hands and dropped into the box with a crash.

Martha whirled toward her, patting her chest. "I hope it wasn't something I said?"

"Yes and no," exclaimed Addie, not being able to contain her excitement. "You gave me the perfect solution to both of our problems."

Martha stared blankly at Addie.

"Saturdays might be an issue, but we could definitely work around Tuesdays . . ."

"What are you on about?"

"Nikki. Don't you see? With her background in library sciences and sales, she'd be the perfect addition to my staff for the summer! You know, since we bought that bookmobile last year, and it's finally ready to go this season as a traveling bookstore. Not to mention the coverage I'll need in the actual store while Paige and Catherine are away with it at festivals, especially since I'm off for the next few weeks and, well, we had to cancel a couple of festivals because I was going to be in Hawaii, but we could do them now with Nikki's help, and—"

"Take a breath, child, you're babbling," said

Martha, dropping her mop and scurrying over to Addie's side. "Simon said something like this could happen when it all hit you, and it looks like he was right." She rubbed Addie's back.

"Simon? He has nothing to do with this, and when were you talking to him about me?"

Martha backed away and shook her head.

"No, I'm not babbling or having a nervous breakdown. Don't you see, for the first time since Saturday, I'm thinking clearly. I could hire Serena's cousin part-time, and she could still work for you when you need her. Of course, we'd have to negotiate Saturdays but maybe—"

"Yoo-hoo, anybody home?" Serena's voice drifted up the attic staircase.

"Up here!" Addie called and then refocused on Martha. "So, what do you think?"

"I think you'd better talk to Nikki before you go planning her life, that's what I think."

"Yes, yes, I know, but would you be willing to work out a schedule between our two shops?"

"Ah, there you both are," said a relieved-sounding Serena as her red hair appeared over the top step of the attic staircase. "You can't imagine my shock when I couldn't find either of you downstairs." She stepped into the attic.

"Ah yes." Martha swallowed and gave Serena a look filled with concern. "We were just about to take a lunch break." She dropped her voice to a whisper clearly intended for Serena's ears only. "I think it's all been a bit trying on one of us this morning."

Given their close proximity, Addie couldn't help but overhear. "What do you mean?" She swiped her hand around the attic. "Look at all we've accomplished."

"Yes, yes, there's that and . . ." Martha bit her lip and nodded at Serena. "I think we need a break, if you know what I mean."

Addie shook her head. "I wasn't babbling, like I told you. It's a worthwhile plan and one we should consider."

"Then it's a good thing I brought fortification."

"What do you mean?" asked Addie.

"Didn't you get my text? I said I'd be by with lunch as soon as I got the twins and my mom set up for the afternoon, and stopped by the tea shop to check in with Vera and Elle Hollingsworth to make sure they have enough of the special tea blend to get them through the day. Afterwards, I'd pick up lunch and then Martha could head back to the bakery if she wanted."

"No, I didn't see it."

"Where's your phone?"

Addie shrugged. "It must be downstairs or in my bedroom."

"Addie Greyborne, without her phone in her pocket? Now I know something is wrong." She obviously tried to lighten her tone but Addie didn't miss her fleeting glance at Martha.

"I'm fine, I'm not carrying my phone because I'm tired of Simon constantly texting and calling and having to decline his calls."

"So you haven't talked to him lately?"

Addie shook her head.

"Addie, he needs to talk to you as much as you need to talk to him."

"I will," Addie choked out. "I'm just not ready yet."

Just when Addie thought the morning had gone so well, and she'd actually managed to focus on something other than her and Simon's predicament, and she felt like her old self for a few short hours, her best friend slapped her in the face with reality.

Perhaps she *was* that delicate, wilting flower they all perceived her to be, because as hard as she tried, she couldn't stop the tears from flowing down her cheeks. She wanted nothing more than for Simon to take her in his arms, hold her tight, and tell her everything was going to work out, but . . . she was still so dang mad at him.

Chapter 4

"So what do you think?" asked Addie later, as she scraped her plate of the last dregs of the Cornish pasty Serena had brought from the tea shop and popped it into her mouth. She laid her fork on the side of her plate and glanced from Serena to Martha. "Well, do you think it's a good idea?"

"I think," said Serena, "that Martha is right. You need to talk to Nikki before you go making any grandiose plans for her life."

"Just don't put the cart before the horse here." Martha heaved her plump body up from the kitchen table and cleared their plates away. "The girl is in a fragile state right now, and she's where she needs to be to start healing. Let Serena's mom, her auntie Janis, help her through this, then in a couple of months you can run your idea past her. But that's just my opinion and all I'll be saying in the matter," added Martha as she loaded their lunch plates into the dishwasher.

"It's just that it would be the perfect solution," said Addie, looking mystified by their reactions. "She needs a job, and I have one to offer her. She can't live with your parents forever, Serena, and I have the apartment over the garage that's just sitting empty. It's a win-win for both of us."

Serena reached across the table and took Addie's hand in hers. "Look, sweetie, I know it makes sense to you right now, but Martha's right. My cousin is in a very fragile state, and, in all actuality, you only need the extra help in the bookstore for the next three weeks. I think a better solution to having the traveling bookstore sit idle right now is for you to cut your planned time short and go back into work earlier, so Paige can take the bookshop bus and attend the Salem festival next weekend."

Addie recoiled and pulled her hand away.

"I know it's scary considering what just happened, but—"

"I can't do that, not yet. There's no way I could stand all the sympathetic glances my customers would be giving me, and then there's the lookie-loos who'll just come in to get a look at the woman who was stabbed in the heart at the altar like something out of a Shakespeare play." Addie shook her head. "No, I can't, not yet."

"Okay, I get it, but think about it. What happens when you do go back and there's four of you working in the shop? You'll be tripping over each other and then you'll feel bad about having to let Nikki go, and to be honest, I'm not sure she could take that right now. Besides, if she was living in the apartment too, it could make things really uncomfortable for both of you then."

Addie sat back and folded her arms across her chest. "It really did seem like a good plan."

"Yes, it might work out, in time, but I'm not sure this is the right time."

Addie rubbed her temples. "It's just that . . . everything in my life is spiraling out of control, and it seemed like a logical solution, you know, for some stability."

"That's why you need to talk to Simon. The two of you have to make a plan, together. You'll feel more in control and then you can move forward. If it still seems like a good idea to hire my cousin, go for it, but until then . . . remember that you and Simon had planned to turn the apartment into a home office and man cave for him. What would he say about you renting it out from under him? This is going to be his home too, and you just can't go off and make quick-fix plans that don't involve him."

Addie stared out the kitchen window as the spring winds lashed at the trees. Being a victim of a wind that blew every which way was something she could relate to, but it brought her no comfort. The plans she and Simon had made all seemed like a surreal dreamscape at the moment, but Serena was right. It was time she put on her big girl pants and faced the man who broke her heart and her spirit. "Okay," she whispered. "I'll call him later."

She didn't miss the look of triumph that crossed

both Serena and Martha's faces, nor the sinking feeling that accompanied her words, but it had to be done. She really did love him, and if they were to salvage anything out of recent events it was going to take working together on it . . . eventually. "But don't you see? I can't get past Simon lying to me."

"He never actually told you he was never married before, did he?" said Serena.

"He lied by omission. He knew all about David. He even knew about my high school boyfriend Tony Radcliff. You're telling me, in all the time we discussed my past loves, he never once thought to tell me about Laurel and the fact that they were married, even for a short time?"

"Well," Serena said and shifted in her seat. "That's why going back to the shop now might be good for you. It would give you something else to think about, and then talking to him might be easier."

"Look," said Martha, "I know it's not my place to get involved. After all I'm only the crotchety old baker in your eyes, aren't I?"

Addie opened her mouth to speak.

"Don't bother." Martha waved off Addie's look of protest. "I know what everyone says behind my back. But did you ever stop and think why I got that reputation? It's because I do know a thing or two about the heartache a man can cause a woman. What you don't see, Serena, is that Addie is hurting, and I think you're wrong about her going back to work right now. Oh, I know you want her to have her happy-ever-after moment the way you did, and anybody can see how much she and Simon love each other, but she's hurt right now, and she has a right to be. He shared that moment with someone else, and she didn't know about it."

This time it was Serena's mouth that opened to protest.

"Don't bother." Martha waved her off. "You don't want her to make the same mistakes I did and end up a bitter, resentful old woman, do you?"

Serena's cheeks turned the same fiery red as her hair.

"You want Addie to jump back into work, hoping it will help her take her mind off what happened, but you didn't see the way her face lit up this morning when she was unearthing her aunt's books and knickknacks. Your cousin Nikki isn't the only one who needs healing right now. Addie has been hurt deeply, and she needs to heal too." Martha harrumphed. "There, I've said my piece and with that, I'll leave the two of you to figure this out. Since you're here for the afternoon, Serena, I think I'm going to stop by the hairdresser's and pamper myself with a new do." Martha grabbed her handbag from the island counter, bustled out of the kitchen, down the long hallway, and out the front door.

"You're both right," said Addie, glancing awkwardly at Serena as she got up from the table and retrieved her phone from where it sat in sleep mode on the island. "I'm not ready to go back, but I do need to talk to Simon to try and figure out what the next steps are." She tapped out a text. The reply came within seconds, and she set her phone back on the counter. "He'll be here when his shift is over in emergency. He figures about eight tonight."

Serena crossed the brick floor and wrapped Addie in her arms, giving her one of her big old bear-hugs. "I'm sorry. She is right. I just wanted you to be happy because I hate seeing you like this, and I know how much you love the bookstore and how happy it makes you, but you're right. Some people in town seem to have nothing better to do than gossip. We can only hope that when you do go back, they've moved on to talk about someone else." She looked down at Addie's phone, with Simon's text still displayed. "Feel better?"

Addie shook her head. "But I have to make a start, don't I? You know, in forgiving him for not being totally honest with me."

"It's a good first step though," said Serena and then fumbled for her phone as it pinged out a text alert. She drew in a deep breath and checked the message and then grinned at Addie. "So, if cleaning the attic is what's making you happy today, I'm here to help, okay?"

Addie looked at her and grinned. "Really, you can stay the whole afternoon and help me?"

"Yup, my mom just texted me and she's all squared away with the twins for the rest of the day, and dear Uncle Marc is going to pick up take-out fried chicken for their dinner and then help her get them down for the night, and by then Zach should be home from the clinic."

"Is Zach always that late getting home?"

"No, but Tuesdays are crazy for him. He has his

regular daytime office hours with his naturopathy patients, but then they also host a wellness group in the evening. So, it looks like everybody is taken care of and I'm free, and I'll leave when Simon gets here."

"Just like old times!" Addie grinned, clasping Serena's hands in hers.

"You mean old times like when I was footloose and fancy-free before my life-changing event." Serena laughed and rolled her eyes.

"Which life-changing event would that be, the marriage or the kids?"

"Not the marriage. It's great, it's just that . . ."

"Come on, you know you wouldn't trade little Addie and Ollie for anything."

"Well, except for maybe a few more hours of sleep every night and way more than two hours a couple of days a week to spend at my tea shop." Serena snorted out a short laugh. "But no, life is pretty perfect now. So let's make yours perfect too, and get you back to your happy place. We have an attic to finish cleaning, my friend."

Addie deposited the last of the stack of books from her afternoon finds that she was donating to the Boston Library into a crate and caught a movement out of the corner of her eye. "Don't you dare try to move that bookcase by yourself!" she shouted, dashing toward Serena in the far front corner of the attic. "Do you want to put your back out and be useless to the twins for the rest of the week?"

"Yeah, you're right," panted Serena, leaning her

shoulder against the top shelf. "It's heavier than it looks and seems to be wedged in here. It's definitely a two-person job to move."

"Of course it is! The last bookshelf in this corner couldn't be easy, could it? Murphy's Law or something," said Addie with a soft chuckle as she slid her hand behind the case. "Okay, you grab that side and we'll walk it out, one corner at a time. If we get it at least to the center of the room then I can ask Marc and Zach to carry it downstairs."

"Do you think Simon's sister Carolyn would ask her husband, Pete, to lend you his truck to move it, and those other pieces you're keeping for the bookstore?"

"Yeah, I'm pretty sure she would, because I'd love to have this and a few of the others to replace a couple of the taller bookshelves in front of the counter and have a more open view into the front part of the shop."

Serena grunted walking her corner out. "Judging by its weight, I'd say this one is solid oak, or am I just getting old and tired?"

"You're definitely not old, tired possibly; it's been a long afternoon, but yes," grumbled Addie, working her corner out from the wall, "it's solid oak."

The two of them inched the bookcase away from the wall and heaved a sigh of relief when it was placed out of the way in a line with the other cases and cubby shelving that Addie intended to keep, sell, or trade.

"There, done," puffed Addie. "I can't tell you how happy this makes me. That jam-packed corner has been driving me nuts since I discovered the small office back there." She gazed at the space they had just cleared and gasped. "Oh my, do you see what I see?"

Serena lifted her head from where it rested on the top of the bookcase as she struggled to catch her breath. "What the—"

But Addie had already darted toward the far corner and stood mouth open in disbelief.

"Can you believe this door was hidden behind the bookcase, and you never knew?" Serena slid up to her side. "And is there another door into wherever this leads to from the small office and book room next door?"

"No, it's such a long, narrow room and this wall backing onto the main attic is lined with bookshelves. I just assumed the end wall was the house exterior. I had no idea a whole other room was on the other side."

"It can't be that big, judging from where this little door is tucked under the eaves, and the actual exterior house wall. What do you think, about ten, twelve feet wide?"

Addie nodded and reached for the brass door knob. "But with my aunt's penchant for hidden compartments, why should a hidden room surprise me?" She gave the knob a turn but it wouldn't budge.

"Now what?" asked Serena, her gaze scanning the bookshelves running alongside under the eaves to their left. "Do you think there's a key hidden somewhere?"

"Maybe, but knowing what I do about my aunt after living in her house, my thought is it's more likely a puzzle to be worked out. Remember her writing desk and the puzzle box?"

"Yeah, but how many puzzles can there be for an old door?" asked Serena, pressing on the two top raised door panels and then the lower two. "Nothing, now what?"

Addie scanned the original 1880s beadboard wall on either side of the door. "Hmm . . . maybe it's a combination of a puzzle *and* a key." Her fingers began working their way around the old boards, searching for one that loosened under her grasp. She worked her way from the door to the exterior wall and then moved the next row down and worked her way back to the door. Addie followed this pattern until she reached the wider plank just above the floorboards and gave a squeal when the corner piece moved under her hands. She sat back on her haunches and gingerly worked the smaller square of wooden beadboard away from the wall surface, revealing a small opening.

"You're not going to put your hand inside that, are you?" Serena glanced over her shoulder.

"No, I hoped you would," Addie said, looking mischievously up at her friend.

Serena danced a step backward and only just avoided stumbling over an equally startled Pippi, who had left the comfort of the makeshift bed Addie had created for her out of an old blanket by the top of the attic stairs and had come over to investigate the commotion. "Yikes, I'm sorry, Pippi," she cried as she fought to keep her balance and not come crashing down on the little Yorkipoo.

Pippi darted away, shook her little body as if to

say, *Whatever*, trotted back over to her bed, and gave a deep sigh as she lay back down, keeping a watchful eye on Serena.

"She's fine—are you? That was quite the dance you just performed."

"What can I say, I finally get to live my childhood dream of performing in front of an audience."

"Yeah." Addie gestured with her head toward Pippi. "But I'm not sure how impressed that audience is with you at the moment."

"I hope she knows I nearly dislocated my hip trying to avoid stepping on her."

"I'm sure she's most grateful, but come on. We have a mystery to solve."

"I'm not putting my hand in there, no matter how guilty you try to make me feel about almost hurting Pippi."

"Aw, but just look at her eyes. She can't believe her auntie Serena nearly stepped on her."

"Addie, I mean it."

"Okay, okay, I'll do it."

"Wait!" Serena raced over to her side. "Before you go being all macho and brave, have you seen any signs of rats or other vermin up here? You never know what—"

"You mean like this?" Addie grinned, dangling a brass key ring in the air above her head directly in Serena's line of sight.

"Yeah, like that," said Serena sheepishly.

Addie rose to her feet and went over to the door, slipped the largest of the three keys into the old lock and gave it a jiggle. The doorknob turned easily in her hand. She sucked in a deep breath, glanced over her shoulder at Serena. "We need light, give me your phone."

With a shaky hand Serena turned on the phone's flashlight feature and gave her phone to Addie, who shone it at her feet. The last thing she needed was to step into a black abyss. Relieved to see the attic's wooden floorboards extended past the doorway, she aimed the light in front of her, ducked her head to fit through the short door, scanning the area in front of her, then stepped inside the hidden room. "Oh my . . ." she gasped.

"What, what is it?" Serena pushed in behind her. "There's a string, it must be for a ceiling light." Serena gave it a tug and the entire room was instantly illuminated by the soft glow of the overhead bulb dangling from the beadboard ceiling. "Wow!" cried Serena. "What the heck is all this?"

Addie glanced blankly at her and shrugged. "You tell me," she said, turning off the flashlight.

Chapter 5

Addie's legs ignored her brain's messages telling her to investigate. It wasn't the books on the shelves above the small writing table, or the old oil lamp on the desk. It wasn't even the antique, brass-bound wooden steamer trunk that short-circuited her brain waves. It was the garment covering the mannequin that had her frozen to the spot.

"Does that look like a wedding dress under the garment bag?" whispered Serena.

Addie nodded, and finally finding the strength to make her legs behave as her brain commanded, she took a step toward the remarkable sight. "As best I can tell. The bag, although clear, is fairly discolored with age, but . . . yes," she said, unzipping it, revealing a yellowing white dress.

"Wow, that means it must be your great-grandmother's then. What a find!"

Addie let the garment bag drop to the floor, exposing the dress in its entirety. "I don't think so. She would have been married sometime in the late 1920s, but this style is more recent than that." Addie fingered the lace appliqués of the illusion neckline on the satin and tulle fabric, eyeing the cinched waist of the A-line gown on the dressmaker's form. "No, look at the waistline and the length of the full crinoline-enhanced skirt. This style was popular in the 1950s."

"Was she married twice? Or maybe they had a vow-renewal ceremony?"

"I doubt it, my great-aunt Anita's father, my great-grandfather John, wasn't a romantic at all from what I've read in Anita's journals. According to her, he was very stiff-upper-crust and all, and very old-fashioned in his thinking, so I can't see him doing anything as heartfelt as a vow renewal."

"Anita's brother was your grandfather, right. Maybe this was your grandmother's?"

"No, I've seen photos of my grandparents' wedding and this is nothing like the dress she wore." Addie shrugged. "But you know it does add to the mystery of that wedding-cake topper I found downstairs in the old china cabinet."

"What topper?"

"The one I gave to Martha to put on the wedding cake she made for your wedding."

"Oh right, the one I never got to use."

"Yes, that one." Addie's fingers traced the outline of the dress on the form. "I did find it odd since Anita was never married, and now this adds to the mystery even more. What's this?" Addie said, sliding her finger under the neckline and flipping out a piece of paper on a string. "It still has the price tag on it!"

Serena leaned in and took a look. "Lou Lou's Bridal of Boston. Maybe they have a record. It could be a lead?"

Addie glanced at Serena's phone, which she still held in her hand, and tapped in the information. "Nope, dead end, they closed in 1973."

"Okay then, maybe there's something in the trunk that can give us a clue about who this belonged to?"

"Let's hope so, because it sure has me baffled," said Addie, eyeing the brass key ring still looped around her finger. She slid it off, inserted the next larger key into the lock on the trunk and the lid opened easily under Serena's eager hands.

"Yes, look!" cried Serena. "Here's one of those old wedding books. You know the ones where the bride records all the events leading up to and through the day of her wedding. I bet there's something in here." Serena excitedly removed the large book with the satin-embroidered wedding bells on the cover and began flipping through it.

But Addie was more focused on the leather-and-cloth-bound books that lay underneath where the wedding book had been. She picked up one, read the top entry on the first page and gasped. "These are my aunt's early journals, the ones that are missing from her collection that I found in the outer attic."

"Good," said Serena, setting the wedding book on the floor beside where she knelt in front of the chest. "Because the wedding book is blank, there's nothing in it. Not even an early entry about any of the plans for the big day, not a wedding invitation, or bridal party members, a list of invitees. There's absolutely nothing in it."

"That seems odd, doesn't it?"

"Yeah, my mom has one of these, and it's full of every detail of her big day and all the events like wedding showers and who gave her what gift, every detail that led up to the big event. She even has a piece of lace from her dress tucked inside it. Mom said whenever she's feeling nostalgic she likes to pull it out and relive one of the happiest days of her life."

"Hmm." Addie scanned down the journal page in her hand. "Well, if there's going to be any clues to the dress, I think I'm going to have a lot of reading ahead of me. This book's first entry is the summer of 1948, and it reads like a typical eighteen-year-old teenager's muses and daydreams." She snapped the journal closed and removed another from the trunk, flipping to the first entry. "This one is 1949, so I guess I have my evening cut out for me."

"Don't forget, Simon's coming over so you can talk and work out a plan for your next big day."

Addie slid from her crouched position to sitting on her bottom with a thud. "Right, Simon," she said, gazing up at the wedding dress, choking back a tear as Serena continued to rummage through the chest.

"Wow, look at this nightdress," said Serena, folding back the tissue wrapping. "It must be pure silk. I bet it was for the wedding night."

Addie eyed the pale pink nightdress with the pearl beaded neckline as Serena held it up, and she frowned. "Okay, now I'm really curious. That most definitely is pure silk, and those, if I'm not mistaken, look like real pearls. Not cheap even by 1950s standards. Who did this chest belong to?"

"Here's a photo album and a scrapbook," cried Serena excitedly as she lifted the two large leather albums from the trunk.

"And a shoebox," added Addie, her excitement rising as she retrieved the box from the trunk and flipped off the lid. "Look at this. It's old Valentine's Day cards, Christmas cards, a couple of what look like letters, and a photo of a rather handsome young man."

"Let me see," said Serena, slipping the picture from Addie's fingers. "Ooo-oo, whoever he is, he's a looker, isn't he? Very much like a young Rock Hudson."

"How do you know about Rock Hudson?"

"I'm a classic-movie buff, remember?"

"That's right." Addie nodded, recalling her friend's passion for old films. "Is there an inscription on the back, a year, name, anything?"

Serena flipped it over and shook her head. "But if I'm not mistaken, these smudges on the photo are"—she squinted, studying the picture closer—"lip marks?"

"Like someone was kissing the picture?"

"Exactly. Do you think this is a 1950s movie star that some superfan was crushing on?"

Addie studied the photo over Serena's shoulder. "I don't know. See—there's a Harvard crest on his sweater, and I don't think many movie stars back then were Ivy League graduates. I could be wrong though, but . . . there is something familiar about him. Around his eyes and his jawline." She shook her head. "So maybe he was a celebrity of some sort? There must be something in here that will tell us what all this means," she added, rummaging deeper into the trunk. "Ouch, rats!" She yanked her hand out of the trunk. "Something near the bottom—"

"A rat bit you?"

"No, silly. Something hard snagged one of my nail extensions that I got put on for the wedding." She examined her fingernails. "And look." Addie waved her hand in Serena's face. "It broke the one off on my ring finger. How fitting, hey?" Addie shook her head in disgust. "You know what. There's so much to dig through in here and I'm getting hungry. Let's take the shoebox, journals, and albums downstairs, order a pizza, and start digging through them before we get overwhelmed by what's in here."

"Wow, I've never known you to leave a mystery unsolved."

"I know, but it seems the more we pull out of here, the more questions than answers we have. The trunk has been here for years and isn't going anywhere tonight. I think if we're going to find any answers, then we need to start with this"—she shook the box—"and the journals and photo albums."

Serena's tummy picked that exact moment to let out a low rumble.

"See, it's time to refuel and take a look at what we have so far." Addie chuckled and helped a giggling Serena to her feet.

*   *   *

Serena pushed her plate away and let out a contented sigh. "Best pizza I've ever had."

"Really," said Addie, eyeing the half-eaten slice on her own plate. "I found the crust a bit greasy. I think it was all that extra cheese we had them add."

"Let me tell you, after over two years of wedded bliss and cooking seven nights a week for a finicky husband and two picky one-year-olds, any meal I don't have to cook is the best dinner I've ever had."

"My grandmother used to say that," laughed Addie, clearing the table.

"I tell you, the cooking and cleaning and constant picking-up gets old after a while, and evenings like this, for me anyway, are like taking a mini vacation. And as much as I love my family, I hate to see this evening end." Serena glanced at her phone. "But, like they say, all good things must come to an end, and I only have an hour of this freedom left before I told Mom I'd be back. So"—Serena plopped a photo album on the table—"let's see if we can solve the wedding-dress mystery." She flipped open the cover of the album and grinned. "Is this your great-aunt Anita?"

Addie leaned over her shoulder and peered at the photo Serena pointed to. "It looks like her, I mean I've only ever seen pictures of her when she was older, but I'd say yes. It's the same face only younger."

"She looks like Doris Day, and if that other picture we found of the guy was her boyfriend, wow! Wouldn't they have made the cutest couple," swooned Serena.

"Ah," Addie scoffed. "What's suddenly up with you and Rock Hudson, now Doris Day, too?"

"On Sunday night Zach and I watched that 1959 movie of theirs, *Pillow Talk*. After what happened to you Saturday, I needed a real-world romantic escape, and the movie was so cute and fun that I guess my mind kind of got stuck on a loop about it. Sorry, but really look at her. She really does look like Doris Day, maybe it's the smile and hair style, but wow . . . I wonder who these other people are in the picture."

"It looks to me like it might be her high school graduation class. You know, one of those silly, candid yearbook shots they used to take out on the front lawn of the school. Is there a date on the back?"

Serena carefully removed the photo from the four black adhesive holders in the corners of the page and flipped the photo over. "Yes, it says *graduating class of 1948*." How did you know what it was?"

"I have a similar one from in front of my school," chuckled Addie. "Except, of course, when I graduated, poodle skirts and bobby socks weren't all the rage, and there were a few middle fingers raised." She returned her attention to the album page, searching for any images of her great-aunt snapped repeatedly with one particular boy who might be a clue to the wedding dress.

From where she grazed on her bowl of kibble beside the kitchen island, Pippi perked her ears and let out a yip.

"What's the matter, girl? Did you hear something?" asked Addie, rising, but Serena beat her to the kitchen door.

Serena cocked her head and listened as Pippi yipped again, darted between her legs and raced down the corridor to the front door, where she did her gopher stance, dancy-prancy thing on her hind legs and barked.

"Ah," said Serena with a short laugh. "It's someone knocking. She has way better hearing than I do." Serena set off to the door as Addie checked the time on her phone. *Five past seven.*

"It must be Catherine," Addie called out. "She texted earlier and said she'd drop by after dinner." But when Serena didn't respond, Addie shrugged and continued to scan down the page.

"Addie?"

She glanced up from the photo album. "Simon? You're early, aren't you, or did I read your text wrong?"

"No, you read it correctly. Something came up, so I got the nightshift doctor to come in a bit early."

"Okay," she said, closing the photo album. It was so unlike him to leave a shift early, he must've been really anxious to settle this once and for all; the problem was . . . she still didn't know how she felt about what happened on Saturday, or . . . if she had gotten past it and was ready to move forward again.

Simon crossed the brick floor and leaned into her, but his lips brushed across Addie's cheek as she instinctively turned her head in order to avoid his lips. Since she still wasn't certain she had forgiven him, a kiss on the cheek was all she could muster at the moment. He frowned as he hung his jacket over a counter stool.

"Um." Serena popped her head around the door frame and glanced from Simon to Addie. "I have to get home now, so I'll call you later?"

"Yes, that sounds good, and thank you for today," said Addie, grateful for the momentary distraction as she regrouped her thoughts.

"See you, Serena," Simon said with a wave of his hand, but she had already started down the hall, and when the front door clicked shut, he glanced at Addie and shrugged. "It looks like I'm now on the frenemy list with her."

"I wouldn't say that. She's just as confused by the turn of events as I am."

"That's why I left work early. My friend in New York, the lawyer I was telling you about, Nigel Berman? He emailed me the annulment papers today that Laurel and I have to fill out. They have to be notarized by a notary public who is certified in the Commonwealth of Massachusetts, and since her aunt is still in town visiting her from Pen Hollow, I'm going to drop by there in a while so we can get this started. Nigel wants to file them tomorrow so we can get a court day as soon as possible."

"Can Valerie notarize for her niece?"

"No, she's considered family under Massachusetts law, even though Valerie has nothing to gain by the transaction. She arranged for an old friend of hers, a man named Sam Waters to do it. He is also a notary public and lives here in Greyborne Harbor. We're meeting with him at eight, because he's apparently leaving for California tomorrow for his daughter's wedding, so it has to be tonight."

"I see. Then you just dropped by to tell me that you'll be spending the evening with Laurel?"

"Yes, and her aunt Valerie, and Sam. It's all for our benefit, Addie, don't you see?"

"What I see is you having to bend over backward to look after something that should have been taken care of sixteen years ago. And that something ended our plans for a happy-ever-after."

"We can still have that. It's just that we have to get over this little bump in the road first. I have no choice if I want to make this right."

"You want to make this right?" she scoffed. "Then begin by telling me how all this happened in the first place and why you never said a word about Laurel in all the time I've known you."

"That's exactly what I've been trying to do since Saturday afternoon."

"And now, after the shock of a lifetime, I'm ready to listen. So please, explain it all to me." She gestured with her hand to the empty chair across the table from her.

Simon took a seat. "Okay," he said, raking his fingers through his wavy black hair. "Like I told you, I graduated from high school a year ahead of my class. I was only seventeen when I got accepted into NYU."

Addie nodded. "That part you did tell me about. It's the rest of your time there you appeared to omit."

"It wasn't intentional. You see, I was so young and immature, and so lost those first few weeks on campus. Then after a particularly confusing lecture in organic chemistry, Laurel and I began talking about it on our way out of the lecture hall. It turned out we had a few other classes together too, even though we were heading down different medical paths. Then I joined a study group, and she was the first face I recognized in the group and I kind of latched on to her. After that, we just clicked, at first as friends and study partners and then . . ."

"It's the *and then* part I need to hear about."

He reluctantly nodded. "I know." He took a deep breath. "For the first couple of years we both continued to live separately in student housing, but spent every moment we could together, either in study group or . . ." His voice trailed off and then he cleared his throat. "Then when I thought I had grown up so much and matured"—he chuckled and shook his head—"we decided to live together off campus."

"And that's when you got married?"

"No, we didn't take that plunge until the last year of our undergraduate studies. We were applying for scholarships and entrances into graduate schools that were close enough together so, even though she was going into veterinary medicine and I was heading off to a medical school, we might see each other, either by living halfway between our two campuses or on evenings and weekends. Then the unexpected happened."

Addie sucked in a deep breath, afraid to hear the words that were sure to follow—Laurel was pregnant.

Chapter 6

"What happened?" Addie asked guardedly and hit *silence* as her phone pinged out a text from Catherine telling her she heard Simon was coming over so she'd call later.

"You're lucky. You have such caring and loyal friends to have helped you through all this these past few days." He gestured with his head to her phone on the table. "I know it's been a shock, but please believe it was for me too."

"Simon! What was the unexpected that happened between you and Laurel?"

"I got my dream full scholarship to Johns Hopkins in Maryland, and she got a full ride to UC Davis in California."

Addie slowly released the breath she'd been holding and softly exhaled with relief.

"Remember, we were young and naïve, so we decided that to cement what we had, even though we'd be a country apart, we should get married. So we did. Then it didn't take long for the reality of what we'd done to sink in as we tried to work out the logistics of making a long-distance marriage work when we both would be working such long shifts and we . . . Well, we decided what we'd done was impulsive. Her uncle was a lawyer and said he'd file annulment papers for us since we were only married for a few weeks. He did, or so I thought, and we both went on with our separate lives."

"And since then you've never had any contact with her?"

"At first, for a few months we stayed in touch, but then with classes and my crazy med student schedule . . . and she . . . well, we just drifted apart. If anything, it proved to both of us that the decision we made to annul the marriage was for the best because we never could have made a marriage work out under those conditions and with the distance." He reached across the table and took Addie's hand in his. "Don't you see? I never mentioned it because my life since then has been so much more than what it was for that twenty-one-year-old who I don't even recognize now as being me."

Addie pulled her hands away. The fading sunlight out of the window caught the splash of tiny diamonds that encircled the emerald stone in her engagement ring. The burst of light reflecting from it momentarily took her back to the day Simon had placed it on her finger and asked her to be his wife. "Did you get down on one knee when you proposed to Laurel?"

"No, we were in one of the campus watering holes. Like I said, it was very impulsive."

"Okay," she said, twisting her ring on her finger. "Then I guess you'd better get over to Laurel's to sign the papers so we can get this done and start planning . . . our next wedding."

"Really? You understand now why I never thought to mention it?"

"I wouldn't say that." She poked her leg around under the table, searching for Pippi's warm little body that always brought her a deep sense of comfort, and finding it when her furry little friend nestled into her leg. "But . . . I know I'm not the same young girl who promised to marry Tony, my high school boyfriend, should we both still be single when we turned thirty-five, am I? Then, of course, you knew all about that, didn't you?" Her gaze pierced his. She knew her last words were more cutting than they should be, but she couldn't help getting one last dig in.

"Yeah," he said, hanging his head. "I did. As far as I know you were completely honest with me about your past and I was . . . not as transparent, it seems." He raised his head, meeting her gaze. "I promise *nothing* will be left unsaid or unrevealed from this day forward. Addie, you are my life and my soul. Please know how much I love you."

The sincerity expressed in his eyes was enough to bring tears to hers. Fair enough, his punishment was over. She could forgive and hopefully with time, forget—although that might take a little longer, but right now she ached to hold him in her arms.

She leapt up from the table, raced around to his

side, and flung her arms around his neck. He turned his face to hers, and she planted soft butterfly kisses from his cheek to his lips, and then she kissed him like she'd never kissed him before. Yes, this was still the man she wanted to spend the rest of her life with.

With the inner battle that had been raging inside Addie for the past couple of days somewhat abated by her and Simon's conversation, Addie poured a glass of brandy and snuggled in beside Pippi on the large, overstuffed, antique sofa in her living room. Beside her on the eighteenth-century marquetry coffee table sat a stack of her great-aunt's recently discovered journals. Simon probably wouldn't be back to update her for a few hours, which was plenty of time to make a start on trying to solve the mystery of the wedding dress.

However, that wasn't the only reason Addie eagerly anticipated delving into the journals tonight. There was also Addie's insatiable curiosity to learn all she could about the enigma that was her great-aunt Anita. Addie only had flashes of memory of Anita from when she was young, when her father used to bring her to Greyborne Harbor to visit. That was, of course, before her grandmother had discovered his relationship with Catherine Lewis while they were in town visiting. That had apparently begun while Addie's mother, who had been hospitalized since Addie's birth with a post-delivery stroke, lay lingering for a few years in a vegetative state before eventually passing away. But, with the discovery of her son and Catherine's blossoming relationship before Addie's mother had ultimately passed, her grandmother, who was helping him to raise Addie, forbade him to take her with him to Greyborne Harbor ever again.

According to Catherine, he had told her then it was because of his mother's fears about how the discovery of the relationship he was having with another woman while his wife was still alive, even though she was dying, might affect an impressionable child. So, he complied with his mother's wishes, and given that he'd since died, Addie couldn't ask him now about that time. She'd never know if he did so because of the guilt he felt then, or if her grandmother told him that she wouldn't continue to help him raise little Addie if he carried on with the relationship.

Either way, it didn't really matter now, and any memories Addie had of Anita from back then became mere smoke-like wisps in her young mind. Even though Addie had learned a great deal about her aunt since moving to Greyborne Harbor, and Addie did owe everything in her current life to her, the woman herself and what made her tick were still very much a mystery to Addie. The discovery of her journals from her younger years was an exciting glimpse into the early days in the life of the woman Anita had later become.

For the next hour she read through her aunt's senior year of high school adventures. The plans she had after graduation and the dreams the young woman had for her future, her general musings over life and the meaning of it, similar to those that a young woman in today's world might have. It cemented in Addie's mind that no matter

what changed in the world, people back in 1948
were not much different than they were today—in
other words, the world might change, but deep
down, people really didn't.

There were a few mentions of a young man
named Billy Douglas, who worked as a shipping
apprentice in her father's company. However,
nowhere could Addie find any mention of a romantic relationship between the two, unless it de-
veloped later, as it seemed it was Anita's father,
and not Anita herself, who was pushing the two
young people in that direction. Addie paused.
Could that be the reason her aunt never did
marry? Had her father pushed for the union but
Anita couldn't go through with it, and backed out?

Addie was intrigued, especially when she read
the entry for July 15, 1948:

*I'm beyond excited. I just received my letter of
acceptance to the new Arts Program at Garland
Junior College in Boston.*

"Garland?" Addie reread the sentence. She was
confused. In all the later journals of her aunt's
that Addie had read, Anita mentioned receiving
her master's in literature from Goldsmiths, Uni-
versity of London. She'd used her flat in London
as a home base and spent the next decade traveling throughout the Continent and Far East. She
didn't return to Greyborne Harbor until her mother
got ill, ultimately passing away, which was soon followed by her father's demise. A broken heart, the
doctors had told her.

By this time Anita's brother, Addie's grandfather,

had a successful accounting practice in Boston, and he wasn't interested in relocating back to the family home in Greyborne Harbor. He'd then signed over his half of the house to Anita, and she stayed on living in this very house until she passed, and she'd ultimately bequeathed it to her great-niece, Addie, her only living relative. *Hmm, Garland—interesting.* Addie shook her head in amazement as she read on.

Mama is so happy for me and she is already starting to plan what I should pack and what we can buy in the city for my room in the student residence housing. I'm over the moon with the news!

I called Bernice right away to see if she got in too, but I didn't know what to say when she told me she had been rejected. I told her then I wasn't going either, but when I told Mama, she said that was being silly. A young woman of today needed further education. She can't depend on a man to take her through life and just because my best friend won't be there with me, doesn't mean I won't make new friends, and besides if I do well, I can transfer to the literature program at Boston College in the future, which is what I really want. She's right of course, and when I called Beatrice back, she said she had decided to go to secretarial school right here in Greyborne Harbor anyway. Her father thinks that's best so she can come to work for him at the news-paper office after she graduates.

I wish Father was as happy about the news. He got really quiet at dinner tonight, then, as we were finishing our meal he set his fork beside his plate, cupped his chin in his hands and gave me that look he gives me when he's displeased. You know that one that nails you to your chair from under his bushy eyebrows, then he said, "Anita, the only reason your mother and I agreed to allow you to apply to Garland was for you to take the home-makers courses." Mama cleared her throat and flashed him a look of annoyance. "Why I allowed you to apply," he corrected himself. "I know you have your head full of fanciful thoughts as some more brazen young women of the day do, but there is no need for a young woman to pursue any other form of education." My eyes must have gotten as big as saucers I'm sure because he then said, "Homemaking is the only education a young woman needs, especially when there is a perfectly good man who is capable of taking care of her. Remember, my dear, that man was put on this earth to serve God and woman was put here to serve man. So, there will be no further discussion about arts college for you, young lady, especially when there's a perfectly good man to take care of you, and Billy Douglas is that good man. He will make you a fine husband, so put all this nonsense out of your head. You can attend their home-makers classes, and then we can begin planning your wedding."

I heard Mama gasp, and he flashed her a look of disdain. By the look on her face, I thought she was going to have a stroke just like Beatrice's grandmother had last year, and then without an-other word, he rose from the table and went into his study, and closed the doors with a bang.

It took Mama forever to stop my tears, but she assured me she would talk to him and for me not to worry. If arts college was what I wanted, then arts college was where I would go.

The row Mama and Father had tonight was horrible. I could hear it all the way up in my bedroom. I stayed out in the turret with my hands over my ears and tried not to let Father's angry words inside my head. But it wasn't until his car drove up the driveway and onto the street that Mama came in. Her cheeks were flushed, but she smiled and told me it was settled. I could accept my entrance to the arts program at Garland College.

Father didn't come home for two whole days after they argued. I heard Mama ask him on the telephone where he was, and he must have said he was staying at the office because then she said, "As far as I'm concerned, you can live at the office until you come to your senses." When he finally did come home, he barely spoke to me or Mama. He acted as though we were invisible and walked right past us.

Addie jumped with a noise at the door that sent Pippi flying off the sofa yipping and yapping as she raced to the front door. She shook her head to clear the time jump she had taken from 1950, and stumbled toward the commotion. "Who is it?" she called out.

"Simon."

Addie glanced over at the mantel clock and gasped; it was fifteen past eleven. Where in the world had the evening gone? She flung open the door, grinning, but her grin quickly faded when she saw the look on Simon's face. "What is it, what's happened?"

"We need to talk," he said, motioning inside to the foyer.

"Of course, come in." Addie stepped aside, and he entered, keeping his gaze not on her or Pippi dancing at his feet but straight ahead toward the kitchen door.

"Did you want to go into the kitchen to talk?"

He shook his head. "No, I think we're both going to need a drink."

She wasn't sure she liked the anxious look on his face as he poured himself a scotch, knocked it back, and poured a second one. Another shoe was about to drop, she could feel it in her bones.

"Simon? What happened at Laurel's? Didn't you get the papers signed?"

Simon dropped onto the sofa, laid his head on the back cushion, and closed his eyes. "Yes, we signed the papers."

"Then why do you look the way you do?" Addie collapsed on the arm of the sofa. "Are you having second thoughts about annulling the marriage?"

"No, not in the least." He set his tormented eyes on her confused gaze.

"Then what is it? Because you're scaring me and earlier this evening you promised that nothing will be left unsaid or unrevealed from this day forward."

Simon sat upright, took the last swallow of his drink, and set the empty glass on the table. "I know, and I want you to know that what I'm about to tell you changes nothing between us. Our marriage will go on as planned. It's just that there's been another hitch." He rose and made his way to the liquor cart, poured another scotch, and knocked it back.

"What kind of a hitch? Did Laurel refuse to sign the papers?"

"No, nothing like that, but . . . well. Valerie waited until we'd both signed them and then she said to Laurel, 'Now you can tell him and he won't think you told him just to keep the marriage together.' "

"What did she mean by that?"

"That's exactly what I asked her," Simon said, coming around to the sofa and taking his seat beside Addie, still perched on the arm. "Then Laurel explained that after she got to Davis, she discovered"—he swallowed hard—"that she was pregnant."

Addie's head began to swim with all the possibilities of what he was about to say next.

"Since she assumed we were divorced she didn't tell me because I was so happy at Johns Hopkins, and she didn't want to ruin my life. She had the baby and arranged for a private adoption with a couple who happened to be professors at Davis College."

"And she never told you about any of this?"

Simon shook his head. "Then about two years ago she heard from the lawyer who had arranged for her baby—our baby—to be adopted. It seemed that both the parents were killed in an avalanche when on a ski trip in Switzerland. He wanted her to know that the boy was being taken care of by his grandparents though. Then last month, the lawyer reached out again to inform her that the grandmother passed away last year and the grandfather recently had a stroke and was in long-term care. Since the boy has no other relatives, he is now in the child welfare system."

Addie's heart ached for the boy. She had friends who had grown up in the foster system and some hadn't fared well.

"Laurel petitioned the courts and, as his birth mother, she was just granted temporary custody while she files for adoption. The lawyer is flying with him to Boston on Thursday for Laurel to pick him up." Simon took a deep breath, laid his head on the back of the sofa, and stared up at the tray ceiling. "His name is Mason Keller . . . Mason Simon Keller, and he's my son."

Her ribs squeezed against her heart, sending it into a hammering rhythm.

Simon reached for her cold hand and gave it a squeeze. "Don't worry, this won't change our plans, I promise. But before I send the papers to Nigel to file, I have to talk to him. After I left Laurel's this evening, I drove around for a while and tried to clear my head. I called Nigel to ask what I should do. You know, since we've just discovered that we were still married when the baby went up for adoption without my consent—"

"Or awareness, it seems."

"Yes, and that too." Simon twisted his hands together and leaned forward, resting them on his knees. "Anyway, I don't know what any of it means now, and I can't file the papers until I sit down and go through it all with Nigel to find out what other papers have to be submitted along with the divorce papers, like my parental rights, custody or financial obligations, which I have no issue with, of course. He's my son, but right now I haven't a clue how to proceed so you and I can go through with our plans for our future."

"Okay, I get it. Just do whatever you have to, to make this right with your *son*." She swallowed hard. "And then we can worry about making it right with our plans later."

"I am so sorry. It's just such a mess right now, and Nigel can't meet until sometime next week because he's wrapped up in a big court case and he's not certain when he can clear his calendar to fit me in." Simon sat back and rested his head on the back of the sofa, his eyes on Addie's. "But don't worry. We'll get this all sorted out just as soon as we can." He clasped her hand in his, brought it to his lips, and kissed it. "It'll be fine, we'll be fine. It's just going to take a bit more time," he whispered hoarsely.

Addie forcibly pasted what she hoped was a semblance of a smile on her lips. "Well, it has been a week of surprises hasn't it?" That was an understatement, and all Addie could think of was she needed time and space to process this new information. "I think what we both need right now is a good night's sleep, and we can talk again tomorrow." She rose shakily from her perch on the sofa arm and glanced over at the liquor cart. In reality, a stiff brandy was what she really needed to help her digest all this.

"Yeah, you're right. We can talk tomorrow morning," Simon said, as he levered himself up from the sofa.

"Aren't you still on day shift tomorrow?"

"I've got a replacement to cover me for a few days while I sort this all out and can get my head around it," he said, moving into the foyer. "I should know a bit more after I go to Boston on Thursday with Laurel to meet Mason at the airport."

Addie paused in the living room doorway. "You're going with her to Boston?"

"Yes. She and Mason have chatted in the last month by video call, but I thought now, since I'll be in his life too, I should probably be there and let him meet me and know that I'll support him any way I can during his transition to Greyborne Harbor and his new life here."

"Yes, yes, you're right, of course. He should meet his father at the same time he's meeting his mother." She almost choked on her last word.

"By the way," he said, pausing with one hand on the open front door frame. "On Sunday, Valerie is holding an open-house tea so she can introduce Mason to some of Laurel's new patients and friends here in Greyborne Harbor."

"Like a baby shower? Are you going?"

"I think I should, at least for a little while, to show the boy some fatherly support, don't you?"

Addie reluctantly nodded.

"She wanted to hold a big event and invite everyone Laurel knows from Boston and the Pen Hollow peninsula area too, but thankfully Laurel vetoed that idea, and they settled on a tea for now. Although, Valerie is so excited by all this and can't wait to show Mason off, that I'm sure she's on the phone as we speak, calling everyone in Laurel's contact list." He gave a soft chuckle. "Another reason I thought I should attend. Nothing like male support in a room of strange women."

"Yes, I suppose if it's a tea and not a party then it's most likely to be ladies who attend."

"That's my thinking. So, I thought we might leave after the introductions and I'd take him out for a burger or something and then he and I could have some one-on-one time together. But we'll see how it goes." He leaned in and gave Addie a soft kiss, and tilted her chin up until her eyes met his. "It'll all work out the way it's supposed to, just be patient, my love."

Addie closed the door behind him, pressed her back against it and slid to the foyer floor, where Pippi climbed onto her lap and nestled into Addie's arms. Her fingers absently stroked the fine fur behind Pippi's ears as she cradled her furry little friend's head to her aching heart. Pippi stretched up and licked her cheeks but then let out a soft whimper. "No, my friend, no tears tonight for you to kiss away, I think I have none left to shed."

Pippi nestled her cold, wet nose into Addie's neck as she continued to cradle her dog close, knowing deep inside her whole world had once again been turned upside down and sideways.

Chapter 7

Over the following days a cold numbness settled into Addie's limbs. It was as though a frigid hand had wrapped around her heart and began slowly squeezing the life out of her. Of course, this sensation could only come because she knew full well what all this recent news meant. It was bad enough that her dream life with Simon had been smashed by the news that he was still married to his college sweetheart, and that their short union had produced a child, a child who would very soon be in the picture and a part of his life going forward.

She sucked in a ragged gasp as she struggled for a breath. In her heart she knew that she could accept the boy, he was part of Simon. Even though her only experiences with children came in the form of Paige's little girl, Emma, and Serena's twins, Oliver and Addison, she did well with them.

As Auntie Addie, she got to indulge and spoil them for a few short hours and then she could go home and retreat to her normal carefree life, leaving the children she'd spoiled with sugary treats in their parents' hands.

After all, it wasn't like Mason was a baby that she'd have to learn how to swaddle and feed in the middle of the night. He was a young man, and yes, she could make him a part of her life too. He was Simon's son. Her misgivings came, though, with the realization that the situation meant she'd have to accept Laurel into her life as well. As Mason's mother she was going to be there for the rest of his life, and that meant part of Simon's life too, forevermore.

As Addie grappled with these thoughts and the erratic emotions they produced, she couldn't even muster up the interest or energy to take on the mystery of the wedding dress in the attic. When she gazed at her own wedding dress, now hanging on the back of her bedroom door—thankfully, fully dry-cleaned by way of Serena—she couldn't help but wonder if the owner of the other dress had stored it away in the attic, unworn, after some equally traumatic event. Was Addie's dress destined to hang beside it?

As the next few days unfolded, Addie became more and more convinced that was her dress's destiny. Every time she and Simon made plans to get together, Laurel intervened by way of a new crisis that she needed Simon to help her with. The latest was the condition of Mason's clothing he'd brought from California. It seemed since his grandmother passed, the boy's elderly grandfather hadn't kept up with his growth spurts and all his shirts were too short in the sleeves and his pants too short in the legs. Of course, she needed a man's touch to help her and Mason select a new wardrobe. Addie couldn't stop the eye roll over that excuse.

Then there was the crisis of furnishing his new bedroom. Laurel had no idea what a boy of fifteen, almost sixteen, would like or want in his room—like Simon would, pfft—and she needed Simon to assist her and Mason with that shopping adventure too.

It was one thing after the other it seemed. Addie had even pointed out her fears to Simon, who had brushed off her concerns and told her that Laurel just wanted Mason to settle in and be happy and that's exactly what he wanted too. None of it meant anything more than that. Addie chewed her bottom lip. Things felt off, and she just wasn't certain about anything anymore.

By Sunday, Addie was exhausted with worry. It was the day of Valerie's tea and social to introduce Mason to the good people of Greyborne Harbor.

"Good people, my foot," snarled Addie after hearing Serena, Paige, and Catherine on their Addie-welfare-checks report that half the town planned on attending the event. The same people who had been *her* friends were now going to take Simon's first wife—his only wife—and his son into their circle. A sense of betrayal overcame her, she couldn't even force herself off the sofa, and binged on the BBC's *Miss Marple* television series for the day.

When a knock came to her door, it was all Addie could do to unwrap herself from Pippi's sofa snuggles and make her uncooperative legs take her to the door to answer it.

"Hi." Serena grinned, waving a bag in her hand. "Paige asked me to drop your dinner off to you."

"Okay, sure, come in. Is she busy tonight?"

"Didn't she call you?"

"No," Addie said, closing the door behind Serena. "She just told me earlier that she'd stop and grab me something for dinner, then come over and tell me all about Valerie and Laurel's tea today."

"Ooh . . . then I guess you haven't heard."

"Heard what? Did something happen to her, or Emma?"

"No, no, nothing like that. It's just that . . . Valerie Price died this afternoon."

"What? How?"

"I wasn't at the tea, but from what Paige told me, she just fell over dead."

"A heart attack?"

"I guess, but Paige is pretty broken up about it and Catherine too. They've known her for years, so Paige asked that I come and bring your dinner."

"Yes, yes, they would be hit hard by this. Catherine and Valerie have been friends through one committee or another for years, and Paige's sister was Valerie's next-door neighbor in Pen Hollow."

"I know. I never met the woman when I was there last year, but it's still sad. Especially for . . . Laurel, isn't it?"

"Yeah . . . Valerie was like a mother to her, so it's like losing her mother all over again." What Addie wanted to ask Serena then was if she knew if that's where Simon was now and the reason he hadn't been in touch today. Was it because he was consoling Laurel? Instead, she asked, "Is anyone with Laurel now to help her cope with it all?"

Serena shrugged as she pulled the food storage containers out of the bag and lined them up across the kitchen island.

"Hey, those are yours, aren't they? Not take-out food containers."

"Yeah, when Paige called, I'd just made dinner, so you got some of my famous spaghetti and meatballs. I hope that's okay?"

"Of course, but I'm not an invalid. You should be at home with your family and could have just called to tell me what happened. I could have fixed myself something to eat."

"Really?" Serena pinned her with a look. "I've seen your fridge lately. Tell me, when was the last time you got groceries?"

"You have a point, but in my defense, I wasn't planning on being here for three weeks, remember?"

"Then I guess it's a good thing I dropped these off. So, say *thank you, Serena,* and with that, I will go home and rescue Zach from two one-year-olds that think spaghetti sauce is finger paint."

After Serena left to go home and finish dinner with her family, Addie glanced down at Pippi. "I don't know about you, my little friend, but after that news I need some air. Let's go for a run near the cliff top, what do you say?" Pippi gave a yip as Addie slipped into her running shoes and clipped Pippi on her lead and they headed out the back door.

Just because Addie had made herself a prisoner in her own home and mind this past week, there was no reason to keep Pippi locked within the same walls. Besides, she needed time to digest the news about Valerie. It was so sad. She was such a sweet woman.

The fresh air and sunshine were exactly what they both needed, and when they were done she was panting as much as Pippi, who'd headed directly to her water dish. Addie followed her lead, gulped down a glass of cool water and then loaded her plate with Serena's homemade spaghetti and meatballs. After heating her dinner in the microwave, she settled on a counter stool to enjoy the first home-cooked morsels of food she'd had in days. However, she knew Serena well enough to know that the marinara sauce most likely came from a jar and not from hours of simmering in a pot. It hit the spot in spite of that and gave her the satisfaction she was looking for.

After chewing her last meatball, Addie grabbed her phone and searched for any breaking news on Valerie Price's passing. Maybe it could give her a clue as to why Simon had gone silent. A photo, anything of the grieving Laurel would at least let her know where he was and explain the silent treatment. Instead, what she found was a missed call and voice message from him.

"Hi, Addie, it's me. I'm not sure if you heard but something terrible happened at the tea today and Valerie Price . . . well, she died. Laurel is taking this really hard, not to mention Mason. The poor kid, strange place, new people, and now this. It's such a mess, and things have taken an unexpected turn, so I'll call as soon as I can, but gotta go now, love you."

And there it was . . . one more reason for Laurel

to monopolize Simon's time. Even though Addie knew this latest crisis wasn't of Laurel's making, and she wouldn't wish the circumstances on anyone, it still didn't settle well.

Addie could kick herself. She was the one last year who told Valerie about Doctor Timmons's plan to retire and told her to have her niece contact him about taking over his practice. When, oh when, would she ever learn to keep her mouth shut and stay out of other people's business? She couldn't help but think it was her fault that Doctor Laurel Hill had ended up in Greyborne Harbor. She had literally thrown Laurel back into the arms of Simon, and now Addie was a victim of the fallout.

But who was she really kidding? Whether or not Laurel had ended up in Greyborne Harbor wouldn't have made any difference. The fact was, Laurel was Simon's wife, and if she hadn't met Valerie and Laurel last year, that meant Addie and Simon might have been married last weekend in an illegal marriage ceremony. How would she feel finding out years later, and what if they had children of their own by then? Addie shivered with the realization of all the implications that it could have led to. No, she was a victim of circumstances way beyond her control.

Victim? Me? No, never! Enough self-pity and moping about, Addie. She hadn't played the part of victim when her first fiancé, David, and her father were murdered, and she'd made the decision to pack up her life in Boston, leave all her friends, and move to a town where she didn't know anyone, to start a new life. So she certainly wasn't going to start now.

She tapped out a short, curt reply to Simon, read it . . . deleted it, and then slammed her phone down on the counter. If anyone was a victim here it was her eighteen-year-old great-aunt Anita at the hands of an overbearing, narrow-minded father with archaic self-righteous Victorian morals, who was trying to force her into a loveless marriage. That was the only victim who would get her sympathy from now on.

She glanced down at Pippi. "Okay, girl, it seems Simon's going to be busy for a while longer, so why don't you and I start on that trunk again to try to find out about that mystery dress."

Pippi stood on her hind legs and barked.

"Good. I'm glad you agree, because we need a distraction right about now. Let's go." She started for the kitchen door, then remembered she'd need a flashlight to find the light cord, grabbed her phone, and with Pippi close on her heels, trotted up the stairs to the attic.

Addie kneeled reverently on the floor in front of the trunk. "Fingers crossed I can find something in here that's going to answer this mystery," she said, glancing at Pippi keeping watch by the small attic room door. Addie closed her eyes and lifted the lid, then opened them and gazed inside.

"Hmm, where to start, where to start. Trinket boxes, some 1950s hair scarves, a pair of women's saddle shoes. No, no." She pulled them from the trunk and laid them on the floor beside her. "Ooh . . . a scrapbook, now this might be something." She eagerly lifted it from its resting place and gasped. "What do we have here?"

Addie squinted into the trunk, trying to wrap her head around what she was seeing. On the bottom was an ornately hand-carved wooden box, about the size of a bread box. But it wasn't the exquisitely carved, hand-painted birds and flowers that adorned the small chest that caused her breath to come in short, rapid succession. It was the engraved silver plate on the top that said *To My Beloved Granddaughter.*

"Pippi! My great-great-great-grandmother must have given this to Great-Aunt Anita. Can you believe it? What a find!" Addie said, and lovingly pulled it from the trunk and sat back, placing it on her knees. "Wow." She admiringly stroked her fingers over the smooth wooden finish of the box and tried to force the lid, but it was locked. Addie pulled the key ring from her pocket, slipped the smallest key into the lock, and turned it until it clicked.

"Okay." Her fingers itched as she raised the lid, and her heart beat erratically. She counted, "One, two, three, four, five," as she ran her fingers over the clothbound spines. After picking up the nearest book, she opened it to the title page. "Whoa! Pippi, do you know what this is?" Pippi lifted her little head from where she napped, let out a soft sigh, curled her head back into her tail and closed her eyes. "Well, if you did, missy, your heart would be jumping out of your chest like mine is." Addie picked up the next book and laughed as she took a look inside it, and the next and the next.

"This is a complete first edition set of A. A Milne's first four Pooh books. See, here's *When We Were Very Young; Winnie-the-Pooh; Now We Are Six;* and *The House at Pooh Corner.* Oh, Pippi, I can't believe this." She scanned the cover of the last book still in the box and frowned with disbelief. "This can't be what I think it is, can it?" She opened the book to the title page, and her heart squeezed against her chest wall. "I can't believe this. It's a 1922 copy of Margery Williams Bianco's *The Velveteen Rabbit.*" Her eyes scanned the page and she struggled to catch her breath as she read the inscription across the bottom.

For my beautiful granddaughter on her first birthday . . . this book was given to me by your grandfather on the day I told him I was expecting our first, and only, child. I now pass this token of his love for this story on to you.

Love, Grandmamma Anita.

"Grandmamma Anita?"

Chapter 8

It was interesting for Addie to discover that her great-aunt Anita was named for her grandmother, considering that when Addie had her family tree traced a few years ago, that information hadn't jumped off the page at her. Surely, she would have noticed something that significant, right?

Confused, Addie dug through her files in the desk in the living room and flipped through page after page of the information she had gathered for a previous case about her family. There were her findings about the Greyborne-Davenport feud. Her early family links to the pirates who once inhabited Greyborne Harbor, and the beginnings of her family's mercantile business and how it led to the establishment of the upper part of Greyborne Harbor and the lower old town by the original harbor town site.

Then she came across some of the microfilm copies in the *Greyborne Harbor Daily News* that she'd made at the time and scanned through the pages, stopping when one article in particular caught her eye. It was the one about the daughter of one of her early ancestors in Greyborne Harbor, a young woman named Emily Greyborne. Addie recalled that this was a woman she had wanted to know more about. The *Daily News* had reported her as a bit of a detective, and that had intrigued Addie then as it did now. According to the newspaper, Emily Greyborne was responsible for discovering the identity of a man the police had sought in regard to the theft of a first edition Bible on loan to one of the local churches.

"I bet she would have figured out the mysterious wedding dress by now," Addie muttered, and continued to search through the file box. Finally, at the bottom of the file box, was the family tree she had commissioned a local historian to complete for her.

And there it was in black and white. Her aunt Anita *was* named after her grandmother Anita née Barrows, who had married Roger Greyborne. "Well, I'll be." Addie continued to read over the names on the branches of the family tree and she did notice this time, that naming following generations after preceding ancestors was common practice in the Greyborne family. But Addie noticed something else. Her great-aunt Anita's father, John, was the first one listed but he was followed by three other children's names.

Addie dashed over to the coffee table, retrieved

The Velveteen Rabbit from the chest and opened it to the title page, rereading the inscription at the bottom.

For my beautiful granddaughter on her first birthday . . . this book was given to me by your grandfather on the day I told him I was expecting our first, and only, child. I now pass this token of his love for this story on to you.

Love, Grandmamma Anita.

"Our first and only child?" Addie glanced back over the papers on her desk and then back at the book in her hands. That didn't make sense. It clearly states that Anita *one* had four children with her husband, Roger, and their names and years of birth and death were listed.

Addie wrestled with these thoughts as she tried to settle in for the night. She played over a dozen different scenarios and the only one that made sense was her great-great-great-grandmother Anita perhaps had only planned on having one child, or she had been told after a difficult delivery she couldn't have any more and then the other three came along unexpectedly.

That must have been it, right? Addie pounded her fist into her pillow and fought to find the sleep she desperately needed. It was going to be a trying day dealing with the Simon and Laurel issue, and she'd have to be at her best mentally and with a clear head to handle whatever fresh crisis Laurel threw her way.

After a sleepless night, Addie grabbed her phone from the bedside table, and trotted down the stairs to the kitchen to make coffee and feed Pippi her breakfast. Then she headed to the living room to retrieve the photo albums on the coffee table, took a sip of her fresh morning brew, sat down, crossed her legs, and settled into the sofa's comfy cushions. After a quick check of her cell, where she hoped to find a message from Simon, she frowned when there wasn't one and tossed her phone on the sofa beside her, then pulled the first album onto her lap, and began scanning photos.

She skimmed through the first few pages as they were mainly a recap of Anita's high school friends: a few of Anita's mother, Amelia, and one particular one of her father, John, such a sour-faced man he was. However, she paused when she came to a photo of a young woman who looked exactly like the portrait of Maisie Radcliff that she'd seen last year in Pen Hollow—Addie's high school boyfriend Tony Radcliff's grandmother. Now she was getting somewhere and the inscriptions in the books she'd found signed by Anita made complete sense. They *were* friends.

Addie set the photo album beside her and reached over to the stack of her aunt's journals on the table. In her reading, Anita had only arrived at the college in Boston and hadn't made any mention of Maisie. It was clearly time for Addie to do some speed reading, certain that the key to the dress must come from her aunt's three years spent at Garland, since it had been a while since she'd even mentioned the name of Billy Douglas. He couldn't possibly be the one she'd intended to wear the dress for. She must have met someone new after she left Greyborne Harbor, and her friendship with Maisie might hold a clue.

Addie jumped when there was a thumping sound from the front foyer. Pippi yipped, leapt up from her bed beside the sofa, and raced to the front door. Addie looked at the mantel clock. Twelve o'clock. It was too early for Serena to stop in. She said she couldn't be here until later because her mom had an appointment in Salem this morning. Paige and Catherine were both supposed to be at the bookstore, so it must be Simon. She laughed, a sense of relief gushing through her, and grinned as she flung the door open.

"Marc?"

"Hi, I hope I'm not disturbing you?" he asked, removing his police cap, causing tufts of his chestnut-brown hair to stand on end. "But Serena can't make it today. Ollie has a bit of an earache it seems, and she has to take him to the doctor, so she asked me to stop in and check on you."

"You're kidding?" Addie shook her head in disbelief. "I'm not sure why she thinks I need someone to keep vigil over me."

"You can't blame her. She told me about the other bombshell that got dropped on you this week, and she was just worried about how you're dealing with it all."

"As you can see, I'm fine, but . . ." She stood back and gestured to the foyer. "Did you want to come in, just to make sure so you can make a full report back to my nursemaid?"

"Sure," he said with a chuckle and stepped inside. "I would have come earlier but things are crazy at the station right now, you know the whole Valerie thing. This is the first chance I've had to slip out, and I'd love a cup of coffee right about now." His brown eyes implored her with a hopeful glint.

"What do you mean *the whole thing with Valerie?*" asked Addie, following him into the living room.

"I'm sure Simon has told you what happened yesterday?"

"You mean about Valerie Price dying?"

"Yeah, it's just this case has us baffled," he said, taking a seat in one of the chairs by the window.

"What do you mean this *case* has you baffled?" asked Addie, perching on the sofa across the coffee table from him.

"I mean we can't figure out how the poison was administered."

"Poison?"

"Yes, I thought Simon told you. He's been in the lab all night testing everything we took in as evidence from the scene, but we're no farther ahead."

"Evidence? Scene? I thought she died of a heart attack." Addie rose to her feet and pinned him with a mystified look. "Marc, what are you saying? That Valerie was murdered?"

Marc averted her questioning gaze. "I guess you never heard the rest of it, did you? I'm sorry to spring this on you because I know you were fond of her, and I just assumed you knew, you said Simon told you."

Addie slid back down onto the sofa and shook her head. "It appears he left out a few details." She glanced at Marc. "And you say he was in the lab all night testing items taken into evidence from the crime scene?" Now there was a small blessing, at least he hadn't spent the night holding Laurel in his arms trying to console her, but still . . . "Valerie? Murdered? Who would want that sweet woman dead?"

"Well, yesterday a few of the attendees we interviewed threw out your name, for one."

"I beg your pardon. I never wanted the woman dead."

Then Addie reminded herself that sweet woman's news had been exactly what sent Addie's life hurling sideways. *Don't kill the messenger* she reminded herself when she could feel pressure building at the base of her skull.

"Look, Marc, I hope you're joking because killing Valerie wouldn't change the fact that Simon and Laurel are married. As my father used to say, don't kill the messenger; she didn't cause this, she only stopped an even bigger mistake from happening."

"Good, and I was joking. You were one of the few people in town who didn't drop by that day, so unless you gave her some slow-acting poison last Saturday at the church right there under everyone's noses . . ."

"Actually, I doctored her tea last year in Pen Hollow."

"What?"

Addie couldn't stop the internal eye roll from happening when she saw the look on Marc's face. "That was the last time I've seen her since that little incident in the church, so it must have taken a year to have its effect, right?"

"Right," he said, sitting back grinning, "which is why you are one of the few people not on the suspect list."

"That's good, but I just can't imagine who would

want that lovely lady dead. It doesn't make sense. Are you certain she was poisoned?"

"Yes. It's clear she was murdered, and it was poison."

"So, an autopsy was done? That's usual for someone with as many health conditions as she was suffering from, isn't it? She told me all about it last year."

"Yes, normally it would have been put down to natural causes, but in this case . . ."

"What else did you find at the scene?"

"It's not what else we found. It's who else was there. In this case the coroner was a guest at the tea."

"Simon was still there when she collapsed?" Addie tried to wrap her head around what Marc was saying. "But I thought he was going to leave with Mason and go for some father-son bonding time."

"Apparently he didn't." Marc shrugged. "He said there was lots of commotion, as you can imagine, when she hit the floor, and by the time Simon got over to her she was already gone and there was nothing he could do. However, later, when Catherine told him that Valerie had grabbed her throat, not her chest, as you'd think someone with a heart condition would do, it made Simon curious, so he decided to do an autopsy just to be certain of the cause of death."

"And he found poison in her system? That's just so weird. As far as I know everyone loved Valerie. I can't imagine anyone wanting her dead."

"It seems someone did because he discovered a very high, extremely toxic amount of something called tetrahydrozoline in her system."

"What's that?"

"It's an active ingredient found in some brands of eye drops."

"Could the overdose have been caused by her overusing eye drops maybe?"

"No, Simon said something like that could have made her sick, but the amount and concentration in her system tells him it was definitely ingested."

"You mean something as common as eye drops in her . . . say, tea, is what killed her. That's scary because eye drops are sold over the counter, and anyone can buy them."

"Yup, and according to Simon, the amount he found in her system was equivalent to two ten milliliter bottles. He said normally that amount could take hours to kill a healthy person or just make them very ill. However, combined with her various health issues and her other medications, she was dead within about fifteen minutes of ingesting it."

"So, someone doctored her tea or something else she ate?"

"Since eye drops are a liquid, it was more than likely the tea, but the problem is he's tested everything—the teacup she drank from, the tea itself, and there are no traces of the poison."

"Did you check everyone's handbags before the guests left, you know for empty bottles?"

"No, at that point we were just there because a death had occurred and no one suspected foul play, until the autopsy was done later due to Simon's curiosity."

"Well, you do have a tough one to solve then, don't you?"

"What do you mean?"

"I'm sure, given the age of many of the guests in attendance, over half of them carry eye drops in their handbags all the time, right?"

"Yup, we have the means, more suspects than I care to count, but until I can figure out a motive, not one of them is viable."

These were all Addie's friends, and everyone loved Valerie; no one she could think of would have had a motive. It was hard to see anyone as a suspect, but yet there was a dead body proving otherwise.

"What makes it tougher is that since it was an open house, some people just dropped by, got a look at Mason and Laurel, said their hellos and then left without signing the guest book. It looks like we'll have our hands full tracking down all the guests to get statements."

Addie shrugged. "Yup, like I said, you've got a big suspect pool because dry eyes and allergies are common this time of year. Nearly everyone I know uses them."

"I'm starting to see that, and what makes it more complicated is Simon said that a certain age group would need eye drops for something called age-related macular degeneration and there were a lot of that age group in attendance."

"Did Valerie use them?"

"Apparently, at least there was a bottle in the bathroom and her niece confirmed they belonged to her."

"Is there any way Simon can find out exactly what brand killed her?"

"No, they all have roughly the same ingredients, so it could have been any of them."

"All I can say is good luck with this one. It appears to me that you may have a gray-haired killer on the loose in Greyborne Harbor."

"It sure looks that way, doesn't it?" Marc's eyes narrowed as he scanned her living room, darting from the crumpled chip bags and candy wrappers strewn across the coffee table and onto the floor. "If you'll forgive me, but you are looking a little pale and those dark circles under your eyes tell me you haven't been out of the house much this past week."

"Pippi and I went for a run this morning."

"A run?" He chuckled. "That's a new activity for you, isn't it?"

"*Run* might not be the correct word. I guess we could say more like a light jog, but yes. It helps clear my mind."

"Hum, now I know you're not doing well, no matter the stoic face you're trying to put on for me. The Addie Greyborne I know doesn't run or *jog*," he said with a soft laugh and a head shake. "So I've got an idea. Why don't you come to the station with me?"

"As one of your hundreds of suspects?" She leaned forward. "Let me save you some time, Police Chief Chandler. I don't use eye drops."

"No . . ." he said thoughtfully, staring at her. "But clearly you need to get out, and I could use a set of fresh eyes on what little evidence we do have."

Addie was taken aback. "Seriously? You want me to help you out with this?"

"Yes, I'm serious. I've looked at the photos we've collected so far from everyone's phones at the tea until my eyes crossed, and I can't see anything out of the ordinary or how it would explain the eye drops she ingested."

"First, I think I'm too emotionally involved with this whole family to be considered impartial, and second of all, after all the times you've told me to keep my nose out of police business, now you're asking for my help?"

"Just your fresh eyes. Please, will you take a look at the crime scene photos and see if you can spot anything I'm missing?"

Addie recalled her great-great-great-great-aunt Emily finding the stolen bible, and the other stories she had read about in Anita's later journals, pertaining to some of Anita's own detective work in tracking down first editions she wanted to purchase. Then there was the time Anita assisted a museum curator in France in finding some stolen paintings and artifacts that were lost in World War II. Maybe it was the discovery of the mysterious wedding dress, or the fact that Marc had always told her to leave detective work up to the professionals, but she'd come to see that was impossible because the more she read, the more she could see it was in her blood. She owed it to the long line of Greyborne women amateur sleuths to keep up the family tradition, didn't she?

"Of course I'll help you," she said and sat back. A soft smile touched her lips as she cast a glance at Anita's photo album on the coffee table.

Chapter 9

Marc led Addie up the metal staircase to the rear door of the old sandstone police station, punched in the access code on the security keypad and stepped back to allow her to enter. "I'll meet you in my office. I just want to go downstairs and check on any latest developments with Lieutenant Fowley."

"Could you tell Jerry thank you for the beautiful crystal vase and let him know I'll be returning it to him and his wife sometime later in the week?"

"You're going to return all your wedding gifts?"

Addie paused in the doorway leading into the front of the station house. "Um, yes. It seems like the proper thing to do."

"But aren't you and Simon just rescheduling the wedding?"

"Yes, but . . ." Addie hesitated. "With all the latest developments it might be a while and . . ." She raised her shoulders in a helpless gesture.

Marc's chocolate-brown eyes softened and he nodded his understanding. "Okay, I'll be back up in a minute," he said and trotted down the stairs to the lower offices and holding cells.

"Chief Chandler wants me to wait in his office," Addie responded to the desk sergeant's curious look when she came around the doorway behind him, and smiled when, with a hand gesture, the young man motioned for her to go ahead.

The murmur of the unfamiliar voice of the desk sergeant on the telephone behind her made Addie yearn for the days when she knew all the staff here. She never realized, until now, how much she missed seeing a recognizable face like Jerry's or Simon's sister Carolyn's behind the desk.

Yes, things had changed over the years, but as she slid into one of the two chairs in front of Marc's desk and ran her fingers over the smooth wooden armrests, there was a small comfort in knowing not everything had changed. This still felt like her chair. The chair she would sit in for hours and discuss her latest theories about a case with Marc. It actually felt good to be here today, and at his invitation too, and not because she barged in and demanded he hear her out, even though he had warned her to stay out of a case. She shook her head in disbelief that she could have been so brazen and wondered what he must have been thinking all those times. Her pang of guilt was quickly replaced by a sinking sensation in the pit of her stomach when Marc sauntered into the office and took his seat behind the desk.

"Are you sure you want my help with this and you're not just saying it because of some obligation you feel as my best friend's brother and the need to distract me from my own issues?"

"No." His head snapped up and he pinned his gaze on hers. "I told you I needed a fresh set of eyes on this."

"But what about Ryley Brookes? You were with her at the wedding. Wouldn't she be a better choice?"

"Ryley? No, I wasn't with her."

"But we saw you two together in the church."

"Yes, she stood with us, but we're not together."

"You're not?"

"No, Ryley and I are ancient history. She's dating that fellow you hired as the photographer for your wedding."

"Paul Green?"

"Yeah, I think that's his name. He has a studio in Salem?"

Addie nodded.

"Yeah, I guess he does some work for the Salem Police Department and they've been a thing for about a year now. She just didn't want to sit alone while he was busy taking pictures and"—he shrugged—"so she joined me, Mom, and the kids."

"I see." Addie shifted awkwardly in her chair. "So, you didn't ask me here out of—"

"No Addie, there is no ulterior motive. Since you are one of the few people not on the suspect list and since you've helped"—he cleared his throat— "solve a case or two in the past, I was just hoping that . . ." He dropped his gaze to the file folders in front of him.

"Then even after all you've said to me in the past, you do need my investigative skills?" A glow of triumph swept through her.

"I wouldn't go that far." He squirmed uneasily. "More like your keen observation skills."

"I'll take that. What exactly is it you want me to *observe*?"

"You knew the victim—"

"I only met her last year, and we chatted some, but I wouldn't go so far as to say I knew her."

"I get that, but you knew her well enough to have gotten to know some of her behaviors and mannerisms, right?"

"I suppose."

"What I want is for you to look through some of the photos we've collected so far from the phones of people who attended the tea on Sunday."

"Yeah," she said, not able to contain the hint of sarcasm that edged into her voice. "I guess that would have been one of those events that *everyone* would be snapping pictures of."

"Yes, it seems most people who went wanted to get a picture of the woman who . . . and the . . . boy . . ."

"Who is Simon's wife and Simon's son? That's okay, you can say it."

"I'm sorry, Addie. Considering the circumstances, I know this must be very hard for you."

"Yes, it is, and because of those circumstances I'm not sure I'm the best person for you to be asking for any help with this case."

"That's exactly why I am asking you. You are one

of the few people who wasn't there, and you knew the victim. Not as well as say Catherine or Paige, but since we can't rule anyone out at this point—"

Addie pinned Marc with her look of shock. "You aren't seriously considering them as suspects in this murder, are you?"

"Like I said, at this stage we can't rule anyone out, and they were both in attendance for the entire afternoon."

Addie started to rise to her feet. "I can't help you with this witch hunt. I'm sorry. Catherine and Paige both cared for Valerie a great deal." She started for the door. "And there is no way I'm going to help you build a case against one or both of two of my dearest friends."

"Wait, Addie," Marc called, rising to his feet. "That's exactly why I need your fresh eyes to look at the photos, to help me rule them out, not to implicate them."

She paused at the door and drew in a deep breath, keeping her back to him. "Are you sure you're not using me to make an assessment of their close interactions with Valerie so you can wrap this up quickly? I know that DA Wilson is facing an election soon and would probably like nothing better than this notch on his belt before he heads onto the campaign trail."

"Addie, seriously? I said there was no ulterior motive, and I meant it. I don't give a hoot about the DA's reelection hopes. We have a murder in Greyborne Harbor, and I'll be darned if I'm going to be as cavalier about it as Sheriff Turner was last year in Pen Hollow."

Addie couldn't stop the shiver that niggled up her spine with the recollection of the most botched murder investigation she had ever been associated with. "Okay," she said, turning to him. "As long as this isn't a witch hunt and you're not trying to score points."

"I swear." He crossed his heart. "Now please come back to the desk and take a look at the photos and tell me what you see that I don't."

Addie settled back into her chair as Marc slid the file folder across the desk to her. "I want you to look at the photos we've collected so far from some of the phones and tell me if you can spot anything unusual or out of the ordinary in Valerie's behavior. Is there anything you can see from her interactions with people that might give us a lead on who could have slipped the eye drops into her tea and then maybe cleaned up after, which is why we can't find the source?"

Addie flipped open the file folder and scanned the first image. There was Valerie, clearly making introductions of a devastatingly striking Laurel Hill, who, with her cascading waves of long, dark hair looked like a glamorous 1940s movie star. Then Addie's breath caught. Beside her was a young man, the spitting image of Simon—shocks of black hair, piercing sea-blue eyes, and the same dimples in his cheeks that Simon got when he grinned. This was going to be harder on Addie than she'd first thought. Her hand hesitated as she began to flip to the next photo.

"Are you okay?"

She nodded and studied the next picture in the

stack. It soon became clear to Addie as she examined one photo after the other, that their next book club meeting might be interesting. They were all there: Catherine and Paige, of course, she knew they were attending the tea, but she also spotted Ida Biggs; Connie, the clerk from the courthouse; even the local real estate agent Maggie Hollingsworth was there with her mother, Vera, and her daughter Elle, who worked for Serena.

She glanced over the next image. Of course, Doctor Timmons and his wife were there. Laurel had bought his practice, so that stood to reason, but she was surprised to see a photo of all of them talking to Martha and Bill alongside Martha's daughter Mellissa. Wow, was Addie the only one in town who didn't attend?

"I'd say all these photos are from early in the afternoon. "See"—she pointed—"in all these, there's a small group in the room and Valerie appears to be greeting newcomers." She paused at the image of Simon standing beside Mason, beaming like a proud father. "I wonder why Simon changed his mind about leaving early with Mason?" she said in a stage whisper as she studied the image of a glowing Laurel beside him, and then with a brusque flip of her wrist scanned the next image in the pile.

"Actually, my cousin Nikki overheard Laurel and him talking and she encouraged him to stay because she . . ." Marc's words trailed off as he studied Addie's flinching gaze.

"Because she what?" Addie snapped, and flipped over another photo.

"Nothing."

"It's okay, you can tell me. There's not much I haven't already heard about Laurel's needs for Simon this past week."

"I assumed she meant that she needed his moral support because she was nervous about meeting so many new people, that's all." His voice dropped off to a whisper.

"So, even your cousin was there?" Addie tried to force a hint of lightness into her voice as she abruptly changed the topic. "But she doesn't know anyone in town, why would she attend?"

"Moral support for my mother, who went because . . . she was curious, I suppose."

"Yes, I suppose she was just like everyone else in these photos, but I don't see anything in these. My guess is it was too early in the event and you need to find some photos taken as the afternoon wore on. That's where you might find something to give you a hint about who the murderer might be." Addie dropped the photo she held and shoved the stack back across the desk to Marc, but took a quick glance at it again and edged forward to retrieve it. "Wait, here's something."

"What is it?"

"It might not be much, but look at the way Elle's holding her camera in these last three photos. I'd say she's taking a video for her social media. She's not holding it like people do when they're taking a still photo."

Marc slipped the pictures from Addie's fingers and studied them. "You might be right. Like I said, we've just started to collect what people have on their phones. Let me check with Jerry"—he pressed the intercom button on the desk phone—"and see if anything from Elle has turned up yet."

Addie leaned back in her chair and stared around the office. It had been a while since she was in here, but not much had changed. The old clock still hung on the wall behind the desk, the file cabinet doors appeared as though they'd had their fair share of being slammed shut. She recalled the time Marc caught her going through one and darn near took her hand off. When he hung up from Jerry she quirked an eyebrow. "Well, what did he say?"

"He said they're just downloading the latest batch now and when they're done, he'll email them to me."

"Okay," she said, rising to her feet. "If there's anything on there you want me to look at, you can forward them to me, but I have to go. I really hate leaving Pippi on her own too long; she's used to going out with me, and I have a mystery of my own I'm working on too."

"A murder mystery?" Marc asked with a chuckle as he rose to his feet. "Because I certainly didn't ask for your help today so you'd run off half-cocked and start investigating this on your own. I only told you what I did because I know Simon will fill you in anyway when you see him, so—"

"Relax, Chief, this one's all yours. No interference from me. Mine is something a little closer to home and less nefarious."

"Did Pippi lose Baxter again? You know I could help you look for him—that is, if you want some company?"

If Addie wasn't mistaken, the tips of his ears reddened with his words and she chuckled softly. "Thanks anyway, but I think you have your hands full with this case and besides, unless 1950s wedding dresses are your specialty, I'm not sure you can help."

"Now"—he folded his arms and perched on the edge of his desk—"I'm intrigued. Please tell."

"There's not much to tell. Serena and I discovered an old wedding dress in my attic and I'm trying to track down who it belonged to and figure out why it was never worn."

"Hmm, now that would be a mystery worthy of your detective skills."

"Why, because it doesn't involve a dead body for once?"

"Because you said it was from the 1950s and your aunt was never married, so it stands to reason it was hers and the real mystery would be as to why that wedding never took place."

"Yeah." She glanced back over her shoulder, grinning. "Or maybe there's no mystery and someone cursed the Greyborne women, which is why now we're collecting unworn wedding dresses."

Chapter 10

Karma or cursed? Addie wasn't certain, but as she pulled up in front of her early 1800s, three-story Queen Anne Victorian home and turned off the ignition, she wondered about the latter. She used to think she was paying for something that she had done—like when she was ten and ran away from home, even though it was only to hide inside a moving box in the basement. When her father and grandmother eventually discovered her, her grandmother told her she would pay one day for causing them such a fright.

It was natural for Addie to believe later in her life, when her fiancé, David, was murdered, and then her father was killed in that somewhat suspicious crash on the switchback above the Pen Hollow peninsula, that perhaps her grandmother had been right. However, with the discovery of the mystery wedding dress in her great-aunt's attic, a whole new light had been shed on Addie's recent beliefs. Maybe when she jokingly referred to a Greyborne curse, she hadn't been wrong.

She stepped out onto her driveway and gazed up at the apartment above her three-car garage. She missed the days when Serena and Zach were her tenants. It was times like this she would have trotted up to their door, knocked, and said, *Let's have a drink, I need to talk.* Serena would oblige and they'd go into the main house and spend hours solving the problems of the world, then Serena would toddle home across the driveway.

Yes, so many changes. She sighed and closed the door of her Mini Cooper. "Except you, old girl," she said, patting the roof. "I need to keep a few constants in my life, don't I?"

Addie shored herself up to shake off her melancholy and trotted up the double-wide steps to the covered porch, turned the key in the lock, and flipped on the foyer light as she stepped inside.

A yip from her furry little friend broke the silence in the house and the click-clack of tiny feet could be heard as they left the area rug and raced across the wooden floor of the living room. A grinning Pippi did her dancy-prancy greeting and twirled around at Addie's feet. She picked her up and cuddled Pippi in her arms. The little Yorkipoo responded with a lick across her cheek and another yip of excitement.

"Are you ready for your dinner?"

Another yip as the little dog squiggled and squirmed in her arms. Addie let her down and she raced down the wide corridor into the kitchen at the back of the house. "Okay, I get it, you're starving. So am I. It's been a long day."

Addie set her handbag on the corner of the island, then retrieved the bag of kibble from the pantry and filled her little friend's bowl. She proceeded to forage through the cupboards to find something for her own evening meal. She grabbed a box of cereal, shook it, got a clean bowl out of the dishwasher, opened her fridge, seized the jug of milk, removed the cap, sniffed, nodded, and poured the last of it into her bowl.

"Now here's a homemade meal." She chuckled and strolled back down the hallway into the living room. She eased onto the corner of her large sofa, careful not to spill the last remnants of something that passed as food in her house, and gingerly edged her phone out of the side pocket of her blouse. She tapped a note to *buy groceries* into her calendar and sat back savoring every morsel of the cinnamon-sugar-coated dinner in front of her.

When she was finished, she glanced down at the screen of her phone beside her and saw her phone ringer was on silent and that she'd missed a call from Catherine when she was enjoying her *dinner.* She clicked on voice messages and listened.

"I know I said I'd be by today with your dinner but I got busy with Laurel and the Timmonses. We went to her aunt's house in Pen Hollow to pick out a burial dress for the funeral. Sorry, but it's been a trying day and now I have to try to get some food into Laurel. It's all so sad and she's such a mess. Maybe call Paige and see if she can bring you something, but I know she was busy at the

bookstore this afternoon. I felt bad about leaving early but she told me to go. Laurel really couldn't have coped with everything herself and the Timmonses are no help because they are as broken up about it as she is. It's hard on them too, as they've known Valerie for so many years. Anyway, Simon is supposed to be dropping by later to update us on further developments, maybe that will help settle her. I'll call you again later, bye for now."

"Hmm, so he's seeing Laurel tonight too?" Addie scowled at the phone. "Well, I'm glad he found time to fit me into his obviously busy schedule. That is, if he even shows up like he said he would," she snapped, and tossed her phone on the coffee table.

Then a pang of remorse hit her. How could she be so selfish? She reminded herself that a very nice lady had been murdered. "It wasn't Valerie's fault she just happened to be the aunt of his . . . *wife*"— she gulped—"and the great-aunt of his . . . *son*." And to make it worse, the boy had only just met Valerie. Addie couldn't help but feel bad that he would never get to know, like she had, what a wonderful person Valerie Price truly was.

Addie blew out a deep breath and got a grip— for the umpteenth time today—on herself and all the erratic emotions the whole sordid situation had sent bubbling up inside her. "Okay, Pippi, ready for a run? Heaven knows I need it, even if you don't."

Gasping and fighting to fill her burning lungs with much-needed oxygen, Addie stumbled through her back door into the kitchen with Pippi panting at her feet. "Simon? You made it," she managed to wheeze, patting her aching chest.

"Hi, beautiful, I hope you don't mind. I went home and had a quick shower, but of course my cupboards are bare as I didn't plan on ever having to cook there again."

"Yeah," she gasped, finally slowing her racing heart by downing a glass of cold water. "Neither of us planned on being here, did we? Speaking of which, did you talk to your landlord to see if you could stay in your apartment after the first of the month?'

"He's rented it out already."

"What are you going to do? I mean, all your stuff's in boxes isn't it, so that when we came back from Hawaii all we had to do was load it up and move it in here?"

"I guess I just assumed that we'd still go ahead with that plan, but meanwhile I'm starving, so what can we make for dinner?"

"There's some dry cereal"—she pointed to the pantry—"and half a pound of butter, so knock yourself out."

"Um, I don't think so, thanks. Gotta watch my girlish figure as I'll still have to fit into that tuxedo." He leaned over to kiss her cheek just as she moved to set her glass on the counter.

"Let's try that again." She tipped her head up and his lips brushed over hers. "That's better," she murmured, "and yes. I can't wait to see you in that tux again." Her fingers slid down the collar of his shirt. "It's all a blur to me now," she said demurely, "but if I recall, you looked extremely handsome that day. So, I'm relieved to hear that you're still planning on going ahead with our wedding."

"Of course I am. Why wouldn't I be?"

"It's just that with everything . . ."

"You don't want to?"

"It's just that we don't know when the wedding will be rescheduled."

"But it will, Addie, and as soon as the annulment is granted, everything will work out as we planned. What's this really about? Don't you want me to move in now?"

"I don't know." The back of her hand swiped across her forehead. "I'm not sure. Everything has changed so much. It's not just the fact you're married to another woman but that you also have a—"

"Child?"

She winced and nodded.

"It changes nothing between us. You are my soul mate; the love of my life. I've known that since the first day we met for dinner at the Grey Gull Inn and over appetizers you quizzed me about a murder," he said with a soft chuckle.

"Maybe I'm just having a wobble because of all that's going on and—"

"Now, enough of this crazy talk. Kiss me again to remind both of us why we fell in love in the first place."

She wrapped her arms around his neck and stood on tiptoes, her lips hungrily searching for his.

His phone rang out an emergency alert. He cringed and pulled away, checking his phone. "Sorry, it looks like I'll have to take a rain check on dinner. I told Laurel I'd be by later tonight to update her, but if she needed me before then to call, and it seems Mason has taken off and she can't find him."

His words cut the moment like a knife, and a wall of emotions hit her in the face as he pulled away. Even though his work involved shifts and long hours, the times when they could be together had always been special and belonged only to them. But things had changed. Even if he couldn't see it or wasn't experiencing the same roller coaster of emotions that she was, the day Valerie Price shoved the papers into his hands, her life—their lives—had changed.

A barrage of the very images she had grappled with since Laurel came back into his life flashed through her mind like a newsreel being played out right there in his apologetic eyes, and she could see their future.

"You know what? I can't do this right now." Addie danced a step back. "I thought I could when I got over my initial anger and shock, but . . . no." She nodded in resignation. "I can't because when I told you I loved you that first time, it was the hardest thing I've ever done because I was so scared that you would die if I did."

"I remember." He looked at her curiously. "Are you saying now that you really don't love me?"

"No, that's not it at all. I guess, I'm saying I realized later my fear of telling you I loved you was for nothing because you didn't die like David and my dad . . . but now you're gone nonetheless. The fact is, you and Laurel have a son together, and she brought him back here to live with her. You and she are still married, and you're his father."

"That changes nothing between us."

"Yes, it does, can't you see that? Simon, you have always been the man who does the right thing. You waited until I put all my ghosts, dead and alive, to rest, but this time you're the one wrestling with a ghost, and yours is still very much alive, and you have a lifetime connection."

"I don't understand. What are you saying, Addie?"

"I'm saying," she took a deep breath, "that you have to see this through with Laurel, and this time, I will be the one to take a step back, just like you did when Marc and I were trying to figure out what we had and if we had a future together."

"But this is different. Laurel and I are ancient history."

"Not so ancient, Simon. Go, be with Laurel and find your son. They need you."

In silence, Addie walked him to the door, where he turned to her with a helpless look of regret.

"Look, Simon. I don't know where we're going or what the future holds for us, but I do know where you need to be right now, and it's not with me."

"I'm sorry about tonight."

"Oh, Simon." She shook her head. "It's not just about tonight. It's about all our future nights."

"What do you mean?"

"I mean Laurel is the mother of your son, and through him, you and she are bound together forever. If it's not this tonight, then it's something else, and always will be. Like I said, you've always been the man who does the right thing, and that's what I love most about you . . . but go, she called and they need you," she whispered.

"I'll be back as soon as I can, I promise," he said, caressing her cheek with his hand.

"No." She pulled away. "This, us, just isn't working right now. We both need time to figure out where we're going and how Laurel and Mason fit into our lives."

"But I love *you*," he murmured, his eyes glistening under the porch light.

"I know, and I love you, but . . ." *Just breathe, keep breathing.* She closed the door, muffling out the rest of his words.

Her shoulders heaved as she struggled to catch her breath. Then Pippi yipped from the back of the house. Her little nails clickety-clacked on the brick floor in the kitchen—the dance she did when she had to go out to relieve herself. Addie shored herself up, braced her wobbly knees, and marched toward her constant companion, but paused at the dining room doorway.

The table laden with gifts taunted her from where her friends had stored them out of her view last week. As she closed the double-wide pocket doors on the last remnants of her once happy-ever-after future, the crushing pain in her chest that she'd experienced earlier was replaced by a void that grew out of the pit of her stomach.

Chapter 11

Addie yawned and stretched, wiping the sleep from her eyes, and slowly opened them, gazing toward the brightly backlit bedroom curtains. If it was morning already, and she wasn't dreaming, this meant she had slept through the whole night for the first time since her almost wedding day.

She flipped back the duvet cover and stuffed her feet into the slippers at her bedside, peered out the curtains to confirm her awakened state and stumbled into the bathroom. She braced her hands on the vanity counter and peered at the bulging, red-rimmed eyes that reflected back at her. "Great, fish-eyes, just what I need this morning." She quickly splashed cold water over her face, in the hope it would reduce some of the puffiness in her eyelids. "That's what you get for crying yourself to sleep, girly."

She stood back and took another look. "But, what do you know. For the first time in weeks the dark circles under my eyes are barely noticeable and I don't recall tossing and turning all night." She glanced over her shoulder at Pippi, still stretched out on the bed, her little ears perked. "And you know what, my little friend?" Pippi raised her head and stared at her. "I actually feel refreshed this morning. Hmm, weird, hey?" She flipped off the light. "Okay, ready for breakfast?"

Pippi having gone outside to relieve herself, and her kibble poured, Addie sat on a stool at the island counter and settled into her morning routine. Well, as best she could since she didn't have a scrap of food in the house to enjoy with her morning coffee, something she'd made sure was always kept well stocked.

"Mmm," she sighed, and took another sip of her morning elixir. "Okay, here's the game plan, my friend." She glanced down at her furry companion finishing the last of her breakfast. "First, a much-needed trip to the grocery store, then we finally solve the mystery of the dress in the attic. How does that sound?"

Pippi sat back on her haunches and barked.

"I guess you're only agreeing because you know that means you get another hour of sleep while I'm out, right?"

Pippi let out an agreeable yip.

"Okay." She grabbed her handbag, headed for the front door, patted her friend on the head, with last-minute instructions to behave while mommy went to replenish the pantry, and flung the door open.

"Marc? What are you doing here?"

Marc stood with his hand raised in readiness to knock, and slowly lowered it. "Good morning." His face reddened. "I hope I'm not intruding?"

"I was just heading out to get groceries."

"Okay, well." He shuffled his feet and glanced back at his patrol car. "I can wait in there or come back later?"

The look on his face told her he wasn't just passing by and being friendly. "That's okay. What's up?" She stepped aside and gestured for him to enter.

"We've finished going through the guest list and tracking everyone down who signed in at Valerie's open house on Sunday."

"And?"

"And, I made a copy of all the photos and videos we've gotten off their phones so far." He held up a flash drive. "There's still a few more to go, but time's a-ticking and we're still not any closer to figuring out who killed Valerie, so I was hoping you could go through the rest of what we have, to this point."

She glanced into the living room at the stack of journals and the photo albums on the coffee table and inwardly cringed; so much for her plans. Then her tummy took that opportunity to moan out its own objections. "Oh," she said, rubbing her stomach. "Excuse me. Um, yeah, I could later, but really, I have to go buy something that passes as food first. My cupboards are completely bare and . . ." She couldn't muffle the repeated groaning and growling. "Sorry."

"No, it's me who should be sorry. I can't expect you to change your plans. I should have called first. You know what, I'll just go and you can call me later when you have time to review them."

Addie studied his taut face and the sheepish look in his eyes. This wasn't the same Marc she'd known since she moved to Greyborne Harbor. Where was the man full of bravado and confidence who would place an investigation above all else? "Are you okay?"

"Sure, why?"

"You just don't seem like the same Marc I know."

"I don't?"

She shook her head.

He puffed out a breath and lowered his gaze. "Truth be known, Addie, since . . . the whole scene in the church that day, and with all that's happened since, with Valerie and Simon and Laurel and now Mason, I really don't know how to talk to you anymore."

"What do you mean?" She dropped onto the arm of the sofa with a thud. "I'm the same person, or do you see me like some wilting delicate flower just like everyone else seems to think I am?"

"No!" He emphatically shook his head. "I definitely don't see you as that. It's just that . . ."

"What?"

"How do I put this?" He shuffled from one foot to the other, avoiding her questioning gaze. Then he raised his head, his eyes meeting hers. "I'll just be blunt."

"I would expect nothing different from you."

"Good, then it's just that since you've been dating Simon you and I worked out a relationship, friendship, whatever you want to call it, and then you were engaged and supposed to be married and we still managed to muddle through and be civil with each other, putting our past in the past."

"Yeah, so what are you saying?"

"I guess I'm saying that we managed to make that work and by now you were supposed to be married to him and we could continue to be the way we had made it, and now that you're not . . . Oh, I don't know what I'm trying to say. Just that everything has changed now and I don't know where that leaves us anymore."

It was Addie's turn to expel a deep breath as she struggled to grasp what he was saying. "I'd say, in all honesty, it leaves us exactly the same place as we've been for the past couple of years. We're friends, Marc, and since you asked for my help, I guess that also means we're coworkers, but as for anything else . . ." She gazed down at the floor and whispered, "I still love Simon and . . ."

"Okay." He braced his legs in a proper police stance. "Then this investigation is a priority, so I'll call Jerry and have him pick up two breakfast specials from the truck stop on the highway and we can eat while we scroll through the photos. You'll have to get groceries later."

Now there was the old take-charge Marc she knew, and she saluted. "Aye, aye, sir, but . . ." She pulled out her phone. "While you place the breakfast order, let me"—she tapped on her screen—"place a small grocery delivery order to tide me over. There . . . all done. Now, I'm all yours for the morning."

There was no mistaking the reddening of his

ears this time and she replayed her words back in her mind. "I mean, I will be at your professional disposal for the rest of the morning if that's what it takes." She dropped her gaze. *Must remember to choose my words more carefully next time.*

"Yum, yum, I'd forgotten how good their breakfast specials are," said Addie exchanging her empty plate for her laptop in front of her. "Now, back to these." She clicked the touch pad and started scrolling again through the images on the screen. "I can see why it took so long to track everyone down who dropped in to the tea. A few of them don't appear in more than one or two photos, but it looks like everyone in town was there at one time that afternoon."

"Yeah," said Marc, refilling her coffee cup. "I have everyone on the force taking their statements too. Like I said before, there's hundreds on the suspect list, just because they all had the opportunity to administer the poison. I'm just hoping we, *you*, can discover something that might give us a means, so we can narrow the pool down."

"I don't know," she said, clicking through images of Bin and Bev Thomas, the sisters that owned the Greyborne Point B&B, and Tara Wylie, the hairdresser from Tresses by Tara. "So far all I can say is Valerie appears happy and proud in all the photos she's in. I can't see any body language that she's exhibiting that might indicate tension or a problem with anyone in particular. You said you had videos, are they on here too?"

"Yeah, here . . ." Marc reached over her shoulder, clicked the mouse, and opened a new file. "It seems Elle wasn't the only one topping up her social media platforms. I think we have a few others too, including Paige's."

Addie hit play on the first one. It was short, but had a good angle shot of Valerie introducing Mason to what appeared to be a packed room. Addie's chest constricted when the shy-appearing young man raised his head and sheepishly smiled and said, "Hi, everyone. Glad to meet you all." His words didn't match his body language, as he looked like he wanted to run for the nearest door, but it was the look he gave Simon off to his left standing by the kitchen door that really tore at her heart strings. It cried, *Save me and get me the heck out of here!*

Addie clicked play on the next video. It was Paige's, and she was giving a soft, play-by-play commentary on who was who in her video. There were the usual announcements of guests as they arrived, and Mason's introduction, then a good shot of the floor that made Addie chuckle, but that's where this one ended.

"I'm still not seeing anything in these that gives any clues as to who the killer might be."

"Try Elle's; she seemed to have caught most of the event on hers. It's really long, so let's fast-forward a bit," he said, clicking and dragging the button on the bottom of the video. "There, this is a bit later in the afternoon and closer to the time of death."

"So, you've looked through these already?"

"Yeah, until my eyes crossed, but I didn't see anything. That's why I'm hoping you can spot something out of the ordinary in Valerie's behavior or someone else's that I've missed."

"Okay." Addie rubbed the back of her stiffening neck as she leaned into the screen, trying to focus again. Blurry vision and crossed eyes was something she could definitely relate to about now. Thankfully Marc had put the groceries away for her when they were delivered earlier, but right now, she would have loved that menial distraction.

"See anything?"

"No." She shook her head and then paused the video, squinting at the still image and then slid the button back to rewind a couple of frames, and then played the scene again. "Here's something." She pressed pause again and zoomed in on the still frame. "Look, see here, this woman with the long red hair, who I'm assuming is your cousin Nikki, is talking to Laurel by the kitchen door."

"There's nothing unusual about that, is there?"

"Look past them into the kitchen. See Valerie talking to Mrs. Timmons as they're, by the look of it, making more tea?"

"Yeah, I imagine with all those people there they went through a lot of tea that day, but since Valerie's making the pot, I doubt she poisoned herself, if that's what you're getting at?"

"No, it's too early in the afternoon for the poison, but look at the expression on her face. She appears perturbed, doesn't she?"

Marc leaned closer to the screen and then nodded. "You might be right. I wonder what they're talking about."

"I don't know, but look at Mrs. Timmons in the next frame." Addie pressed play, then pause. "See, she looks uneasy to me about whatever Valerie is saying to her." Addie glanced up at Marc hovering over her shoulder. "How techie are the officers in your IT department? Is there any way they can isolate that particular conversation from all the other noise in the room?"

"Ooh, I don't know. I'd have to check with them. I think that takes a higher quality of audio-visual equipment than we can fit into our budget."

"Well . . ." Addie glanced back and studied the screen, focusing on Valerie's tightly knitted brow. "It might not be anything, but on the other hand, it could mean a lot. Since it's the first indication we've had in all these images that something happened or was said that day that rattled her."

"Okay, I asked for your help, so I'll take your word for it that this might be a clue to what was brewing under the surface of this seemingly celebratory gathering."

Addie pulled the flash drive out of the port and handed it to Marc.

"That's okay," he said, waving it off. "I have a copy on my computer. You can keep that to look over again later."

Addie inwardly cringed. Even though there was nothing she liked more than a good mystery to solve, this one was a little different. It wasn't because she didn't care enough about Valerie to help find out who killed her. On the contrary, it was just that . . . She drew in a deep breath to steady her emotions. The whole Laurel and Simon situation had sent her world spinning sideways, no matter who the murderer turned out to be . . . unless, of course, it turned out to be Laurel. Then how would it look if Addie was the one pointing her finger at Simon's *wife*? She gulped. No, she needed a distraction right now, something to focus on that didn't involve a constant reminder of what happened that day in the church when her whole life seemingly came crashing down around her. "Okay, but remember, I have my own mystery to solve, so I might not get to this again for a while."

"Whenever, I just really appreciate any insight you can give me. Like I said before, this case has us baffled because everyone there that we've spoken to loved Valerie. No one seems to have had a motive, despite us having a dead body that was clearly poisoned by one of them."

Chapter 12

After Marc left for the station, Addie took a much-needed break and went for a brain-clearing run with Pippi along the cliff top behind her house. She paused on the path overlooking the harbor and tried to imagine her young aunt standing in this very spot over seventy years ago, grappling with her feelings about her demanding father and his wishes for her future. The vision of the mysterious dress hanging in Addie's attic taunted and called to her.

"Come on, Pippi, let's take a shortcut home through the trees. I'll be darned if I spend another night speculating. I need answers." She dashed off through the thick grove of trees. Pippi charged past her, leading the way through the back garden and up the stairs, where she danced gopher style, waiting for the treat she knew would be on the other side of the door.

Treats dispatched and Pippi clearly tuckered out after her run, Addie settled with a steaming cup of coffee into the corner of the sofa with the latest Anita journal in hand and began reading.

What a fab day today! I can't believe that my new friend, Maisie Chase of THE Chases of Boston, invited ME to go with her to Pen Hollow for the Christmas party season. Maisie and her boyfriend Arnold Radcliff have a friend they want me to meet. Maisie says he's a dreamboat and she thinks we'll hit it off. Even if we don't, I can't believe that I'll be spending the entire week at Windgate House with the Radcliffs.

Mama is not pleased. She says I should be in Greyborne Harbor because Christmas is for spending time with family, not with strangers and wearing a week's worth of party gowns they can't afford to buy me. But Father told her to hush, this was a chance of a lifetime and he's thrilled. He said I'll be rubbing shoulders with the best-of-the best from Boston, and he would make certain I was dressed as well as all the other girls. I'm over the moon that Father actually approves of something I want to do.

"Hmm, interesting. The old goat was probably only agreeing because he hoped she would find a rich husband to take care of her," Addie murmured, taking a sip of her now tepid coffee, and continued reading.

From there her aunt described preparations for the upcoming week and how Maisie hoped Arnold would ask her to marry him over the holidays. There

were pages and pages about dress shopping with
Maisie. Then, finally, Addie got to Anita's arrival at
Windgate House and paused, recalling her own first
impressions upon seeing what was referred to as
the holiday house for the Radcliffs.

> *I can't believe this house, and Maisie says their
> house in Boston is four times bigger and even more
> fab. I thought our house in Greyborne Harbor was
> big, but from the circular driveway and the columned
> entrance, this three-story Georgian mansion makes
> ours look teeny-weeny and the inside is just as
> glamorous. The housekeeper took us up a wide
> staircase that led up to a landing where two single
> staircases branched off to the left and right. Our
> rooms were to the right and guess what? We each
> got our own room for the week. With so many
> guests expected, I thought we would have to share
> for sure, but I guess since Maisie is Arnold's girl-
> friend, we're receiving the royal treatment, and I'll
> tell you, standing in the three-story grand foyer
> looking at the French doors into what Maisie
> called the ballroom on the second floor, I sure do
> feel like royalty today.*

"Yup, it truly is an amazing summer home, isn't
it, Pippi?" Addie said, glancing over at her little
friend curled up on her bed in front of the fireplace.

Pippi quirked an ear, let out a snort, and continued to snore softly.

Addie laughed, shook her head, and continued
reading more about Anita's first impressions of the
house: the massive orangery across the entire back

portion, and the Radcliff family's and the girls' preparations for the first party of the week that night. However, when she got to the part where Anita said, *Maisie was right, David Winthrop is a dreamboat!* Addie paused. She had heard of the Winthrops of Boston; they were old money and at one time owned most of the property in the business district.

> *Maisie was furious tonight with both David and Arnold. When she introduced me to David, she swears she saw sparks fly when he took my hand in his, smiled and said how nice it was to meet me. That was until this floozy—as Maisie called her because of her too-red lips and way too much rouge on her cheeks—showed up and ruined the moment. According to Maisie this girl is a local from the peninsula and the younger sister of one of the local boys they sometimes hang with. She said for the past two years, this girl has found an excuse every time she could to get close to David, and when her brother was invited to the parties this week, she took it upon herself to come too. When David handed me a refreshment and we were all chatting about how great the party was, she just sashayed up to him, draped her arm around him and pulled him onto the dance floor. That was the last time tonight that I talked to David. So much for us being a good match. But it didn't matter, I was just moon-eyed over the whole evening, I've never been to any parties like this in little old Greyborne Harbor. It really was a blast until I heard Maisie and Arnold arguing later in the grand hall. Maisie asked him if he had told*

*David about their plan for him to meet me this
weekend and he said yes and that was probably
why he spent the evening with Lucinda. He really
was shy around women he liked and he probably
didn't want to appear desperate. But he told her
not to worry, there was a whole week left of parties
and he'd make sure David and I had plenty of
time to get to know each other.*

*When Maisie and I headed up to bed, I told her
not to have a cow about David, because I found
their friend George Price kind of yummy.*

"Hmm, Pippi, this is interesting. I wonder if this
George Price is the same one that was married to
Valerie."

Pippi yawned, stretched, turned around in circles on her bed, and collapsed with an *oomph* and
began snoring again.

"Okay, I get it, you're napping and I'm interrupting, nah, nah, nah, but you're missing the best
parts." Addie shook her head and read on about
the week of partying. It was like she was watching a
soap opera unfold before her eyes. She couldn't
wait to find out if David became the man Maisie
and Arnold thought he was, or if the femme fatale,
Lucinda, made another appearance, throwing a
wrench into everyone's plans for him and Anita,
or if George and Anita became a couple.

Addie stared at the page. Was the dress in the
attic meant for her marriage to George, but at
some point Valerie came into his life and he called
off the wedding with Anita? *Oh my, this is getting interesting.* She frantically began scanning through

the next pages to see if the mystery of the dress had been solved, when she jerked at the sound of a knock on her front door.

"Darn! Just when things were starting to get juicy," Addie said, laying the book aside and glowering at Pippi, who'd leapt to her feet and raced to the front door. She begrudgingly followed her little furry friend into the hallway. Since she wasn't expecting anyone this afternoon, she peered through the side-window panel and grinned as she opened the door. "Catherine, just the person I want to see."

"Is that good or bad? Given the week we've all had, I'm not sure about anything anymore," she said, stepping into the hallway raising a bag. "But I brought dinner, if that helps?"

"Of course, but just so you know," Addie said, following her friend down the hall to the kitchen, "I did get some groceries today, thanks to the market's new delivery service, so I could have cooked for us."

"It's no problem. I needed to get out of Laurel's for a while. Simon dropped by, and I could tell that . . . I was a third wheel." Her voice faded off as she cast her gaze down. "Anyway, what did you need to pick my brain about? Because I think it's been picked clean these past few days, between the news at the wedding and Laurel and Mason and then Valerie's death."

"Did you say Simon dropped by Laurel's?"

Catherine didn't meet her questioning gaze.

"Did Laurel call him to come over?"

Catherine shook her head. "Not as far as I could tell. She was surprised to see him and then kind of

went all schoolgirl-like, so I thought it best . . .
Anyway, what was it you wanted to pick my brain
about?"

"Don't worry, it's nothing momentous." Unlike
Simon being at Laurel's beck and call since Valerie's death, he was the one now doing the calling, and that realization gnawed at Addie's gut. "It was
really nothing." Addie waved her off. "I only
wanted to ask you about Valerie and her late husband George."

"Okay, shoot," Catherine said, setting out
Chinese-food containers on the island.

"When Valerie and George met, was he involved
with my aunt Anita?"

"Heavens no, Valerie was twenty years his junior.
I doubt she would have even been born yet. As I
recall from the stories I heard, she was his second
wife though."

"His second wife? Who was his first?"

"A woman named Charmaine Lyman, I believe.
It was before my time, I'm afraid." Catherine took
the plate Addie handed her and began filling it.
"Why do you ask?"

"It's just that I found some early journals of my
aunt's in the attic and she mentions meeting a
man named George Price, and I wondered if that
could have been the same George that Valerie was
married to."

"Most likely. He's the only George Price in the
area, and he used to run in the same circles as
Anita and her friends back then."

"Did my aunt ever date him?"

"I have no idea, but like I said, that was all way
before my time. If I recall, your aunt mentioned a

fellow named David something or other who . . .
well, let's just say she only had eyes for him, back
in the day."

"David Winthrop?"

"She never said his last name, so that could be
it. All I know is that the way she talked about him
to me, it sounded like he was the love of her life."

"Did she ever mention what happened to him?"

"No, she didn't like to talk about it much." Catherine paused with her fork halfway to her mouth.
"What's up with all these questions?"

Addie relayed the discovery of the wedding
dress, the trunk, the photo albums and journals
she and Serena had discovered in the attic, and
with each mouthful of food Catherine took, her
eyes grew wider in disbelief at what Addie was
telling her about the contents of the journals.

"Remember, this is hearsay as I didn't know any
of them back then, but rumor has it that George's
first wife came from a very wealthy Boston family
who owned three or four of the great estate houses
on the Pen Hollow peninsula. George was a local
Pen Hollow boy and not well received by her family, but he made Charmaine happy, and she was
her daddy's little girl. He gave her everything she
wanted, and she wanted George. After all, George
got a scholarship to Harvard and was on his way to
being a high-powered lawyer, so her daddy eventually approved of the marriage."

"But the marriage didn't work out?"

"On the contrary, to everyone in her family's surprise, they were happy together, so it came as quite
a shock that after she was killed in a boating accident, George soon took up with his secretary . . ."

She glanced at Addie. "A woman named Valerie Rogers, who was much younger than him. Charmaine's family disowned George and completely cut him off. He even lost the house where he and Charmaine had been living in Boston. He had to pack up and leave, and move back to Pen Hollow to try to rebuild his career, which took years. I guess Valerie followed him there and helped make that happen and at some point after the move back, they were married."

"Wow, I had no idea. Do you think Valerie and George were : . . um . . . you know, involved, before Charmaine died?"

"That was always the question the family had, and I'll tell you, they weren't the only ones not pleased when he took up with Valerie and eventually married her."

"Who else wasn't?"

"Lucy Timmons."

"Why would she be upset about it, did she love George too?"

Catherine patted her chest as she choked on her mouthful of food and frantically reached for her glass of water on the counter. "Yes, I suppose she did," Catherine sputtered out, wiping her mouth with a napkin, "because she's George's sister."

"What?"

"You didn't know?"

"No. I had no idea."

"Well, she is, was, and from what I heard, Lucy used to idolize her brother, but she was young and very immature back then. So, I think the split in that family had less to do with Lucy's love of Charmaine and more to do with Lucy's love of the doors that opened for her being related to the Lymans. When George lost access to all that, Lucy would have very little to do with him and less to do with Valerie. That feud went on for a few years."

Addie opened her mouth to speak but it was as though Catherine had read her mind . . . and she snapped it closed with her next words.

"That's all water under the bridge now. You know, after Lucy married Ralph Timmons and they moved to Greyborne Harbor, she was away from that upper-crust group in Boston. She grew up a bit, forgave George, and eventually accepted Valerie."

"I had no idea they were sisters-in-law." Addie's thoughts raced. "Did George and Ralph eventually become friends too?"

"Ralph and George were old college buddies."

"They knew each other back then?" Addie tried to remember if Ralph's name was mentioned in Anita's journals, but couldn't recall off hand.

"They were the best of friends from what I understand. After the fallout over George's choice of his second wife and being snubbed by the aristocracy in Boston forcing George's move to Pen Hollow, I heard that Ralph insisted Lucy move to Pen Hollow too. In a show of support, I suppose, but Lucy refused. She still hadn't forgiven George and had really not accepted Valerie at that point, so they settled on Greyborne Harbor, only fifteen minutes away."

All this was news to Addie. None of it was mentioned in Anita's journals, or at least the ones she'd read so far, and she hung on Catherine's every word.

"The rest is history, as they say. George, with Valerie's help, built a very successful law practice in Pen Hollow, and Ralph and Lucy went on to build a very lucrative veterinary practice here. To be honest, I think the move was the best thing for Lucy as she matured a lot, which helped Valerie and Lucy get along well in later years."

"So, they did become friends?" Addie's mind replayed the video conversation she and Marc watched earlier and the looks on the faces of the two women.

"Oh yes! Actually, to hear Valerie talk, they had grown very close through the years." Catherine looked sideways at Addie. "But it sounds to me like you've gotten a better insight into the early life of your great-aunt, haven't you?"

"That's for sure. When you told me last year that my aunt was a real party girl when she was young, I didn't believe it, but then you said I hadn't read the right journals yet. I've sure had my eyes opened with these," Addie said with a laugh.

Catherine just grinned and shook her head.

Chapter 13

Catherine left to go home—in her words—to a very neglected-feeling Felix, and Addie stood staring at the open journal on her sofa. Her mind replayed what Catherine had told her about Lucy being Valerie's sister-in-law and was still taken aback by the news. That meant that last year, when Addie told Valerie to tell her niece to contact Doctor Timmons because she heard he was looking at retiring and selling his practice, Valerie probably already knew. All this week, Addie thought she was the one who, by opening her big mouth, had brought Laurel to Greyborne Harbor and back into Simon's life; but clearly, that wasn't the case. Valerie must have known then about the pending retirement and sale of his practice. *If so, why didn't she say anything to me then?*

But it didn't really matter why, did it? Did Marc know Valerie and Lucy were related and think that fact might be important? She wondered about the falling-out they had years ago. Their faces and tense body language in the recent video signaled that somehow old wounds must have resurfaced between them.

She dialed his number and waited for him to pick up. "Hi, Marc, it's Addie . . . Yes, yes, I'm fine, but I came across some information you might find interesting . . . Oh?" She went to the window and pulled back the curtain. "Okay, see you in a minute." She clicked off the phone and went to the door, opening it just as he got to the top of the porch stairs.

"I am surprised by this second visit of the day," Addie said, stepping aside to let him enter the foyer. "Does this mean you found something on the video?"

"Yes and no, but another one surfaced that I want you to take a look at, if you have a few minutes?"

"Sure, why not," she said, gesturing for him to come in.

"You just said on the phone that you had some new information?"

"Yeah," Addie said, waving toward the kitchen. "Want a coffee?"

"Coffee sounds perfect, thanks. So, what's the news?" he asked, following her down the hall.

Addie dropped a coffee pod into the coffee-maker and retrieved two cups from the cupboard. "Like I said, I don't know if it means anything, but did you know that Valerie was Lucy Timmons's sister-in-law?"

"That did come out in the interviews. I had no

idea until then, but Lucy and Laurel both mentioned it." He took a seat at the island counter, and dropped his hat on the stool next to him. "Did you find something out about it that might be related to the murder?"

"I don't think so." She shrugged, getting the cream and sugar and setting them in front of him. "But I just found it interesting and wondered if you knew and if you managed to isolate their conversation in the video."

"Yes, that new officer at the desk, Hunter Powell, used to be a DJ and audio engineer, and lucky for us he had it done in a flash. But from what we heard they were just talking about George's old files, and the amount of work Valerie had ahead of her to clear them out. There was nothing off about their conversation."

"So, you don't think it has any bearing on the case?"

"No, and from what both Laurel and Lucy told us, it didn't sound like Valerie and Lucy were best friends, but they were friends, nonetheless. Lucy shrugged off my questions about any unresolved issues in their relationship and said no, and that when they did see each other, they got on well. So, I don't think there's a lead there."

"Really?" said Addie, setting a steaming cup in front of him. "Then she didn't tell you their relationship wasn't always amicable?"

"No," he said, mixing a teaspoon of sugar into his cup. "Why? Do you know otherwise?"

Addie took a sip from her cup, leaned on the counter, and relayed what Catherine had told her about how Lucy was upset when her brother George married Valerie and became ostracized from the Lyman family and how that affected Lucy at the time.

Marc listened, then shook his head. "I can't see that being an issue in the case all these years later. From what I learned after interviewing her, Lucy married George's best friend Ralph, and they've been happily married for over sixty years. I'm pretty sure that fence was mended a long time ago."

"I'm sure you're right," Addie said thoughtfully. "It's just that last year, after I knew Valerie wanted Laurel to move closer to her, from Boston, I mentioned to Valerie that our local vet, Doctor Timmons, was looking to retire. She didn't bat an eye or say anything about knowing him. Not a word about them being in-laws even. Don't you find that weird?"

Marc stared down at the cup he held in his hand. "My guess is you're grasping at straws here. Perhaps the only reason Valerie didn't mention the connection to the Timmonses was because she knew who your aunt was. She thought you knew then about what happened all those years ago, when Lucy was feuding with George, and she felt like she'd have to explain how she knew Lucy. That's a pretty heavy conversation to have with a person you just met casually, isn't it?"

"I suppose you're right," sighed Addie. "It probably doesn't mean anything. I think I'll just stick to my own little mystery."

Marc chuckled and swigged back the last of his coffee, setting his cup on the counter. "I'm glad you're keeping your mind off"—he lowered his gaze fleetingly—"recent events, by staying busy investigating your mysterious wedding dress, but I do have to bring you back to mine for a few minutes."

"Alright, if you must."

"Not only don't we know how the poison was administered but we also don't know how they disposed of the means it was administered by, afterward. That's why I need you to take a look at this latest video turned in to us."

"Okay," grumbled Addie. "Wedding dresses aside . . ." Her mind flashed to hers, hanging on the back of her bedroom door. "Let's go into the living room and you can show me what you have."

Addie settled on the sofa and reached for her laptop on the coffee table. "Who took this one, if you're not breaking any of Marc's rules of investigation by telling me?"

"It was Phil Harper."

"Phil Harper, the reporter at the *Daily News?*"

"Yeah, that's the one."

"That surprises me, since he's of the generation when reporters used a pencil, notebook, and shorthand to make notes for a story, not videos."

"What can I tell you? He's not one of those stuck in the past, but it took a while for him to turn it in, which might be due to the fact that he had to make a copy for his use later before he turned it over."

"Has he run his story yet?"

"No, we've put a forty-eight-hour hold on everything except the death notice. If there's something here to point to the murderer, I don't want them to have a heads-up and do a runner."

"Okay, did you have another flash drive?"

"Yeah, sorry," said Marc, digging it out of his breast pocket and handing it to her.

She plugged it into the port and clicked play. "What am I looking at?"

"It's the moments leading up to Valerie's collapse. Phil covered everything, by the look of it. See here, it's a wide-angle of the entire room of people. There"—he pointed—"is Catherine coming out of the kitchen with a tea cart . . ."

"And she's clearly restocking the dining room table," said Addie as the images moved across the screen showing Catherine replenishing the sandwich platters and exchanging what were probably empty teapots for full ones. "There's nothing unusual about that."

"No, but look. Here, she's taken a pot and is refilling Valerie's cup not long before she clutches her throat and falls to the floor."

"I think you're projecting what you want to see, because if you watch in sequence . . . here"—Addie pointed—"that image was clearly from earlier, because then she also refills Laurel's cup and then Lucy's, who's standing behind Valerie's chair, and neither one of them was poisoned. So, if you were trying to imply that Catherine is the killer, then you're mistaken, aren't you?" She snapped the cover of her laptop down and glowered at him. "I told you before that I wouldn't be part of a witch hunt for a quick conviction, and I meant it."

"No, I'm not, but I can't see anything else there that would point to who killed Valerie and how she was poisoned." He sat back, scrubbing his hand through his hair. "I'm just frustrated by not having come across even one clue yet."

"Talk about me grasping at straws." She shook her head in disgust. "I've never known you to be so cavalier about making an accusation about someone before. Aren't you always the one telling me you need proof, and evidence, and that instincts and suspicions aren't enough to build a case on?"

"I really do hate it when you throw my words back at me." He glanced sheepishly at her.

"Think about it, Marc. Would the DA really issue a warrant for Catherine's arrest based on the fact that you just don't have any leads and she happened to pour tea for half the room just before the woman collapsed? I think not."

Marc leaned forward, rubbing his forehead, clearly showing his frustration, and her heart ached for him.

"Now then, if you behave, we'll take another look at the video."

"Okay." Marc nodded in resignation. "I'll behave, because the killer has to be someone in these pictures, which means there must be something . . . a hint, a clue, as to what is about to take place. And we need to keep looking until we find it. The longer a murderer goes free the more likely they are to get away with it or—"

"Kill again?"

"Exactly, and since we don't have a motive and a sweet old lady is dead, we don't know what we're dealing with." He sat back; his unblinking eyes gazed past Addie at the sidewall. "Of course, it could mean the poison must have been in the cup before she drank from it."

"But look at all these pictures. It appears as though she used the same teacup all afternoon, and as far as all these photos and videos show, no one but her, Laurel, or Catherine refilled it. And you said Simon found no trace evidence of the eye drops in any of the teacups, or pots, right?"

Marc regarded Addie and he slightly shifted on the sofa beside her. "There is one other possibility that we haven't considered yet."

"Which is?"

"She took the poison herself."

"You mean on purpose?"

"Yes." He leaned forward, elbows on his knees. "Think about it. From what Laurel said, her health was an issue, and it was confirmed in Simon's autopsy. Heart disease, she was diabetic, and she had macular degeneration and was going blind. Plus, her husband had recently passed away. Maybe it just all got too much for her and now that Laurel was set up in her practice and her new home, and Mason was back in her life along with . . . Simon, of sorts"—he averted his gaze—"she—"

"I don't know about that." Addie shook her head. "We both heard Valerie in the videos announcing to everyone that she was taking Mason to Boston next week to some rare-comic-book store he wanted to visit. That doesn't sound like someone who was planning to take their own life, does it? You know, making future plans. No." She sat back and crossed her arms. "I don't believe it, not the woman I met. She loved her family too much and had a good future to look forward to with them. Laurel was finally going to be only fifteen minutes away." She tapped her touchpad to bring her laptop to life. "No, there has to be something in these pictures we're not seeing. As you said, the killer is someone in this room, and there are a lot of them, so let's find out who had the opportunity to slip a bottle or two of eye drop solution into her cup."

"You're right. Generally speaking, people who are planning to take their own life don't make future plans. It seems then we're left with the probability that the poison was in her cup before she drank from it."

"Except, as I pointed out, in all these pictures, it looks like she's been drinking from the same teacup all afternoon. It doesn't appear to have ever been replaced, only refilled on a number of occasions."

Marc shook his head. "I don't know then. We have to be missing something."

Addie clicked through the video, pausing it and restarting while scanning each still frame. "Look here. Valerie is dabbing a tissue at her eye—it looks quite red; she leans over, says something to Laurel, and gets up and leaves, then Lucy says something to Laurel and by her face, she seems quite concerned. Then Lucy waits a minute, sets her teacup down and exits out of the shot."

"Wait, turn up the audio. Do you hear that in the background?" Marc said excitedly.

"Valerie are you okay, dear?"

"Yes, I'll be out in a minute."

"Then they come back," said Marc, focusing on the action in the video. "Lucy hands her another tissue from the box on the table beside her. Valerie leans over and says something to a concerned-looking Laurel, but pats her hand, reassuring her, and says something about needing her eye drops. Lucy is back behind her, holding her teacup again, and pats Valerie on the shoulder." He sits back, looking at Addie. "Now do you see why I thought she might have taken the eye drops herself? She even said she went into the bathroom for her eye drops. She could have drunk them then because it's not long after she falls over dead."

"I still don't believe this was self-induced. Maybe she had an eye injection for her macular degeneration recently and, like Martha gets afterward, her eye was dry and she needed to put in a drop, which is why she went to the bathroom to do it."

"Okay." He sat back, eyeing Addie. "But I'm just saying that whole little scene looks iffy to me, since a few frames later she's drinking the tea, which clearly no one has touched, or even been in a position to doctor it, since Lucy is over by the refreshment table here"—he pointed to the screen—"talking to her husband, and then Bin Thomas joins them. Simon is over by the kitchen door laughing and joking with Mason. Laurel gets up from her chair beside Valerie's and goes over to them, most likely wanting to get in on the joke, and then Valerie, sitting all alone now, suddenly dies. It doesn't show anyone near her for the previous fifteen minutes who could have poured the solution in her cup."

Addie tuned out Marc's words as soon as he'd pointed out Laurel joining Simon and Mason's conversation. She couldn't miss the look in Laurel's eyes as she gazed up at Simon, but what made her chest constrict was the return look Simon gave her for a fleeting moment.

"I know you don't want to believe that this was self-induced, but Addie, there's just no proof of foul play."

"Then we have to keep looking," she snapped.

Marc glanced curiously at Addie at the vehemence in her voice.

She closed her eyes with the image of Simon and Laurel burned into her mind, and angled the screen toward him. "Okay, and here on the far left of the image, it still shows Valerie, or at least her knees in the frame, and she's clearly sipping her tea, but here. Look, this is where she stands up, grabs her throat and falls gasping onto the floor. It was in the tea, I tell you. The Valerie Price I knew wouldn't have taken her own life." Addie drew in a deep breath and forced her eyes away from the next images of Laurel and Simon hovering over the body. She counted—one, two, three—and tried to focus on Valerie lying on the floor.

"Okay, I get it. I'll keep looking at this from a murder investigation angle then." Marc looked uneasily at the still shot of Laurel and Simon that Addie had paused the video on. "But if this is too much for you, I understand."

She shook her head. "No, the answer is here somewhere. We just have to keep looking." She glanced uncomfortably at the image she'd captured on the screen.

Marc swung the laptop toward him and hit play. "Yeah, okay. Phil did a great job in making sure he was covering everything, even the gruesome parts with Valerie lying on the floor."

Addie leaned closer to Marc to see and nodded. "Yeah, it's good for us, though, because he's caught all the commotion when everyone rushes toward her."

"It was pure chaos, wasn't it?" added Marc, studying the action playing out.

"Yeah, which means we're going to have to look through each image as a still photo to try to see if anything telling gives us a clue as to how the poison was given to her and then what happened to the delivery means." She squinted, searching through scene after scene. "Her cup comes in and out of view because of people getting in the way, but here, after Simon is crouched over her, it's still there. It's even here, when you guys arrive on the scene. So, it doesn't make sense, if Simon tested it and there was no trace of the eye drops, how was she poisoned?"

"And we're back to square one."

Addie started to close her laptop but paused when the video panned to an image of Simon holding and comforting a distraught Laurel. Tears burned behind her eyes, and she swallowed hard to dislodge the lump growing in the back of her throat.

Chapter 14

Addie rubbed her eyes, trying to dispel the visions of Simon embracing Laurel burned in her mind. She berated herself, knowing he was only comforting her as her aunt lay dead at their feet, but the pain of seeing them together under any circumstances, was just too much. "I'm sorry, Marc. I can't do this anymore today. Leave the flash drives with me, and . . . I'll look at them again later."

"Yeah, I think we both need fresh eyes and it's been a long day," he said, getting up and heading for the door, but he glanced back at her. "Are you okay?" he asked hesitantly.

"I'm fine, just tired."

"Because if this is too much, I understand. I know the timing with the wedding and then . . . well, all this has been a lot for you."

She heaved herself up and met him at the door.

"Which is why I need to refocus on my little mystery; it helps keep my head clear of all the . . . well, you know."

"It breaks my heart, Addie, to see you going through this. I thought helping me out with this murder case might help you keep your mind off, you know, the situation, but from some of the pictures we saw tonight, I can see I was wrong. It made things worse."

"It is what it is, Marc, and I have to accept it. Laurel and Simon have a past that didn't legally end when they thought it had, and they also have a son who will bind them together even after their marriage is finally annulled, and I have to figure out if there's a place for me in all that."

They both jumped when a loud knock came from the door behind Marc.

"Are you expecting someone?"

"No." Addie pulled her phone out of her pocket to check for a missed text and shrugged.

"Maybe it's Simon with an update. I told Powell at the desk I was heading over here with the latest video," Marc said, opening the door. "Serena?"

"Marc? What are you doing here?"

"I might ask you the same. I thought Ollie was sick."

"He is," she said, stepping inside, nodding a greeting at Addie. "But his medication kicked in and his fever broke, and since Zach's gone to Boston for the rest of the week to a naturopath convention with Doctor Lee, Mom came over to give me a break for the night." She held up a bottle of wine and grinned at Addie. "Are you game for some girl time?"

"Am I ever," cried Addie. "Get in here and let's get that open."

"Okay then," said Marc with a chesty chuckle. "I'll leave you two, but promise me you'll behave. I don't want any calls from your neighbors about a rowdy party or anything."

"I can't promise you anything at the moment," laughed Addie, taking the bottle from Serena. Then she realized—from the eager, hopeful look in Marc's eyes, and recalling the conversation he'd had with Serena last year in Pen Hollow when he told Serena he wasn't giving up on Addie yet, even though she was with Simon then—she might have misspoken. "I mean I can't promise anything about tonight or . . ."

"I know," he said, his voice holding a regretful tone. "I know." He turned and started down the stairs but stopped. "When you do look at the photos again, I had Powell put on the filtered audio of the conversation between Valerie and Lucy, in case you wanted to take a listen." He glanced at an edgy Serena and chuckled. "Okay, okay, I'm going now. You two have fun."

"We plan on it," she said, and grabbed Addie's arm. "Come on, get in here, girl." She closed the door with a thud. "I've been walking the floor with a screaming baby for two days and I really need some fun right about now."

"Slow down, girlfriend," laughed Addie. "I think before we delve into that little bottle of cheer, we'd better make sure we have some snack food in our bellies. It's been hours since I had dinner and I don't want my first glass to knock me over."

"Same with me, so where do you want to order

from?" asked Serena, following her down the hall to the kitchen.

Addie paused at the door and looked at her. "I was planning on making us something."

"You actually went out and got groceries?"

"Not exactly. I was on my way out when your brother showed up, and so I ordered from that new delivery service the market has." Addie bent down and searched through the fridge. "Now if I can just figure out where he put everything . . ."

"He put your groceries away for you?" said Serena, plopping down hard on a counter stool. "Wow, he's been at my house when I've come in with bags of groceries and two screaming, hungry kids and the most help I got was him carrying in a few bags, then sitting at the table drinking a coffee while I put them away and tried to get the kids fed."

"I was doing him a favor, so I guess he thought he owed me. How about I make a big platter of nachos? I had Chinese with Catherine, so why not some Mexican now, and make it a real international food fest."

"Sounds good to me. Are you going to make guacamole too?"

"Make, no. Open premade container, yes." Addie gathered up the ingredients needed and spread the taco chips on a baking sheet, then added salsa and covered it all with a heaping amount of grated cheese, and slid them under the broiler. A few minutes later she retrieved the bubbling, gooey mess of cheese and chips out of the oven, dished up two heaping plates of nachos, and set them on a tray.

"Sour cream?" She glanced at Serena, who by the look on her face was already eating with her eyes.

"Of course, and the guacamole, don't forget it."

Addie laid out the two condiment bowls, setting two spoons beside them, and looked at Serena. "Okay, let's take it into the living room and get this girls' night started."

Serena snatched up the last clump of cheese-coated chips from her plate, scraped the guacamole bowl clean and covered her gooey treat with it, popping it into her mouth, then sat back purring with satisfaction. "Okay, mom, I've got food in my belly. Can we please open the wine now?"

"Yes, you can open the wine now." Addie chuckled, handing her a corkscrew. "Do you want any more nachos? I can make another batch, it'll only take a second."

"No, thanks. I'm stuffed. That was great and hit the spot. I was trying to remember the last time I had spicy salsa. I think it was when I was first pregnant, and got heartburn so bad I couldn't sleep for two days. That was perfect tonight," she said, eyeing the journals on the table. "Have you found anything yet to tell you who the wedding dress belonged to?"

"No, not yet. I was going to get back to my reading after I got groceries, but then Marc showed up and asked a favor, so everything else I'd planned for the day got put on hold."

"Yeah, I was surprised to see him here. What did he want you to do for him?"

"He has pictures and videos of Valerie's tea and wanted me to look at them to see if I could spot anything unusual that might give him a clue to who the murderer was, how the eye drops were given to her, and how any trace evidence might have disappeared after."

"And he couldn't have the crime team do all that?" asked Serena, a hint of skepticism in her voice.

"They have, but he thought since I sort of knew Valerie and I wasn't there, meaning I'm not a suspect, that I might be able to see some subliminal communications happening between her and someone else that attended, and it might mean something."

"Hmm, sounds like he was fishing to find a reason to spend time with you."

"Serena. Marc and I are *just* friends."

"I know that, and you know that, but now that your wedding has been put on hold, does he know that?"

"Yes, we discussed it."

"Hmm, well, I bet it was fun for you seeing all those photos of the entire town celebrating the arrival of Simon and Laurel's son."

"No, it wasn't, and neither of us expected to see so many scenes of Simon and . . . Laurel. You can tell that at one time they were very, very close." Addie sat back in her chair. "It's given me a lot to think about."

"I bet it has," said Serena, giving Addie a knowing look as she poured a glass of wine and handed it to her. "I just hope Marc wasn't trying to plunge the knife deeper into your heart."

"No, actually that's why he left. I think he could tell that seeing all those images of the *happy couple* were, well. Let's just say he knew I needed to focus on something else right now, so, if we could change the topic *please*, I'd appreciate it."

Serena reached out and patted Addie's hand. "I'm so sorry this happened to you."

"I know, but like I told your brother, it is what it is, and I have to figure out where my place is now in this cozy little family that's been sprung on Simon overnight."

"Have you spoken to him lately?"

"No, not since I told him I felt his place right now was with Mason and Laurel because they were both struggling with Valerie's death."

"He hasn't called you or anything, since then?"

Addie shook her head.

"Pfft," huffed Serena, grabbing a journal from the table.

Addie gazed into the unlit fireplace, swirling the red wine in her glass. "It's for the best though," she said wistfully. "Like the old saying goes, 'If you love something, set it free. If it comes back to you, it's yours. If it doesn't, then it was never meant to be.'" She shook herself out of the trancelike state the quote had brought on. "But never mind all that," she said, setting her glass on the table, glancing at Serena. "Getting back to the wedding dress, I've been reading through some of what you read, and I couldn't believe how much you skipped over."

"That's true, but I'm not as invested in every detail of your aunt's life, like you are. I want to get to the nitty-gritty facts, so I'm scanning for key words and phrases or it will take weeks for you to unravel this mystery."

"Fair enough, but so much of a sense of who Anita was gets lost in that process, doesn't it?"

"I think it gives us a pretty good picture."

"Really, you think?"

Serena nodded. "Like here, she talks about her and David's first kiss and how she felt it in her toes," Serena said with a giggle. "Your aunt could have been a romance writer."

"It does sound like she and David Winthrop really did make a go of a relationship, didn't they? Okay, we'll use your method because I'm dying to find out if the dress was meant for their marriage."

"Oh, now I have permission to speed-read?"

"Smart aleck!" Addie grabbed a pillow from the sofa and tossed it at her friend. "Yes, read!"

Serena laughed and threw the pillow back, and then fell silent. "Whoa! Listen to this entry.

"February 14, 1952

"I'm over the moon. David asked me to marry him tonight at the Valentine's Day party at Windgate House. Maisie is so excited that she has already started planning the event. She said I can use everything she and Arnold had for their wedding and that she wants to make sure mine is twice as nifty. Arnold's parents have even offered us the conservatory at Windgate for the ceremony and reception. I can't wait to tell Mama and

Father tomorrow when I go home for Sunday dinner."

"That means the dress *was* hers and meant for her wedding to David. That makes sense because of the vintage of it. Does it say anything about the wedding date or what happened, why it didn't take place?"

"Hey, give me minute," said Serena, scanning pages. "First, you tell me I'm reading too fast; now, you want me to get to the end of the story by the next page. Sheesh . . ."

"Sorry," said Addie, edging to the front of her seat, her gaze fixed on Serena. "Well, anything yet?"

Serena shook her head but didn't take her eyes off the page, and then she gasped. "Oh, Addie, your aunt was a thoroughly modern woman," she said and snapped the journal closed, laying it on the table beside her. Her cheeks took on that freckled, red-mottled appearance as she stared down at her wineglass in front of her.

"Why, what happened? You've gone as red as a beet."

"They just . . ." She swallowed and met Addie's probing gaze. "They just . . . *canoodled.*"

"Canoodled?"

"Yes, right there at Windgate House, in Anita's room when they were there for Arnold and Maisie's first wedding anniversary party on August 16, 1952, and . . ." Serena's eyes widened. "I feel like I just read my mother's journal." She shivered. "Did people back then actually do *that* sort of thing? You know, before they were married?"

Addie let out a soft laugh. "I'm pretty sure that wasn't invented in modern times. Back then, though, it was just not spoken of. Remember, they were engaged to be married and this is her private journal, so she's going to write about things that she wouldn't publicly disclose, but," said Addie thoughtfully, "it does mean she must have really loved him, and their engagement was the real thing." The image of the unworn dress in the attic flashed through her mind. "I wonder what happened. Is there any mention of that girl, Lucinda? Maybe she came back into the picture and things fell apart from there."

"I didn't see her name mentioned after that, at least not on that page. Maybe whatever broke them up happened just before the wedding? From your description of Lucinda, she might have coerced him into a liaison and Anita caught them and"—Serena snapped her fingers—"the wedding was called off."

"Yeah, maybe. I guess there's only one way to find out and that's to keep reading."

Serena's shoulders shuddered. "Not sure I can if there's any more of that mentioned."

"Come on, don't be such a prude. It's a fact of life."

"Yes, but like I said, I look at those pictures of your sweet young aunt and then the ones of her when she's older, and I feel like I'm digging into my mother's background. And I'll tell you, I don't want to know anything about whether she and my father did or didn't do any sort of canoodling before they were married. No sirree."

"There you go again, canoodling." Addie grabbed

her stomach, trying to hold back the laugher rising from the pit of her tummy. "I can't wait until you have *the* talk"—she let out a breathy gasp—"with little Addie when she's of age."

"Wait, wait, there's more here."

"There you go, skipping pages again. How will we ever know all the details?"

"The details don't interest me like they do you. I just want to know how the story ends. Listen to this." Serena's eyes widened and she looked blankly at Addie.

> *"October 30, 1952*
> *"David hasn't come back. We went out looking for him but could find no sign. Arnold thinks he might have gone off partying with the people he met up with at the fair, but after the news I gave him, I don't think he would do that. He was so happy that we were going to be parents. I'm worried."*

"What? They were going to be parents?" Addie stood up and grabbed the copy of *The Velveteen Rabbit* from the table.

Serena frantically waved her hand. "Wait. Just listen to this . . .

> *"Sunday, there's still no news of David. The police have been searching but there's no sign of him anywhere.*

"Oh no!" Serena gasped. "Do you remember that story we heard last year in Pen Hollow about the young man that went missing and two days later they found his body strung up on a scarecrow stand?"

Addie nodded, taking a step toward Serena. "Yeah, and Paige tried to tell me the woods around there were haunted." She glanced down at the journal Serena held. "Why, what does it say?"

Tears filled Serena's eyes as she looked up at her. "It was David Winthrop's body they found," she hoarsely whispered.

For the third time in her life Addie could actually say her blood ran cold through her veins on hearing those words. Her knees buckled, and she dropped the copy of *The Velveteen Rabbit* clutched in her hands.

Chapter 15

Addie picked up the throw blanket from the back of the sofa, draped it over Serena, and smiled down at her softly snoring friend. She could remember the time when girls' nights were spent drinking a whole bottle of wine, and talking until the wee hours of the morning. *My, my, how things have changed.* As she settled into the far end of the sofa, she eyed Serena's still half-full glass of wine and chuckled softly. She took a sip of her tea and opened the journal Serena had been reading from.

Her thought was that if she went back and filled in some of the gaps Serena had skipped over when she raced to the bullet points, it might give her a clue about who was responsible for David's death and more information about Anita's revelation that they were going to be parents.

She read through page after page; all she took

away from it was how much her aunt had loved
him, their plans for their upcoming Christmas
wedding, how much help Maisie was to her in
helping make the arrangements. There was even
mention of her old friend Beatrice, from Greyborne Harbor, and how she had pulled strings
with her father at the *Greyborne Harbor Daily News* to
get him to print the wedding invitations. Anita also
mentioned how giddy her father was with the fact
that his daughter was marrying a Winthrop of
Boston. But, in all that, Addie couldn't find even
one clue as to who would have wanted David dead,
and the last entry in the journal left her with more
questions than answers.

*They found David's body today. He'd been
strung up on a scarecrow stand in a farmer's field.
Who, oh who, would have wanted to do that to
him? My heart will forever be broken . . .*

The missing pieces of the puzzle gnawed at
Addie. She frantically flipped through the rest of
the pages in the journal, hoping to find a foot-
note, a hint, something that would tell her what
happened next, but they were all blank—every last
one of them. So that was it? The end of the journal
entries for 1952, and not one mention of the baby
she was expecting anywhere. What happened to
Anita and the baby after David was found murdered?

She grabbed the next journal from the stack off
the table and checked the year—1954? The journal for 1953 was missing. She scanned the first
page, but it picked up when Anita landed in Lon-

don to attend college, and there was no word of any baby. What happened to it?

Addie picked up the copy of *The Velveteen Rabbit* from the table and reread the inscription. *For my beautiful granddaughter on her first birthday . . . this book was given to me by your grandfather on the day I told him I was expecting our first, and only, child. I now pass this token of his love for this story on to you.*

Love, Grandmamma Anita.

When she'd learned her great-aunt was pregnant, Addie immediately decided she had written this to her granddaughter, whoever that was. But now that Anita had gone on with her life in London, which Addie read about in later journals, and there was never any mention of a child, Addie decided she'd been wrong. Perhaps the child died at birth or was adopted out and Anita wasn't part of her child's life and the whole situation was far too painful for Anita to ever write about. However, if the child had died, there would be no grandchild, and if the baby was adopted, Anita wouldn't have been involved in its life and therefore she wouldn't have known about any future granddaughter, right?

At least that was Addie's original thought, meaning the book had to have been given to Anita by *her* grandmother, who would have been Addie's great-great-great-grandmother. But, as Addie studied the penmanship in the journal and compared it to that in the book inscription, it was clear to Addie that there were similarities in the forming of the letters. Was it a coincidence that two different women, generations apart, would have similar penmanship, or not?

Which meant, if Anita was the author of both,

then what happened to her granddaughter and how did she know she even had one? Although Addie had to admit that the idea of having a relative somewhere out there excited her. Perhaps she wasn't the last Greyborne, as she had been led to believe. To think she might have a cousin somewhere, and didn't even know it. "But one mystery at a time," she whispered and closed the journals, looked at two others with 1955 and 1956 written on the spine, and set them all back on the table alongside *The Velveteen Rabbit.*

Now what? The wedding dress mystery was solved; but, just like when she and Serena explored the trunk, everything that was revealed only led to a new mystery to solve. Who killed David Winthrop and what happened to the child? These questions ate at her gut, but she'd run out of places to find the answers. Unless of course—she glanced over to her aunt's puzzle desk—the 1953 journal had been hidden elsewhere in the house.

A flurry of movement out of the corner of Addie's eye caught her attention, as Pippi leapt up on the sofa from her bed by the fireplace, turned in circles and settled onto Serena's chest. Serena stirred and moaned. "It's okay, Ollie, Mama's here," as she wrapped her arms around Pippi and hugged her close in her sleep.

So much for digging through the desk tonight. Addie judged by the burning behind her eyes she should probably call it a day too, until she remembered the copy of the isolated conversation between Valerie and Lucy was on the latest flash drive Marc gave her.

The last thing she wanted to see right now were

any more pictures of Simon and Laurel, so she skipped that video and searched for the file containing the conversation, but paused when she saw the file name, *Phil Harper's Video*. That was it!

Phil Harper had been with the *Greyborne Harbor Daily News* his entire newspaper career. Even though he wouldn't have been there at the time of David's murder, when he did start at the paper as a cub reporter, whoever it was that covered that story might have still been there and Phil might be able to give her some insight as to what they found out during their coverage.

That was her next starting point, and she made a mental note to go see Phil first thing in the morning, which, when she glanced up at the clock on the mantel, she realized wasn't that far away. However, she was curious about the conversation between Valerie and Lucy. Even though Marc said he didn't think there was anything telling about it, she couldn't help thinking something might have been missed, because their body language and facial expressions told a different story. She opened the file, clicked play, and adjusted the volume so as not to disturb the sleeping duo on the other end of the sofa.

"Where on earth did you say you found Simon and Laurel's annulment papers?" said Mrs. Timmons, as she dropped two bags into a teapot.

"In his desk drawer," replied Valerie, pouring boiling water into the pot. *"I couldn't believe it, and then I found another important file crushed in the back of it too."*

"So, what are you going to do?"

"I'm going to have to go through all his file boxes now

to make sure nothing else was missed." Valerie shook her head. *"It's such a bother, but I can't risk this mishap bringing into question any of his other cases."*

"I had no idea George still had all his old files. I thought for sure he would have disposed of them after the legal six-year time period, or ten if it was a criminal case. I mean, there must be so many, after all his years in practice. Poor you to have been left with all this."

"I know, and I told him for years to start shredding what files had passed their legally required retention date, or to at least start making electronic copies, but you know George. He couldn't bring himself to shred anything, just in case he needed it someday, and as far as computers went." She shook her head. *"There's no way he would have trusted the likes of those with his files,"* she said with a sardonic laugh. *"So, judging by the number of file boxes I came across in the locked storage room when I could finally bring myself to go through his office, I'm sure he's got files going back to the first day he opened his practice, if not from even when he was in law school."*

The voices became muffled from there, but judging by their actions, loading up the tea cart and pushing it into the living room, that's where it ended anyway. And Marc was right, there was nothing telling in that conversation. It was clear to Addie that the tension appeared to come because Valerie was feeling overwhelmed and Lucy was being supportive of her. Addie snapped her laptop closed, downed the last of her cold tea, switched off the light, and tiptoed up the stairs to bed.

The next morning Addie followed her nose down the hallway to the kitchen, when to her surprise she found a chipper red-headed woman flipping eggs in the frying pan.

"Good morning." Serena beamed. "I wondered if you'd be able to sleep through the aroma of bacon wafting through the house."

Addie eyed her through her blurry morning state and scowled. "Some of us were up half the night trying to solve a murder mystery, you know."

"Well, I can't believe how great I feel. You know, I don't ever recall feeling this good after a girls' night! It's amazing! I don't even have a headache." Serena slid two eggs on a plate with toast and bacon and handed it to Addie.

"It doesn't surprise me," said Addie, nodding her gratitude and taking a seat at the island. "You only had half a glass of wine."

"No! There's no way I only drank half a glass!"

"Yes way. Look in the fridge. The bottle's almost full."

Serena eyed her skeptically and peeked in the fridge. "I don't believe it, So much for give'ener last night, hey?"

"You know, it doesn't surprise me. I'm pretty sure your sleep deprivation took over, which is understandable having been through two sleepless nights with a sick baby."

Serena set her plate beside Addie's and hopped up on the stool. "I'm sure not the person I used to be, am I?"

"Do you miss her? You know, the old you?"

Serena thought for a second. "I'm not sure. It's harder than I thought it would be, for sure. You know, twins. At first, I thought perfect, we got our boy and girl in one go and I wouldn't have to go through another horrible pregnancy with my feet so bloated and swollen, but now . . . Some days it gets to be so much that I just want to do nothing but cry."

Addie reached over and squeezed her friend's hand. "Oh, sweetie, you know whenever you're feeling like that you can always call me and I'll come over and give you a hand."

"I know, but it's just sometimes in the moment, it all becomes too much and I get overwhelmed. Stuff you don't stop and think about until it piles up. Like when one is up and playing and the other is ready for a nap, then that one wants to play and the other one is ready to go down. I seem to never get a break some days." She sighed. "But then little Addie will do something like push her bowl of Cheerios off her high-chair tray, and I want to scream, but she looks at me with those big brown eyes and says, 'Done.' And I just want to hug her, she's so darn cute. They both are and I love them to death."

"I imagine it's times like that you realize all of this is worth it."

"Yeah, even though there's the matter of having to have two of everything: highchairs, diaper bags, twice the baby laundry that has to be washed separately from ours. But"—she looked pensively at her breakfast—"I know I'm doubly blessed, because when I had the kids at the playground last week, another mother said to me, *You're lucky to have two.* I asked her why she thought that, and she said because they always have a playmate, and with her one, she's on the floor playing with him more than she is anywhere else during the day."

"She does have a point."

"I know. I thought about what she said and she was right. Most days, I can put them both in the playpen and they keep each other happy and then I can get some baking done for the tea shop. So yeah, she's right, of course. So, nope"—Serena shook her head—"I wouldn't change my life now for anything. It also helps me to remember what Paige told me when I was pregnant."

"Which was?"

"When you feel overwhelmed by a stage they're going through, remember it's only one of many phases and will soon pass on to the next one."

"I imagine that when they get to the stage of not wanting naps at all, then you'll be really grateful they have each other to play with."

"My thought exactly, but who knows what else that phase will bring with it." She shook her red head. "There's never a dull moment around my house, that's for sure."

"But Zach's a big help when he's home, isn't he?"

"Yeah, he's the best dad ever, and I know without him and his support, and my mom and dad helping out as much as they do, it would be a lot tougher. But"—she glanced down at her breakfast—"a night off once in a while, even if it's just to catch up on sleep, is going to become a more regular occurrence, so they all better be prepared. This Serena I am this morning. Well, I like her, *a lot*," she mumbled, stuffing her mouth with a forkful of egg.

The more Serena tried to delay the end of her mini staycation, the antsier Addie became about getting to the newspaper office, especially when Serena insisted on doing the dishes, then decided to reorganize Addie's pantry. Addie was exhausted just watching her friend buzz around the kitchen, but she knew this was important for her so she bit her tongue. Phil had been at the newspaper for years; he would be there later. If her best friend needed more mommy time away, then she would support her in that.

Serena stood back, examined her work, and grinned. "There, I think my work here is done."

"All I can say is my kitchen has never sparkled like this before, thank you."

"Oh, I didn't do it for you."

"No?"

"No, this was purely therapeutic, my friend. I needed to create a little control over the chaos in my life and this was strictly for my benefit, and at least I can leave here knowing that little hands won't be following along behind me undoing all my hard work," she said with a laugh.

Addie didn't know what to say, and then she recalled how she'd felt after discovering Simon's past and present were still one, and how digging through the attic unearthing her aunt's treasure made her feel in the moment, and she nodded. "You're right. I guess it's human instinct to try to create calm when we lose control of what's happening around us, even if that means cleaning and organizing." Addie glanced deviously at her friend. "How about we add to that and throw in a little old-fashioned sleuthing like we used to do?"

"What do you mean? Did you find something else in the journals after I fell asleep?"

"No, but I had an idea. Do you want to come to the newspaper office with me?" Addie asked.

"Ooh . . ." Serena looked torn. "Nah, as much as I'd love to, Mom just sent me a text, and she and Dad have the kids back from their morning play in the park. They've been so great about this but I really hate to take advantage."

"I get it."

"Look, Zach's back tomorrow about dinner-time, and then, knowing him, he'll be asleep right after we get the kids down for the night. Why don't I pop back then and you can fill me in?"

"Sounds like a plan."

"Perfect. Chat later." Serena gave her one of her bear hugs. "Thank you for helping me feel grounded again. This was exactly the break I needed." Serena smiled and trotted down the hallway to the door "Thanks again! You're the best!" she called as she left.

Addie dashed upstairs to shower and dress and then raced off to the *Greyborne Harbor Daily News* office. As luck would have it, she arrived on the steps of the newspaper office just as Phil Harper was going in.

"Mr. Harper!" she called breathlessly as she darted up the stairs to meet him at the top. "Hi, I'm Addie Greyborne. I was wondering if we could talk for a minute?"

"Miss Greyborne, of course, I always have time for the subject of the biggest story I've covered in months for the paper. What can I do for you? An exclusive interview with the jilted bride, I'm hoping?"

"No, I have nothing to say about that at this

time. However, it is about a bride whose wedding didn't take place because of a murder."

"Oh dear, you're not telling me you killed Doctor Emerson after you discovered at the altar he was married to someone else."

"No!" She was taken aback and hoped he was joking. "It's nothing like that, but can we talk?"

"I'm intrigued! Certainly, come in," he said, holding the glass door open for her.

Phil led Addie past the reception desk into a small office off to the side that was encased by windows. "We should have some privacy in here," he said, closing the blinds. Then he motioned her toward a chair and took a seat behind the desk. "My apologies for the cramped space, but we don't have room for private offices in this old building and are all in the bullpen in the back room, so we use this room for interviews when we have to." He poised his pen over a pad of paper. "Shoot, what do ya have for me?"

Addie chuckled to herself. She wasn't wrong about Phil being an old-school reporter. Not a cell phone in sight poised to record their conversation. Notepad and shorthand were his style, it made her hopeful he would have been working here when the reporter that covered the scarecrow murder was still here, and he'd be able to give her a lead.

"Actually, I have nothing for you, so you won't need the notebook."

He looked curiously at her. "Then what?"

She shifted uneasily in her chair. "It's just that . . . I have a couple of questions for you."

"That's a first," he said, closing his notepad but

keeping his skepticism-filled eyes on her. "And what exactly is it you want to ask me?"

Addie took a deep breath and relayed what she had read about David Winthrop being the victim in the 1952 murder in Pen Hollow. "So"—she paused, searching for the correct wording—"I was wondering if you happened to remember that story and if you worked here then?"

He tossed his gray, balding head back and let out a deep, chesty laugh.

So much for wording her question right. She inwardly cringed.

"Look, Miss Greyborne, I'm not sure I'm as old as you think I am, but no. I wasn't here in 1952—"

"I meant, you must have heard about it, and I wondered if you knew who the reporter was. I thought they might have still been here when you started, many . . . many years later . . ."

"Nice attempt at a recovery," he chuckled, shaking his head. "No, I mean, yes, I heard about the case, but the reporter in question was a Dan Armstrong and he had sadly passed away by the time I came on board."

"Hmm, well then." The dead end hit her like a brick wall. She'd been so certain Phil could give her some insight other than what she'd find in the released news stories. "I guess I'll just have to be happy with what information I can dig up in the archives. Thank you for your time, I really appreciate it." She started to rise to her feet.

"Hold on," he said, gesturing for her to sit. "There is one person who might be able to tell you more about the story than what was published."

"I'm intrigued." Addie dropped back into her chair. "Who?"

"Bea Harper."

"Is she related?"

"Yes, she's my mother and the editor-in-chief was my grandfather."

"Wow, sure. Where can I find Bea?" The excitement started bubbling up inside her. Perhaps this wasn't going to be a wasted trip after all.

"She lives at the Greyborne Harbor Senior Living Center up at the top of the hill just off Elm Street."

"Yes, I know it. It's only a few blocks over from my house."

"Good. I know she'd probably enjoy the company, and let me tell you, she loves talking about the old days, so be prepared! She can talk your ear off when she gets going."

"Perfect, then I'll stop in there now on my way home."

"Probably not a good idea," he said, checking his watch. "It's just past one and she naps from about noon until two after they have lunch."

"Okay, then I'll go after two."

He winced. "Tell you what. Although she's still as sharp as a tack, she's not quite as bright in the afternoons. I'd suggest you go see her around ten some morning. After she has her exercise class and before she has lunch. That's generally her best time of day."

"Then ten o'clock it is," she said, rising and shaking his hand. "Thank you again, Phil. You've been a big help."

He rose and firmly shook her hand. "Just promise me that if you find something that cracks that cold case open and you discover after all these years who the killer was, I get the exclusive, hey?"

"You got it." She grinned and practically danced out past the reception room and out the front door. Bea Harper was the best lead she'd had yet and, in her gut, Addie knew it might take her one step closer to finding out who killed the love of her aunt's life.

Chapter 16

The next morning, Addie wove her way around the side streets running along the top of the hill overlooking the harbor and pulled into the wide driveway of the Greyborne Harbor Senior Living Center. She checked the clock on her dash and smiled with satisfaction: 9:55. "Perfect!"

She turned off the ignition and made her way through the glass front door and paused. The interior was far more lavish than she'd expected. Directly in front of her was an ornamental table set with an equally ornate flower vase filled with a fragrant fresh-cut arrangement. Beyond that was a sitting area with a stone wall fireplace that was open on either end to what appeared to be a luxuriantly decorated dining room behind it.

"May I help you?" called a ruddy-faced, middle-aged woman from the main desk.

Addie smiled and stepped toward her, reading

the woman's gold-colored name tag, which showed her official title as GUEST RELATIONS COORDINATOR.

"Good morning, Mary. I'm here to see Bea Harper?"

"Certainly, if I could just ask you to sign the guest registry?" Mary replied, pointing to a sign-in book, and nodded as Addie obliged. "Very good, Miss"—the woman glanced down at the name— "Greyborne. I believe Mrs. Harper is having tea with the ladies in the lounge at the moment. You can just go ahead, it's through those double doors there, directly across the foyer."

"Thank you so much for your help." Addie smiled and headed past the table and flower vase in the direction the woman had indicated.

Once through the doors, Addie came to a lurching stop. Clearly, she hadn't thought this through. She had never met Bea before, so how in the world was she going to find her in this room filled with blue-and gray-haired women?

Quickly, she caught the attention of a young server refilling teacups at a nearby table. "Excuse me, could you please point me in the direction of Bea Harper."

"Yes, that's her in the pink-and-blue-flowered dress by the window."

"Thank you so much"—Addie glanced at her name tag—"Heidi." She smiled and wove her way around tables filled with chatty ladies and a few gentlemen who were all deep in various conversations she could hear only smatterings of as she passed. There was a contentious discussion about a recent bridge tournament, another on the recent selection for shuffleboard teams, and a very animated conversation between two ladies about which movie should be shown at the next theater night. Addie decided right there and then, that when she turned a certain age, this was exactly where she was going to come to live.

She arrived at the table just as the three women were rising and preparing to leave. "Excuse me. I'm looking for Bea Harper."

A tall woman who reminded Addie of Maude, in that old television show, turned toward her and nodded her head in the direction of the woman in the blue-and-pink-flowered dress.

"Yes, can I help you?" the flowered-dress woman replied, staring mystified at Addie.

Addie thrust her hand out and reached across the table. "Hello, I'm Addie Greyborne and—"

The woman let out a soft gasp and nodded. "Yes, yes, you would be. It's in the eyes."

"I beg your pardon?" asked a confused Addie.

"It's just that you have the Greyborne eyes."

"Well, we'll leave you to talk," said the tall woman. "Come on, Gladys, let's go see what's on the lunch menu today. I certainly hope it's that chicken pot-pie we had last week. You know I think that's the best meal I've had since I moved in."

"Yes, yes, that would be lovely, wouldn't it, Georgiana," said the smaller, birdlike woman as they toddled off through the morning tearoom.

"May I sit?" asked Addie, glancing back at Bea, who hadn't removed her gaze from Addie since she'd announced who she was.

"Please." Bea gestured to the seat Georgiana had just vacated and sat back down in her own chair.

"I take it you knew the Greybornes?" said Addie, pushing a dessert plate and teacup to the side. "You said something about my eyes?"

"You have her eyes, you know."

"Whose?"

"Anita's, of course. Well, all of them, actually. Her father's and even that horrible brother of hers, what was his name?" She tapped her temple with her forefinger in thought.

"Jack?"

"Yes, that's it. Jackson." She let out a little shiver.

"I take it you were close to the family?"

"Only since grade school, my dear."

"Bea, Beatrice. Of course! You're my great-aunt's best friend that I've read about in her journals." Bea wasn't just a great lead, she was a windfall for the missing information Addie needed about her aunt's past, or so she hoped.

"I'm surprised though," said Bea, "that she referred to me as her best friend in her diaries."

"You weren't?"

"I was, at one time, at least until she went off to Garland and got in with that hoity-toity crowd from Boston."

"I see."

"Yes, then I'm afraid she didn't have much time for me anymore, and then there was that horrible incident with her fiancé—"

"David Winthrop?"

"Yes, that was his name, and then, well . . . she never returned here, at least not for about fifteen years. I heard from her from time to time. You know, a postcard of the latest exotic place she'd visited, but it wasn't until her mother took ill that she came back to Greyborne Harbor. But it, she, was the never the same. That whole David situation really changed her, and we just sort of drifted apart in her later years."

"I'm sorry to hear that. I know from personal experience that grief can change people."

"Yes, yes, you would know better than most, wouldn't you?" Bea said, studying Addie's face. "I heard about your own fiancé's and your father's deaths, such sad news. I met your father, a very nice man he was, and so good to your aunt, that was . . . until your grandmother . . . well, let's leave it at that."

"I'd like that," said Addie, shifting in her chair. This really wasn't the time or place to get into family feuds, especially with a woman she'd just met. "But what I came here to talk about is David Winthrop's murder."

"Why would you want to dredge all that up again?"

Addie shrugged meekly. "Because it's an unsolved murder case that affected someone in my family and that's kind of what I do."

"For fun, is my guess." Bea shook her head. "You know you're just like her. Anita couldn't stand not having all the answers either. She always said there was no such thing as a mystery, it was just a big old jigsaw puzzle that no one had put together yet."

"See"—Addie winced—"I come by it naturally, I guess."

Bea glanced over at the table next to them and leaned in closer to Addie. "I don't have much to tell you about what happened the weekend David died, but this isn't the place to talk about such

things. There're too many big ears around here."
She glowered at the two women at the table who
were obviously listening to their conversation with
great interest. "Why don't you come back tomorrow, about eleven? Right now, I have a pottery class
to get to and then it will be lunchtime. Heaven
knows what they'll be serving today," she said, raising her frail body to stand. "Until tomorrow?" She
looked hopefully at Addie.

"Yes, until tomorrow. I'll be in the foyer at eleven
sharp."

"Very good," Bea said as she pulled over a walker
from along the wall by the window and shuffled off
toward the door.

The woman at the next table to theirs grabbed
Addie's arm. "Don't believe a word that old
woman tells you. She has more than one bat loose
in her belfry and is always trying to stir up things
around here," she scoffed.

"Janine, you stop that right now," said her table
companion. "Why do you have to be so bitter toward everyone?"

The woman harrumphed and crossed her arms
over her chest. "You saw the look that crazy old bat
gave us, and here we were minding our own business," she spat out.

"Oh!" puffed out the other woman, rising and
tossing her napkin on the table. "It's no wonder
no one else will sit with you at teatime, or any
other time, for that matter."

"Huh, you're a great one to talk." Janine's voice
rose as the woman marched toward the door. "No
one wants to sit with the local harlot either, do

they, Lucinda!" she yelled, causing all eyes in the room to cast startled looks their way.

Did she call that other woman Lucinda? Addie hurriedly made her way out, but when she got into the foyer the woman was nowhere to be seen; then she had a thought and stopped at the reception desk.

"Excuse me, Mary. I was wondering if you allow dogs to visit residents here."

"Oh yes, we encourage it. As long as they're housebroken, friendly, kept on a lead and have had all their shots. Do you have one you'd like to bring in to visit with Mrs. Harper?"

"Yes, I do, and I think a few of the other residents might like to meet her too. She really is a friendly little dog and seems to have a sixth sense about people who need her cuddles."

"That"—she clapped her hands excitedly—"would be wonderful. We have a few"—she glanced over to the tearoom doorway just as Janine appeared—"that don't get many visitors. Their families are busy and all that, and they would really benefit by having a furry little one to visit with."

"Great, I'm coming back tomorrow to see Bea again, so I'll bring her with me."

"Thank you and have a wonderful day, Miss Greyborne." Mary waved as Addie headed toward the door.

On the drive home Addie smiled to herself. If her guess was right, Janine was lonely and that was the root of her bitterness. If she was wrong, and the woman was just plain nasty, then she'd find out soon enough. What really struck her was the other woman's name was Lucinda. Could it be there were two Lucindas roughly the right age in the same area? Could this Lucinda have been the one referred to in Anita's journals? But what better way to get the woman to open up and talk than with a furry little friend in her arms. All Addie knew, when she pulled up in front of her house and saw Paige's car parked there, was that tomorrow might be a rather informative day, and in more ways than one. Not to mention what she feared was about to take place here, right now.

"Paige," she called as she got out of her car and made her way up the porch steps to where Paige sat in a white wicker chair by the door. "What brings you by at lunchtime? Is there something wrong at the store? You aren't here to tell me that you've quit, are you?"

"What, quit? Why would you think that?"

"It's just that it's the middle of the day," said Addie, taking a seat in the other wicker chair next to Paige's. "I take it Catherine is working then?"

"No, she called and asked for the day off. There were some arrangements she had to make with Laurel. I guess the body has finally been released." Paige fidgeted with her handbag on her lap. "I hope you don't mind that I told her it was no problem. I had no idea she and Valerie were such good friends. She's really stepped up and has taken mothering Laurel to the extreme, lately."

"No, I don't have an issue with it, and you are the assistant manager, so you have to make those calls yourself when I'm not there. Knowing Catherine, she wouldn't have asked for time off unless she felt it was necessary." Addie sat back and stared off over her front yard. "I guess Simon must be a big help to Laurel now too, then?" Her voice was barely an audible whisper.

"Actually, he really has been when he's there. You know how comforting he can be in a time of crisis."

"I guess, yes." Addie recalled the time when her cousin Kalea had needed his soothing therapeutic support.

"But," added Paige quickly, averting her gaze from Addie's, "from what I've heard, he's been in the lab a lot trying to figure this whole thing out. Is it true they don't have any leads yet?"

"I guess. I'm not really sure."

"Really, I thought you'd be up to your eyeballs in this one by now."

"No." Addie waved off Paige's words. "This one hits a bit too close to home for me to get involved, so I've been working on my own murder mystery."

"Wait! There's another murder you're trying to solve? Who, when? Why didn't I hear about this?"

Addie laughed softly and explained to Paige what she'd found in the journals about the wedding, the baby, and then discovering David Winthrop had been murdered just a few months before Anita's wedding was to take place.

"Wow," whistled Paige. "That's one for the puzzle board, isn't it?"

"I haven't started one yet."

"You're kidding?"

"No, but one's coming. I think I have a good lead, but it leads to more questions, and it's getting all muddled in my mind. So it's time to get one started, I think. But anyway, you never said what brings you here over your lunch break or what's happening with the bookstore since you're here?"

"It's just been so good talking to you again after this crazy week, I forgot completely that I'm here to ask your advice"—her gaze dropped to the porch floorboards—"or permission, I guess."

"Permission about what?"

"Well . . . yesterday, I called in a phone order to Martha's Bakery for my lunch, but then I got swamped in the store—"

"Catherine wasn't working yesterday either?"

Paige shook her head.

"I had no idea she was taking that much time off. Well, I can't have you burning out. I'll just cut my vacation short and get back in there."

"No, you need this time off. You've had a rough go and you need time to heal, and I think I have a solution."

"Okay, shoot." Addie sat back and waited for Paige to continue.

"Anyway, a little while later, Serena's cousin Nikki delivered my sandwich. She took one look around the bookstore, ripped off her bakery apron and started assisting customers on the floor. It was great. I got caught up at the cash register and customers were thrilled with her knowledge about books and recommendations. When I rang their sales through, they all commented about how wonderful she was."

"Martha did tell me she has a degree in library science."

"And it shows. She's fantastic and I guess she used to help her ex out in his sporting goods store, so she has customer service experience too," Paige said excitedly.

Addie smiled inwardly. "Go on?" she said, feeling a bit like a cat that ate the canary. She knew exactly where Paige was going with this because she'd had the same idea, but had been shot down by Martha and Serena.

"Today, out of the blue, Nikki came in and offered her services for a few hours, without me even asking if she could help with coverage, and when I asked her how much she would want to be paid, she said *nothing*. She's just bored and she knew I had my hands full here because she'd heard what happened to you, and . . . Well, I'm going to give her a couple of books instead of her pay for the day. If that's okay with you?"

Addie nodded in agreement.

"But what I'd really like to do, is hire her part-time for the rest of the summer, at least."

Addie sat back and studied Paige. "So, you think she'd be a good fit, and we have enough hours for her, because I will be coming back in about another week and a half?" It was hard for Addie not to throw her arms around Paige and give her a hug because this was exactly what she'd wanted to do, but Paige needed, for her own self-confidence, to think the idea was all hers. "I mean, she has a good background, perfect for the bookstore, so . . ."

"I know in the fall, after the festivals are done for the summer, it might get a bit crowded in there, but Nikki is hoping to get on with the public library then. They have nothing right now. They told her to check back after the holidays. No one else in town is hiring right now, because they already have their summer staff. But I thought with us having the traveling bookstore, and with Catherine's schedule, it might be something that would work for all of us. What do you think?"

"I think, if you can create a schedule that will keep everyone happy, and you like Nikki, and think she'll work out, then you're the assistant manager, so it's your call."

"Really?"

"Really." Addie grinned. "You know, for example . . ." Addie tried to word it as though she hadn't given the idea a great deal of thought herself. "Maybe you could have Catherine and Nikki split Mondays. They could do four hours each, and then have Catherine work full days on Tuesday when Nikki is working for Martha, and then they can each do four hours shifts on Wednesdays and Thursdays. Then, because Nikki works for Martha on Saturdays, Catherine can work for us and Nikki can cover the Friday shifts . . . or something like that."

"Perfect! That would work. Of course, I'd have to run it past Catherine first, but if she agrees, we'd have full coverage because this summer is shaping up to be a busy one and we're going to need all the help we can get."

"See, your first major decision as a manager, and you rocked it, girl."

Paige sat back, a look of self-satisfaction crossing her face, her blue eyes sparkling in the sunlight, and Addie couldn't have felt prouder of her young protégé. Yes, little Paige had come a long way since she'd first started working for Addie, and what was best about it, was the two of them seemed to be in perfect sync over the direction the bookstore should be going.

Chapter 17

Addie threw together sandwiches for her and Paige, which the two enjoyed on the porch, along with tall glasses of sweet tea. As Addie hadn't actually been involved with the day-to-day operations of the bookstore since just before the *planned* wedding, there were a few things Paige needed to run past her before she hurriedly drained her glass and rushed back to Beyond the Page to check in on Nikki.

Addie crossed her fingers that all had gone well in Paige's absence, and the woman hadn't headed for the hills by now, because with luck, Paige was going to ask her if she was interested in the part-time work she and Addie had discussed.

Addie knew the offer would be met with some resistance from Martha and Serena, as they'd both made their opinions on the matter very clear to her when she'd brought it up previously. However, it sounded to Addie as though Nikki had a mind of her own, and if she was willing to show up today and offer her services for free, then she wasn't afraid to go after what she wanted. Without even having met the woman, Addie liked her already. She was a woman after her own heart, and she had a hunch that Nikki was going to fit in very nicely.

Now back to another topic Paige and Addie had discussed. A crime board, or as Paige referred to it, a puzzle board. It was a name Addie thought fitting since Bea had mentioned that her aunt liked mysteries and said they were jigsaw puzzles that no one had put together yet. She laughed to herself as she retrieved masking tape and a roll of brown paper from the bottom cupboard in the living room bookcase, and tacked a large piece to the wall on the right of the fireplace mantel. Then she stood back, armed with a black marker, and stared blankly at the makeshift puzzle board.

"Puzzle board is right," she mumbled, and glanced down at Pippi, sitting beside her feet as though waiting for a treat. "So where do we start?"

Pippi yipped and wagged her tail.

"Yeah, that's easy for you to say." Addie chuckled, eyeing the blank paper. "Write what you know . . ." She began scribbling.

> *Wedding dress Anita Greyborne–David Winthrop marriage to be held December 1952*
> *Anita pregnant*
> *David murdered Halloween weekend 1952*
> *Body discovered on scarecrow stand in farmer's field Pen Hollow peninsula*
> *Anita . . . ???????*

"Anita what?" Addie glared at what she'd written. "We have nothing, Pippi. Nothing to tell us who the suspects in the murder were, what happened to the baby, what happened to Anita after that horrible weekend, or what happened to her for the entire year of 1953!"

Pippi sighed and laid her head down on her front paws with a *harrumph*.

"Now do you see my dilemma? I just hope that Bea can fill in some of the blanks tomorrow." She scanned over the notes she'd made. "Or . . . I can find the missing 1953 journal. It must be here somewhere." Addie glanced over to her right and studied her great-aunt's desk seemingly taunting her from the far side of the room. "Yes, that's it."

She dropped the marker on the table, scooted around the sofa, got down on all fours, flipped onto her back, and wiggled into the kneehole. Addie commenced tapping and clicking anything on the wooden slats of the underside of the desk that might disguise a button. She knew from her past experiences that her aunt's desk in its entirety was truly a puzzle box in itself, but after an hour of finding one secret compartment after another, all empty, she gave up in frustration. She tapped a few floorboards, knowing her aunt's love of also using those as hiding places, but ultimately, she dropped back down onto the sofa while continuing to scan the living room.

"Okay, I'm twenty-two years old. I'm getting married in two months and I've just discovered I'm pregnant. Then my fiancé is murdered and the wedding can't take place. Where would I hide a diary? . . . Or would I even bother writing in one?"

Addie eyed the stack of journals on the coffee table, and then recalled the boxes and boxes of them she'd found over the last few years in the attic. "Yes, it's my passion to journal my thoughts and experiences. I would have written one, so where would I have hidden it? Perhaps to keep it from my overbearing father's eyes or because what I wrote in it was too painful for me to be reminded of, even years later . . . Hmm . . ." Addie snapped her fingers and raced upstairs to the small turret bedroom.

"Of course! Anita had mentioned in her earlier journal that this was her bedroom. Where else would a young woman hide something she wanted to keep, but not be reminded of what it contained?"

Addie stood in the doorway, not knowing where to begin. She'd never used this room herself, or offered it to any of her overnight guests. It had an aura surrounding it, which in Addie's mind had made it sacred. Now that she knew this had been her great-aunt's childhood bedroom, she understood where that feeling came from. Seeing as most of the house had been charmingly restored to period, and rooms like the kitchen even modernized somewhat over the years, this room appeared as though time had stood still.

Addie ran her hand over the faded floral wallpaper and surveyed the room. The bedroom portion contained a single wrought-iron bed frame finished in white porcelain, and a dresser. But the real character of the room came from the turret room, to the far left. Beside it, French doors led out onto a large sleeping porch that would have been used during hot, humid nights.

Addie's eyes focused on the window seats built around the octagonal windows as she made her way to the turret room. It was as good as any place to start. She eagerly flipped up the cushion and, just as she'd hoped, there was a lid revealing a storage area beneath. "Whoa, what do we have here?" She dropped down onto her knees and began removing boxes of vintage board games.

Sorry, The Game of Life, Chutes and Ladders, Uncle Wiggily Game, Concentration, Park and Shop, all in their original edition boxes. But it was the last one that brought a smile to her face, the original, British version of Cluedo—The Great Detective Game. She read the promotional blurb on the box and her smile widened. *Cluedo is a detective game that would delight any sleuth* . . . and knowing what she did about Anita, she could clearly envision her aunt playing this one with her family and friends. She decided that although these were a glimpse into her aunt's youth, they would also be of great interest to a collector and made a mental note to contact a colleague of hers in Boston.

Addie jumped and dropped the box in her hand when Pippi began frantically barking downstairs. She set the games aside and retreated into the hallway, listening from the top of the steps. There it was—a faint but definite knock on the front door.

"Okay, Pippi." She laughed, descending the staircase. "I hear it, I'm coming," she called and flung the door open. "Simon? What are you doing here? Aren't you working today?"

"I know you asked me to stay away, but I couldn't any longer because I miss you too much," he said, shifting his weight from one foot to the other, looking like a sheepish schoolboy.

"Me too, wanna come in?" She breathed a soft sigh. It was comforting to know that, in spite of everything she'd said to him before, he was missing her too.

"Yes, I do."

She steadied her voice to keep her erratic emotions in check. "So, how's it going?"

"Laurel's such a mess right now, but all things considered, I think she's coping as well as can be expected."

"I meant with the case."

"Sorry, guess I'm just so caught up in everything else that happened too—you know, Mason."

"And how's that going, you being a new dad and all?"

"That's the tough part," he said, strolling into the living room and taking a seat on the sofa. "The poor kid landed here with people he doesn't know and then this happens, but I think making sure Mason is kept on an even track is what keeps Laurel going. She's a great mom and works really hard trying to not let this get the best of him since he's already had so much tragedy in his young life. You know, first losing his parents and then his grandmother, and now his grandfather being so ill."

"Yeah, that's a lot for anyone to go through, let alone a sixteen-year-old." Addie took a seat in the chair by the window, across the coffee table from Simon. "What about you? How have you been through all this?"

Simon met her questioning gaze and shrugged. "As well as you'd expect for someone whose entire life became unraveled overnight, I guess, and you?"

"About the same, but I have found something to keep my mind off things, and it's kept me busy."

"What's that?"

"A seventy-year-old murder mystery I've been trying to solve."

"Talk about a cold case." He chuckled and glanced over at the makeshift crime board. "Is that what you've started to work on there?"

"Yes, and as you can see, I haven't gotten very far. The problem is finding people who were around then that can give me a little more insight than what was printed in the papers at the time."

"It sounds interesting and if I can help in any way, let me know."

"Thank you, but I think you have your hands full with Valerie's murder, don't you?"

"Yeah, and all we have so far is dead ends. This one might end up going down as a cold case too."

"I think that's what Marc's afraid of."

Simon's jaw clearly tensed. "You've spoken to Marc recently?"

"Yes, he asked for my help."

"He did?"

"Yes, he wanted me to look at the pictures and videos from the tea to see if I could spot anything out of the ordinary."

"And I take it you didn't?"

"No, but I haven't looked too closely yet."

"Well, I have time to look through them with

you now. That is, if you want to?" He looked hopefully at her.

"Sure, why not. Two sets of eyes are better than one." Addie stood up, grabbed her laptop from the table, settled in beside Simon on the sofa and opened the file named *Phil Harper's Video*. It immediately went to the still frame Addie had looked at the last time she had opened it, the image of Simon embracing a distraught Laurel. "I was wrong. I thought I could look through these with you but I can't."

"But it's perfect that I'm here. I can explain what was going on with Laurel and why there are images of me holding her."

"I know what was going on with Laurel. Her aunt just died in front of her and you were doing what you do best as a comforting doctor and a friend. But can't you see what looking at those images does to me?"

"Addie, please, she and I are just friends."

Addie glanced at the image again and then quickly looked away. "Close friends, by the look of it."

"Addie."

"What am I supposed to think when I see pictures like this all over the internet? That one I can understand, but . . ." She scrolled through Phil Harper's videos of one, then two, then three times Simon was embracing Laurel at the tea. "These ones here were taken *before* Valerie collapsed."

"There's an explanation for those too."

"I know there is, but they still tear my heart in two. I am only human, Simon, and to see the look in her eyes and yours while you're holding her. It's just . . . too much of a reminder of what the two of you used to have, and clearly that closeness isn't a thing of the past."

"But it is. I love you. How many times do I have to tell you that?"

"Show, don't tell, Simon."

"I'm here, aren't I?"

"Yes, in body, but your mind is with her. You've been here all of five minutes and in that time you've mentioned her constantly."

"She's hurting, Addie."

"I know, I know, she's suffered a great loss, but can't you see what all this time you're spending with her is doing to me? To us? There has to be a happy medium, and it seems that you've chosen her pain over mine."

"That's not fair. Your pain will be resolved when the annulment goes through and we can go ahead with the wedding as planned; hers is lifelong."

"You're right, and maybe I'm being selfish, but yours isn't the only life that's become unraveled with what's transpired since our wedding ceremony."

Simon laid his head on the back of the sofa and stared up at the ceiling. "You're right, and I have to do better."

"You're one person, and as much as you want to, because it's in your nature, you can't take care of everyone else. So, let's make it easier on both of us, so you don't feel torn and I'm not left in limbo indefinitely."

His head snapped up and he stared at her. "What are you saying?"

"I don't know what I'm saying, but actions have consequences, and here we are sixteen years later dealing with those. It's just going to take us time to move forward from everything that's happened, that's all."

"But we will, and then you'll see. We'll both be stronger and so will our love for each other."

"Maybe." She looked skeptically at him. "I guess what I'm saying is, we need to forget about re-scheduling our wedding right now. You need to focus on your son and solving this case, because it will help bring closure to Laurel, and *then* we can see where we are as a couple."

"Stop pushing me away, Addie. I've told you that I don't want to go anywhere that doesn't involve you. I love you."

"To be honest, when I see these pictures, I don't know what to think right now, Simon."

"Addie, with no leads and over a hundred suspects, this murder has everyone in town on edge; Laurel is no exception. Imagine how she feels moving here. Starting a new veterinary practice and then her aunt is murdered in her new home."

"I know, and that's why I'm so torn in my feelings."

"Look at it this way. As things stand right now, the situation is like an open wound with Laurel, and it's festering. Until we solve this case, she isn't going to get any closure and neither are the people of Greyborne Harbor. Everyone is starting to look at their neighbor as a potential murderer, and it's going to tear this town apart unless we can get this solved quickly. So yes, I have to spend a lot of time with Laurel and working on what little I have to go on, because it's just beyond reason to me that someone would want that dear woman dead."

"Someone clearly did, but"—she glanced at her laptop—"I think in your investigation you can start narrowing down the field."

"How? There isn't one clue so far."

"You'd know better than I would, but isn't it true that the poison used was something probably every woman attending the tea had in her handbag?"

"You think it was a woman?"

"Truth is stranger than fiction, and like Agatha Christie always said, women tend to use *cleaner* methods in suicide or murder than men, who are inclined to use more physical means—guns, knives, and brute force. So yes, my guess is the murderer was a woman. That's someplace to start, isn't it?"

"Now we have only about seventy suspects." He groaned and laid his head back. "How and when did the bottle of eye drops get placed in her tea, and what happened to any trace evidence that it was there in the first place?"

She glanced back at the laptop and decided he was right. It was time to put on her big girl pants if there was going to be hope for them in the future; because, until Laurel had closure, she was going to remain the number-one priority in his life. "Like I said, two sets of eyes are better than one. Let's take a look at the videos and see if either of us can pick out something unusual that happened."

"Are you sure you want to look at these again?"

Her finger hesitated over the touchpad. "Yes," she said, and clicked play.

Addie scrolled through the video, pressing play then pause, so they could study each still frame from one point of the action to the next. "This reminds me of those puzzle pictures; you know, the ones that say what's different in these two images."

"Yeah, I used to do a lot of those when I was young." Simon chuckled. "The trick was spotting that one thing that, even so slight, was not the same as in the first picture."

"Yes, like an arm in an ever-so-slightly different position, or shirt cuff not drawn out completely, or a crease in a pant leg that was different, or . . ."

"What, do you have something? Where?"

"Look at this," said Addie as she slowed the motion on the screen and studied the images frame by frame. "It's hard to spot when you first look at the full image, because there's so much else going on in the room. It looks like Phil must have been standing in the front right corner taking a pan shot to get as much in as he could."

"Yeah, like he was trying to record *all* the action in the room at the same time."

"That was probably so when he was writing up his news story about the event, he could see everyone that attended." Addie pressed pause and pointed to the screen. "There's the group talking by the refreshment table." She pressed play. "Here're you, Laurel, and Mason speaking to the Timmonses, and then there're all these smaller groups, Bev and Bin, Martha, Paige, and so on, all moving about the living room, visiting with one another."

"That's the part that's a distraction. There's so much movement happening."

"Yes, but when I zoom in on the far-left front

corner, see? You can just make out the front of Valerie in her chair. Her knees, showing the flowered skirt she was wearing, and then here! Her hand comes into the frame while she picks up her teacup and her arm moves back out of frame. She must be taking a drink of it because she sets it back on the side table, and no one else is around her."

"Okay?"

"Now this is the part I missed earlier when I was looking at it because, like you said, there are so many distractions around her, but look. Here she stands up and moves into frame just for a second and takes a handful of packaged sweeteners off the tray on the coffee table. Then she's out of frame again but we can see her dress when she sits back down. Then look at her hand, putting not one, but three packages in her teacup."

"She was diabetic, so it makes sense she'd use the sweetener not the sugar, but like you said, it was packaged, so it couldn't have contained any of the poison."

"I know, and you said to Marc that the toxic ingredient that killed her was generally found in eye drops, which are a solution, so it wouldn't be in there anyway. But what I'm saying is, this is the scene right before she collapsed, so watch! She took a sip of her tea, as we saw by her hand movement. It must have tasted off, and so she put more sweeteners in it. I've had tea with Valerie and I know she only takes one package in her tea. What I counted out now, makes nearly four that she put in."

"Meaning the first sip containing her normal one package of sweetener must have tasted bitter."

"Yes, or at least something was off with it. Then, see, after she puts more sweeteners in it, her hand picks up the cup and it's not set back down for . . . wait for it. And notice all the people milling around the room, those that stop and talk to her, often blocking the camera view, and there . . . there is Bev and Bin Thomas stopping and chatting, no teacup on the table. Then Martha and Ida join them, and Catherine comes over here with a teapot as she's making rounds asking people if they would like a top-up. She gets to Valerie and her group. Martha holds out her cup, Catherine refills it, Bin shakes her head. Valerie must have waved her off too, because then Catherine skirts around the coffee table and asks those on the right side of the room. She fills Paige's cup, but keep your eyes on Valerie's group. They all disperse and move on toward the refreshment table and we can still barely see Valerie's knees in the shot, but the cup and saucer are still visible on her lap. Her hand comes down, she lifts it out of the shot, for as long as it would take to have a number of sips, then her hand sets the cup back on the saucer, and moves it onto the side table beside her, and ten minutes later, she's on the floor dead."

"That means that none of those who stopped to talk to her in this portion of the video could have put the poison in her cup then."

"Exactly, she had the cup on her lap the whole time, so there's no way. The fact that she had put the extra sweetener in her cup, meaning it tasted off somehow to her, before Bev and Bin, Martha, Ida, and Catherine passed by tells me Marc can take all those people off his list of suspects, because the tea was doctored before this scene was shot."

"Is there anything *before* this that shows when or how the eye drops were poured into her cup?"

"Not that I can see. Earlier, Valerie does get blocked occasionally from the camera angles, when people were still arriving in droves. But other than her cup being refilled by someone who then moves on to top up the next guests . . ."

"Meaning they are all drinking from the same teapot?"

"Yeah, and they didn't get sick." Addie shrugged. "But from this video, I can't see any time when someone might have added a solution into Valerie's tea."

"Then this really doesn't tell us how or who."

"No, but I think it also helps prove that Bev, Bin, Martha, Ida, and Catherine aren't the gray-haired killer."

"Does Marc have a copy of this?"

"Yes, he said he did, that's why he left me the flash drives. Why?"

"Because he should take a look and see what he thinks. It's not much, but it's more than we had before." Simon started to rise to his feet and stopped. "Unless of course you want to go and tell him, since he asked you to look at the videos."

"No, you go ahead. I have my own mystery to solve, remember." She gestured to the makeshift crime board.

"I can't thank you enough, Addie. This might help Laurel out in the sense that so many people are dropping by her house to offer their condolences and leave her casseroles and such that she's been throwing them all away because she just doesn't know who she can trust, and she's afraid that one of the dishes might be poisoned."

"I can see that. There were a lot of people there that day and one of them *is* a killer. But maybe knowing there are a couple, at least, she can take off the list might help her know who she can trust and who she can't."

Simon paused at the front door and turned to Addie. His hand cupped her cheek as he leaned over to kiss her.

His lips, cool and impassionate against hers, sent a little shockwave up her spine, and she pulled back and stared at him as if a stranger had just kissed her.

"I love you," he whispered, "but I better go tell Marc and Laurel what you found."

There it was. The reason for his distance: Even when he kissed her, his mind was still on Laurel. "Yes, you better go update Laurel about at least six of the people that were there."

With his unfeeling kiss still fresh in her mind, she closed the door behind Simon, but she couldn't help but feel that something had changed. With him? With her? She didn't know, but nothing was the same and it made her question whether it would ever be the same again, and if *they* would be the same again.

Chapter 18

Addie sank into the sofa, and Pippi immediately jumped up and laid her head in Addie's lap, nudging her hand with her nose for a scratch. "Yes, I know. I still have your love, don't I, and that's all that matters. Because if I'm honest with myself, I'd say that I was born under an unlucky star, and everlasting love wasn't what the universe had in store for me."

She forced a smile as she gazed down at her loyal companion and stroked the soft fur behind her ear, thinking about the unsettling feelings the afternoon with Simon left her with. It was as though the entire universe had shifted sideways, and everything was off-kilter and beyond her control. Or was it? She sat up and settled Pippi beside her on the sofa, picked up the laptop and opened the Phil Harper video.

If she could solve this, then Simon wouldn't

have to spend his free time with Laurel, and then they could figure out where they stood in their relationship with each other, and figure out how Mason was going to fit into their lives as a couple.

Addie replayed the video, pausing and playing not only it but the other ones Marc had on the first flash drive. However, every image was just as it had been before. There was nothing to indicate someone had doctored Valerie's tea, from what she could tell. Then she noticed something in Paige's video and zoomed in on the cup beside Valerie on the side table. She took a screen shot, saved it, and scrolled through the rest of the short video until Paige had dropped her phone. She reopened Phil's video and zoomed in on the cup beside Valerie and took another screen shot. Then fast-forwarded to when Phil had recorded the paramedics and the police arriving; there was a lot of commotion in the room as Valerie lay on the floor, but Addie managed to find a clear image of the cup and zoomed in on it and saved another screen shot.

Addie opened the file of the three images, laying them out side by side, studied them, and then did an internet search of the history of bone-china patterns. There it was, just as she thought. She quickly reopened the three images of Valerie's teacups and enlarged the pictures. There was no mistaking it. Although similar, very similar in pattern, there was just enough difference to distinguish between the cup Valerie started the day with, and the one she drank from that had clearly been doctored, and then in the third picture, taken after she collapsed, the cup had been switched back to the same one she'd had in the first picture.

Someone had swapped the cups just before she drank from it, and they were so similar it was hard to detect. That's why nothing in the analysis of her cup had any trace evidence. The tainted cup must have been in someone's handbag, and when they left the house after questioning, they and the tainted cup left too.

Addie sat back and stared at the screen. "Okay, Pippi, we finally have means but still no suspect and no motive." She slammed the top of her laptop closed and paused in thought. "Maybe not, Pippi." She looked back over at her little friend asleep on the sofa, her ears twitching with the sound of her name. "That means whoever switched the cups would have to have had prior knowledge of what tea set would be used at the event in order to take one that was almost identical. So, we only have to find out who helped set up before the tea and then left, returning later with a similar cup in their possession, and we have ourselves a killer, right?" Pippi snorted, turned on her back, her four paws in the air, and wriggled into the sofa. "Thanks, friend. I thought that was a good deduction and one Marc should follow up on."

Pippi let out a quiet woof and thumped her tail on the sofa. Addie picked her cell phone up off the table and punched in Marc's number. It went to voice mail so she tapped out a text, knowing he'd read it even if he was busy.

I think I know how the eye drops were given to Valerie. I still don't know by who but it might be a lead as to why there was no evidence at the scene. But I think I have something else that might help nar-

row down the pool of suspects. Call me when you can.

There, at least it was a start in taking back some control in her life, and she grinned at Pippi. "Dinnertime, girl?"

Pippi leapt up and flew off the sofa, her little nails clicky-clacking as she scooted down the hall to the kitchen.

Addie had only just let Pippi out for a run in the yard and was clearing up her dinner dishes when Marc returned her call. He told her that he and Simon had finished reviewing the videos, and Simon was going to head over to Laurel's now to talk to her about what they saw. Addie updated him on her theories about the cup and the switch in patterns. He told her it was a good lead and that he'd join Simon and ask Laurel about the catering, and then thanked her. That was it. Her part in all this was done, and a sense of satisfaction settled in. She crossed her fingers in the hope that she might have given him a lead to whoever had committed the murder, and it would help bring Simon back to her sooner.

Invigorated, she headed back upstairs to resume her quest to find the missing 1953 journal of her aunt's. However, two hours and a number of cuss words later, Addie collapsed on her aunt's childhood bed, muffling her screams of frustration into the pillow. Pippi yipped and darted out into the hallway, barking from the top of the staircase.

"I know, I know. I'm sorry," called Addie. "It's safe now. I'm done, in more ways than one," she muttered, launching herself off the bed and going into the hall to try to decide which of the twenty-one remaining rooms, plus the attic, her aunt might have hidden the journal in. When Pippi howled and pitter-pattered down the stairs, and then stood at the front door, barking, Addie cocked her head to listen. Between the yaps and the barks Addie finally heard the knocking and trotted down to the door, peered through the side-panel window and shooed Pippi back.

"Marc? I hope you're here with some good news, like you caught the culprit?" She looked hopefully at him as he entered the foyer.

"I only wish it were that easy, but I did want to come by and take a look at those images you have of the cups."

"Sure." She waved him toward the living room. "Would you like a coffee?"

"I'd love one," he said, tossing his cap onto the coffee table and taking a seat on the sofa. "This has been a long day and somehow I get the feeling it's not over yet."

"Back in a flash," she said, and scurried toward the kitchen. She quickly made two cups of coffee, added a plate of chocolate-chip cookies to the tray, and hustled back, setting the tray on the table. "If you want more than cookies, I can whip something up for you."

"No, this is great, thanks. I'll stop for a burger later, but coffee is what I really need now," he said, adding a teaspoon of sugar to one of the cups. He took a sip and sat back, a look of satisfaction crossed his face, and he smiled. "Perfect as usual."

"It is hard to mess up those coffee pods." She laughed, picked up her laptop, and settled into the sofa beside him. "Okay." She tapped the touch-pad and brought the screen to life. "Here, look at these." She pointed to the three images of the teacups she'd saved. "Notice the pattern on the first one and the last one; they're identical, right?" He nodded as she enlarged the image. "Now, look at the one from the video that was taken right after Valerie collapsed. See the difference?"

He squinted and shook his head.

She enlarged it again. "Now can you see it?"

"Yeah, but they are so similar. Are you sure it's not the same cup?"

"Positive." She minimized the images and opened the article she'd found about the china patterns. "Read this and tell me what you think."

Marc read the article about the lower quality porcelain set that was popular with many restaurant and catering companies because of its similarity to the original fine bone china set. Addie searched for copy patterns and came across a large manufacturer that used a very similar one to the Royal Doulton collectible pattern.

"They made small changes to it, but it's their biggest seller to hotels, catering and rental companies. So, all it would take is for someone who had a similar pattern at home to have known this and brought their own cup to pour the poison tea concoction into and then exchange the cups at just the right time so as not to be detected. Which would also show premeditation, and that the doctoring of the tea was not a spur-of-the-moment act." She sat back and grinned at him, feeling rather smug by her discovery. "Except they hadn't counted on someone with knowledge of vintage china patterns to be viewing the pictures, did they?"

"I can see why they are popular for catering and restaurants. They'd want to give their patrons the feeling of fine dining."

"Exactly, this is why they use reproductions of the original pattern."

"I asked Laurel, who supplied the dishes and tea sets, and she said they were rented from the local catering and party rental company here in town. She also said that a couple of the ladies came to help set up, then they all left to go home and get ready, and returned later."

"See, there's the lead, as I thought. Seeing the pattern beforehand gave the killer time to go home and get a similar cup they could fill with the poison and then go back and replace Valerie's cup with it, and no one would be the wiser."

"That's what I thought too, until I called the catering company and they told me this is the stock pattern they've used for years. Valerie had also run an open house invitation in the *Greyborne Harbor Daily News* and they used one of the catering company's stock photos in it, which clearly showed the tea sets they rent out for functions."

"Which means anyone with a newspaper could see what the cup pattern was going to be."

"Exactly."

"Back to square one." Addie slumped back into the sofa.

"Don't give up yet. This is a good lead, I just have to follow up on it and I'm pretty certain it will give us a name sooner or later."

"Yeah, it's the later I'm worried about."

He looked questioningly at her, but she brushed it off and gestured to his empty cup. "Do you want another?"

"That would be great. Like I said, I think this is going to be a long night."

She got up and headed for the kitchen, Marc close on her heels. He made himself at home on one of the island counter stools.

"So, Simon and Laurel, hey?"

She eyed him out of the corner of her eye as she dropped a pod into the coffeemaker. "What do you mean, Simon and Laurel?"

"Nothing, it was just when I was leaving, she was starting dinner for all of them and Simon was helping Mason set up his new gaming system." Marc shrugged. "I was surprised he was staying, I thought he'd come over here and tell you what she'd said about the catering."

Just one big happy family. The notion of that settled into the back of Addie's throat and she gulped trying to dislodge it. "I know he's trying to build a relationship with his son, so helping him out makes sense."

"Yeah."

Then she thought about what he'd said. "Why are you telling me this?"

"No reason, I was just surprised. I didn't know him and Laurel were still so close, that's all."

Addie set his cup on the counter with a thud,

and coffee sloshed over the sides. "Are you trying to upset me, or warn me?"

"I was only . . ."

"Please don't, Marc. Simon and I will work out what's best for us after this case is solved, you'll see."

"Sure you will," he said, picking up his cup and eyeing her over the rim.

"No, really, Marc. Simon and I are just fine, so if you think you had to mention where he was and with who to protect me, don't worry. I know Laurel is hurting, and Simon being the type of person and doctor he is, he feels he can be of some help right now. It's all cool, really it is."

Was she trying to convince him or herself? Because, no matter how many times she swallowed, there was no getting rid of the lump in the back of her throat. Even though she didn't completely believe her own words, darn it, she wasn't about to tell Marc that. They had too much history and it was one she didn't care to repeat, if that's what he was hoping by telling tales out of school. Her wounds over recent events were still too raw.

Chapter 19

The next morning, Addie clipped Pippi onto her lead, and they made their way through the front doors of the senior living center. She registered at the desk, and Mary informed her that Bea was waiting for her in the back garden by the gazebo. Mary gave her instructions on how to get there from the foyer, and gave Pippi a pat, gesturing to Addie toward the fireplace. Addie turned and spied Lucinda and Janine sitting on the sofa and slowed her pace as she led Pippi past them.

"What a cute pup. Come here, little one. That's it, come see me." Lucinda grinned, holding out her hand. Addie stepped toward her, letting out the lead just enough so Pippi could sniff the woman's hand first. When she wagged her tail, Addie let her go the full length of her leash to receive the woman's eager pats.

"Keep that flea-bitten creature away from me,"

snapped Janine, rotating on her seat away from the wiggling furry little dog.

"But, oh, look how friendly she is," said Lucinda, scratching Pippi behind the ear.

"I don't want it near me. I can't abide critters, nasty little things."

Pippi perked her ears, cocked her head, looked at Janine and then stood on her hind legs and nestled her head into Janine's lap.

"Get her off!" The woman grimaced and pulled back in her seat.

Addie moved to dislodge her exuberant little friend from the woman, but stopped when Pippi nudged Janine's hand and nestled her head deeper into her lap. Then, tentatively, Janine began stroking her little head and Pippi licked her hand. Addie glanced over at Mary, who was beaming at the scene from behind the desk.

When Addie glanced back at Janine, she swore she saw tears in the woman's eyes as she gently stroked Pippi's head.

It warmed her heart to know that Janine wasn't as nasty as she let on, no matter what she tried to portray to the world. It was clear that all it took was Pippi's comforting cuddles to break through her crusty exterior and reveal the kindhearted woman underneath.

She hated to have to drag Pippi away, but she glanced at the large clock over the mantel and saw that it was nearly eleven, and she didn't want to keep Bea waiting. "I'm afraid we have to go now," Addie said apologetically.

"No!" cried Janine. "Can't she stay for just a few more minutes?"

"I can watch her," said Mary over Addie's shoulder. "She'll be fine. Don't worry, and if there's an issue, I'll have one of the staff come and find you."

"Well, girl"—Addie looked at Pippi—"what do you think? Do you want to stay and visit with these nice ladies while I go see Bea?"

Pippi wagged her tail and snuggled into Janine's neck, her little pink tongue lapping wet kisses across the woman's cheek.

Janine laughed, and pushed her furry little head away, still giggling.

"I guess it's settled then. Thank you," Addie said, turning to Mary. "But, please, if you get busy or there are any changes, let me know."

"I think we'll be just fine," Mary said, grinning down at Pippi playing a gentle game of keep-away with Janine's fingers.

Addie turned to head off in the direction Mary had pointed her in earlier, but stopped and spun back around. "Lucinda, there's something I've been meaning to ask you. Did you ever spend any time in Pen Hollow?"

"Why, yes. I grew up there, why?"

"No reason really, I'd just heard the name mentioned by someone, but I imagine in the 1950s there was more than one Lucinda around this area, right?"

"If this person said the Lucinda they knew was a real flirt, then you got the right girl," said Janine with a chuckle. "There's not a man who moves into this building she doesn't try to get her claws into within minutes."

"I can't help it if I'm tired of all the women who

live here, and men of our age are few and far between because we women tend to outlive men."

"Pfft," snorted Janine, and she went back to stroking Pippi's head.

"Does the name David Winthrop mean anything to you?" asked Addie.

"David, David, I'm not sure."

"She knew a lot of boys back then, I'm guessing," giggled Janine, as Pippi nudged her hand for more pats.

"He was killed the Halloween weekend of 1952?"

"Oh yes! I read about that." Lucinda's gaze flitted to the side. "But no. I don't remember much about it."

"I was just curious when I heard the name. Actually, I'm heading off now to talk to Bea because I think she also knew some of the people from back then on the peninsula, and one of them is a relative of mine that I'd like to find out more about."

Addie didn't miss the paling of Lucinda's complexion when she said that, but Janine shook her head.

"Hmm, good luck getting any straight answers out of Bea." She rotated her forefinger in circles around her ear. "She's a bit off sometimes, if you know what I mean."

"Janine," said Mary, looking every bit like a schoolmarm. "What have we talked about before, when it comes to speaking unkindly about other residents?"

Janine sheepishly retreated and snuggled Pippi into her chest.

"I'll keep that in mind," said Addie, giving Pippi

a pat and telling her to behave while she was gone. Then she headed off down the hallway, searching for the double-wide patio doors that would lead out into the garden, which Mary had said she'd find on her left.

She shielded her eyes from the morning sun and scanned the lavish lawn, with its flower and tree border. Then off to her right, by the small gazebo, sat the petite woman, exactly where she'd told Mary she'd be. "Good morning, Bea," said Addie, approaching her and taking the proffered seat on the wooden garden bench beside her. "It's a lovely day, isn't it?"

"Very nice," said Bea, eyeing Addie closely. "Yes, yes, I see Anita behind those hazel-green eyes. There's no mistaking the family resemblance in this light."

"That's exactly what I was hoping we could talk about today."

Bea nodded, gripping the handles of her walker. "Okay, what is it you want to know? How she dumped me for that crew from Boston, or how she came back and wasn't the same Anita I knew as a young girl?"

"What do you mean, she wasn't the same girl you knew?"

"Hmm, I guess her spirit was broken. Losing David was hard enough, but something else happened. She never said what, but I could guess that's why she left right after he died and didn't come back for over fifteen years. I think she was running from something or someone."

"Running from someone?" Now that was a scenario Addie hadn't even considered. "Do you think she knew who killed David and was afraid that person would come after her too?"

"I have no idea. She never talked about any of it after she came back. Just carried on like nothing had happened and she hadn't spent the last fifteen years traveling the globe."

"I understand that you were working at the *Greyborne Harbor Daily News* when David was killed."

"Working, if that's what you want to call it. I'd finished secretarial school and my father had high hopes for me to manage the office, but gofer and coffee maker was more like what I did."

"Then you weren't involved with covering his murder story?"

"Not really. My father, like most men back then, thought a woman was only good for one or two things, and if they had to work outside the home, then it was acceptable to be a secretary, or teacher, even a nurse, but a newspaper reporter, never. Remember, it was a time when it was frowned on for a woman to want anything more than creating a nice home and raising children. Following your dreams wasn't part of it. But"—a devious glint came to Bea's faded brown eyes and she chuckled softly—"I had different plans and did some snooping around on my own."

"What did you find out?"

"Not much. Since I didn't have any credentials, not many doors opened up to me." She turned and looked at Addie. "You have to remember, dearie, it was different back then and women weren't taken seriously by the authorities. Well," she harrumphed, "by no one, for that matter, least of all the police and my father, who was the editor and my *boss*. But I did manage to find out a few things; sadly they didn't lead anywhere and to this day David Winthrop's murder remains unsolved."

Addie reached over and gently touched the woman's arthritic, gnarled hand. "It sounds like you did everything you could, considering the times. I'm hoping that maybe, after all these years, between the two of us we can finally put this to rest."

"Wouldn't that be something?" She pinned her faded eyes on Addie. "Yes, yes. That's what I'd like too. You know, I'd always hoped I could solve it or find a clue, just to give Anita some peace of mind, but now with you being a relative, I can see that it would bring you some peace also."

"As you said before, I'm like my aunt and can't stand having an unsolved mystery, so it would be nice if we could find closure for Anita and for all she suffered after David was killed."

"And suffer she did. She had moved on, but she was never the same. It was so hard for me, because I still recalled the girls we had been growing up and how we shared everything." Tears replaced the previous glimmer in Bea's eyes and she swatted at her sallow, wrinkly cheek. "If I can be of any help to you, then I will."

"Let's start with the night he was killed. Is there any information you dug up that would give us a lead?"

"I did talk to Maisie and Arnold Radcliff . . . after. Anita was in no state, so . . ." Her fingers tightened on the handles of her walker. "I asked them why they left David at the fairgrounds. You know, the last place he was seen alive that night."

"And what did they say?"

"Arnold told me the same thing that he'd told the police. Anita was feeling queasy and Maisie was worried about her, so they wanted to go back to Windgate House so she could go to bed. They were all piling into Arnold's car when some Harvard friends of David's showed up. Anita told him to stay, that she was just going to go to bed anyway, so he should stay and have some fun. It was the last night of the season and she didn't want to ruin his weekend because she wasn't feeling well."

"Then just Arnold, Maisie, and Anita went back to the house?"

"Yes. Arnold told David he'd be back after he dropped the girls off, and they made plans to meet up in the parking lot, but when Arnold went back, there was no sign of David. Arnold just figured he'd gone off with his buddies and he left again to go back to Windgate."

"Did the police think these friends of David's had anything to do with his disappearance?"

"Who knows. They came from money, lots and lots of money, and the boys' fathers were very influential and made sure their names weren't connected to the murder at all. But I don't think they were involved anyway."

"Why's that?"

"Because when I was talking to other people who were in the parking lot that night, it sounded like David and his friends were approached, shortly after Arnold and the girls left, by another girl and a couple of other fellows. The witnesses said a scuffle broke out between them all, but David and his friends got the better of them with a couple of good knuckle sandwiches. David and his friends were all boxing champions at school, apparently. Then David's group headed back into the fairgrounds. One of the witnesses said they overheard the dark-haired fellow say he wanted to win a teddy bear for his fiancée. I imagine that meant they were going to play some of the games on the boardwalk."

"Any idea what happened after that?"

"None of those people I talked to saw them again. They were in the parking lot because they were leaving for the evening."

"Then we have no way of knowing what happened."

Bea softly chuckled. "I wouldn't say that. A few days later, I was taking a coffee into the reporter at the *Daily News* who was covering the story, and he'd popped out to go and talk to my dad about something. I put his coffee on the desk and . . . let's just say there was a copy of the police report sitting right there in plain sight. I, of course, just happened to read it."

"Of course you did." Addie choked back a laugh. That was exactly what she'd been known to do a time or two herself with a file sitting on Marc's desk. "And what did it say?"

"It said, when the police questioned the Harvard boys, they told them that when the fireworks started, signaling the end of the evening, they talked about going to see if they could find a couple of girls they'd met earlier in the evening, and of course David wanted nothing to do with that. He told them to go have fun and he'd walk back to Windgate as it was only a couple of miles up the road. That was the last time anyone saw him alive."

Addie shifted on the bench, turning toward Bea. "Did the reporter covering the story get any other leads?"

"No, he hit as many dead ends as I did. Everyone involved was either very rich or well connected, or they were under twenty-one and the police wouldn't release any names. The story eventually ran as one of those weird-but-true pieces. *A boy dressed in a scarecrow costume found dead on a scarecrow stand in a farmer's field.* It was front-page news because it was Halloween weekend, but the police were no help at all. They were convinced that because there were so many tourists in town for the fair that it was the work of some psycho killer traveling through, and that was it."

"Did you ever find out the names of the group David and his friends had the scuffle with?"

Bea stared straight ahead, and Addie was afraid she'd lost her. But she shook her head. "Not really, as I recall. Most of the people I managed to track down who saw the altercation between the two groups were from Greyborne Harbor and didn't know any of those involved. But there was one fellow . . ."

"Yes?"

"His name . . ." She tapped her gnarled finger on the arm of her walker. "Oh yes. Kenny, that was it. He was the lot attendant. He said he saw the whole thing and was heading over to break up the fight when the girl there—someone called her Lucinda—managed to end it by yelling at them all."

"Lucinda?"

"Yes, and then he told me he called the police and that the group got all huffy and said they'd rather party instead anyway and they were heading over to the sandspits for a bonfire. Then they got in their car and drove away. David and his friends went back to the fairgrounds. That's all he knew."

Addie recalled the trip she'd taken to Pen Hollow last year with Paige and the drive along the bay side of the peninsula. "That means when David left the fairgrounds, he would have had to walk right past the sandspits on his way back to Windgate, right?"

"Yes, I suppose. It's been years since I've been there, but you could be right."

"And Lucinda and her friends were there partying, after they already had a fight with David and his buddies?"

"But the police questioned them all and didn't think it meant anything. They figured David was picked up by a stranger and it was a random killing."

"But what if it wasn't? Maybe the actual act was random but the killers weren't." Addie looked at Bea. "Could this girl named Lucinda be the same one who is friends with Janine?"

"You mean I could have a murderer living down the hallway from me?"

Addie felt all the blood rush from her cheeks at the change in Bea's complexion. "No, I didn't mean that. If she is the same Lucinda, then, as Kenny said, she broke up the fight, so I doubt she would have had anything to with David's death. But what about the boys she was with? The ones that got into the fight with David and his friends? Maybe they saw David alone on the road, it was late at night, no one else was around, and they decided it was time for some revenge after losing the fight."

Bea chuckled and shook her head. "Yes, you *are* just like your aunt."

Chapter 20

Through the entire conversation with Bea Harper, Addie was all too aware that Bea never mentioned the fact that Anita was pregnant when David died. Perhaps she didn't know. If that was the case, then she certainly wasn't going to tell her. If Bea was just playing her cards close to her chest because she didn't know if Addie knew, then there was no doubt in Addie's mind that fact would eventually come out, but so far . . . Then there was the matter of the mysterious Lucinda. Addie had already made her subtle inquiries to Janine's friend, but the woman had been evasive, to say the least.

All this preyed on Addie's mind as she headed back to the main entrance, only to discover Mary now had Pippi behind the desk. "Even though we don't start serving lunch for another half hour, they're always early to their table, just in case, I suppose," Mary said with a soft laugh.

"I guess when you get older food is still one of things that brings comfort." Then Addie chuckled. "Who am I kidding, it brings me comfort too."

"Yes, but when you're getting on in years and your family doesn't come around anymore, I guess it's the one thing they can count on being there for them every day."

"Lucinda doesn't get many visitors either. I thought she had a brother."

"Not that I've ever met, and I've been here ten years. I figured that's why she and Janine bonded like they did. An odd couple, to say the least. Lucinda has a heart of gold, and Janine, well, it took this little one to break through." She scratched Pippi behind the ear as Addie nestled her into her arms. "Please, feel free to bring Pippi back anytime. She has a way with people who seem to need her. A sixth sense, so to speak."

"Yes," Addie said, gazing down as her little friend snuggled into the crook of her arm. "She does seem to have that." Addie shifted Pippi's position and reached out to shake Mary's hand. "Thank you for today, and the next time I come to see Bea, I'll make sure I bring Pippi too. She seems to have enjoyed herself. Didn't you, girl?" Pippi gave out a short yip. "Thanks again," Addie said with a wave as she headed outside to the parking lot.

On the drive home, Addie replayed in her mind what Bea had told her, and felt as though she hadn't learned anything conclusive about David's death, except that he would have had to pass by

the sandspits on his way back to Windgate. However, if the police had questioned everyone involved,
then it really was another brick wall. She did find it
interesting that Lucinda apparently didn't have a
brother, so most likely she wasn't the Lucinda her
aunt had mentioned in her journal. Unless, of
course, her brother had passed away, and that's
why Mary had never met him. Addie was certain if
that was the case, it's information that would be in
Lucinda's client files and Mary would have known.

"I guess we're back to the search for the missing
journal, little one," said Addie as she tugged Pippi
out of her carrier and trotted up the front porch
steps.

She'd just fished the key out of her purse, while
juggling Pippi on one arm, when a car horn
sounded behind her, making her jump.

"Serena! Look, Pippi, see who's come for a
visit."

"Hi, yay," called Serena with a wave as she hopped
out of her red Wrangler and made her way up the
steps. "Sorry I couldn't get here before, but Addie
is teething and we've had a wild couple of days,
again."

"How's Ollie's ear infection?"

"He's fine now, but *phew*, between the two of
them they keep me hopping. If it's not something
with one, then it's the other one. I tell you I need
some adulting this afternoon," Serena muttered as
she headed toward the kitchen, "and to see food
that isn't minced up for a toddler. What do you
have for lunch in here?" she asked, poking her
head into the fridge. "By the way, I stopped in at

the tea shop to pick up some special blend tea orders Elle got in that I'm going to make up at home tonight, and I ran into Martha."

"How's Martha?" asked Addie, rummaging through the pantry for something her friend might find adult enough to have for lunch.

"She's good, but she asked me when your cousin's coming back from London, because she thought she was supposed to be back last week, and she wants her to make a dress for her. Some fancy dinner she and Bill are going to in Salem next month, the Essex County Bakers awards or something or other."

"I got an email from Kalea a few days ago and it seems she's going to be in London for a while longer. I guess she's been in meetings all week with her European and UK distributors, so she's not sure when she'll be back. I can let her know that Martha is chomping at the bit though, and she can reach out to her. I'm sure one of her other designers could whip up something that Martha would like. Hey, how about I make us a nice cold pasta salad?"

"Um . . ." Serena closed the fridge, clearly mulling over Addie's lunch idea. "No . . . that's too much like toddler food."

"But it's so hot out. The thought of cooking a big meal doesn't appeal to me." Addie pursed her lips and then snapped her fingers. "I got it," she said, scurrying around Serena to open the fridge. "I have a head of lettuce, some chicken breast and sliced ham from the deli. There's also a couple of hard-boiled eggs in here, green onions, and . . . Oh, and some avocados, Swiss cheese, some cheddar, and cherry tomatoes. I can whip us up a chef's salad. Is that adult enough for you?" She turned, grinning at Serena.

"Okay, but I get to cut the lettuce; too small and it will remind me of baby food."

"Deal!" said Addie, retrieving the ingredients and setting them on the island.

Serena pushed her plate away and sat back, rubbing her tummy. "I must say, my friend, you do make one heck of a salad."

"Why, thank you, ma'am." Addie took a bow and cleared their plates. "Do you want coffee or tea now?"

"How about some of that sweet tea I saw in the jug in the fridge."

"Perfect," said Addie, getting down two tall glasses and filling them with ice. "So, what are your plans for the afternoon?"

"I only have a couple of hours, then Mom has to go. Her quilting group is setting up for a big sale this weekend at the community center. It's a big craft fair the town council is sponsoring to raise money to renovate the gazebo in the park. Oh, oh, I know. Zach will be home, so he can stay with the kids. You and I could go."

"That sounds like fun, sure. It will do us both good to spend some time *adulting* out of the house." Addie laughed.

"Then it's a date," said Serena, grinning. "But as for this afternoon . . . I don't know. How's the murder investigation going?"

"Which one?"

"I'm assuming since the one hits too close to home that you've been focusing on the other one," said Serena over the rim of her glass.

Addie couldn't stop her involuntary eye roll. "Think about what you said, my friend."

"What?"

"They both hit close to home. My aunt, Simon and Laurel, duh."

"Oh right. I guess your aunt's then, since you did tell Marc you wouldn't investigate the other one. You did, didn't you?"

"Yes, I did, and I have no plans to look into that one. I think it might end up being a cold case anyway since he hasn't got any leads yet."

"Then in seventy years you can reopen it, like your aunt's fiancé's case, and voilà. We figure it out and case closed." Serena chuckled.

"Yeah, let's see, in seventy years we'll be—"

"Don't even go there." Serena shook her head and took a sip of tea. "But seriously, any new leads on what happened to David Winthrop?"

Addie filled her in on what Bea had shared with her this morning, and her suspicions about Lucinda at the senior living center and how when she'd asked her what she could remember about the murder, she didn't have much to say. "So, you see I haven't made much headway."

"You have to remember," said Serena, "that with older people, their current memories might not be as good, but their long-term memories are like it happened yesterday. Maybe she's trying to forget it. I'm sure since she lived on the peninsula it was a hard time for everyone then. You know, having a murder in their own backyard, so to speak. It would have been really shocking to find out David's body was hanging on a scarecrow stand for days until someone noticed it was a real man and not a straw man, right?"

"True, perhaps that's it, but still, there was something there that didn't sit quite right with me, like she knew more than she was saying."

"Did you ask her outright if she knew your aunt?"

"No, I guess I didn't."

"Then ask her the next time you see her. You are going back, aren't you?"

"Yes, I told Bea I would. She does have a lot of insight into my aunt that I would love to pick her brain about."

"There you go. Take Pippi, she's a great conversation starter, and go from there, gently nudging this Lucinda woman."

"You're right. Yes, that's exactly what I'm going to do, but I still think the answers, if there are any, are going to be found in the missing 1953 journal, but I'll be darned if I can find it."

"Well," said Serena, placing her empty glass on the counter, "I'm here for a few hours, so put me to work, Sherlock. What rooms haven't you checked yet?"

"I'm down to the cellar and the attic."

Serena wrinkled up her nose. "I don't do creepy old cellars, so let's pick the attic."

Addie shook her head, laughing even though she did tend to agree with Serena. There was something about her cellar that she'd never felt comfortable with to explore fully. She wasn't certain if it was the 1800s brick walls, or the root cellar with its earthen flooring, or the fact that there were a number of rooms containing who knows what, but the doors leading into them had become so warped over the years they wouldn't budge. "I agree! The attic it is."

"What about that front office/book storage room you found a couple of years ago? Have you checked it yet?" asked Serena as they headed up the attic stairs.

"No, Simon and I went through that back then. We did find a few hidden compartments, but none of them contained a journal. I'm pretty sure that since my aunt kept all her other treasures in that smaller hidden room, that's where we should start today."

Addie ducked to enter the small room and pulled the light string. "Phew, I don't know where to start in here."

"Think like your aunt," said Serena behind her as she stepped in and stopped. "But yeah. You're right. Do we pull all those books off the shelves to inspect the wall behind them, or tackle all the stuff stacked around the edges of the room? Ooh, look!" She pointed to the back far left corner. "Is that a dollhouse? I never saw that the last time I was in here."

"Neither did I, but then again we were focused on the wedding dress and the trunk," Addie said, taking a step toward it, but was edged out of the way by a giddy Serena, who beat her to it.

"Whoa, it's made of solid wood and looks hand-crafted. Look, Addie! Even the little figures are carved," she said, picking up a mother figurine wearing a housedress in a style common during the 1940s. "This must have been your great-aunt's.

Oh, and look, there's a baby in the cradle up in the nursery! Isn't this all so darling?" Serena cooed and sat on the floor exploring the large wooden replica of a Victorian mansion, complete with lights, furniture, and an entire figurine family along with a black-and-white spotted dog. "Your aunt was a very lucky little girl."

"Yes, I'd say that even back in the 1940s this would have been worth a pretty penny."

"Can you imagine what it would be worth today?"

Addie studied the workmanship and shook her head. "I don't even want to think about it. This is a *real* collector's item, wow."

"You aren't thinking about selling it, are you?" Serena shot her a look of disbelief. "You could have a daughter of your own one day who would love to find this under the Christmas tree when she was old enough."

"A daughter, me? No, sorry to tell you, my friend. I think my years of having any children of my own have passed me by, and that's okay. I'm content with being an auntie to Ollie, Addie, and Emma."

"Don't say that, you never know what the future holds for you."

Addie sputtered. "I've come to the conclusion lately that not everyone is supposed to be married or have children. For some of us it's just not in the stars, and that's okay. I have a good life as it is and, well . . ." She had to push the images of her and David, her and Simon, and the wedding dress hanging on the back of her bedroom door collecting dust out of her mind. "Let's just say, some things aren't meant to be. But that dollhouse, no, I won't be selling it. When Emma comes to visit, she can play with it, and that goes for Addie and Ollie too, when they're old enough. So, help me haul it out of here, and we can start tapping on the walls behind it to see if we can find that journal hidden somewhere."

"It is your life and if you're happy the way it is now, then I'm happy for you," said Serena, taking the far side of the dollhouse. "Does the roof come off?"

Addie gave it a tug. "Nope. It seems pretty solid, but just in case, let's walk it out corner by corner, like we did the bookcase. Okay, you go, then me," she said, placing her hand behind the back wall of the dollhouse. "Whoa! What's this?" Her fingers edged over something soft and leathery on the backboard. "Give me your phone, I need some light." She took Serena's phone, switched on the flashlight app and shone it down the back of the dollhouse. Her knees weakened, and she gasped. "I don't believe it," she cried, her fingers ripping at strips of tape. "Look! It's the missing journal!"

Chapter 21

Addie glanced down at the dollhouse she and Serena had managed to get as far as her bedroom door before they had to stop and take a break. "It's crazy that the journal was taped behind the back wall of the nursery. But knowing what we know, how appropriate, and so like a hiding place my aunt would pick," she said, hobbling into her room, where she dropped onto her bed to stretch out her aching back.

"What's crazy is that we managed to get the dollhouse this far without breaking anything, including us." Serena wheezed, joining her on the bed.

"Speak for yourself, I think my back's gone out."

"It's my knees. Wow, running after two toddlers you'd think I'd be in better shape than this," she puffed.

"You know," said Addie, staring up at the ceiling, "I've been thinking about the mysterious Lucinda—"

"You've been what? All I could think about was not dying by *dollhouse* on those steep stairs."

"Silly." Addie playfully slapped her. "I was the one going backwards down the steps, so if it was going to crush anyone it would have been me."

"Yeah, but then I would have felt bad," Serena said with a giggle.

"Pfft, thanks, but seriously. Mrs. Timmons's first name is Lucy, right?"

"I think so. I've always called her Mrs. Timmons though, because at her age it seemed more respectful."

"Yeah, me too, but I'm sure it is and Lucy is short for Lucinda, if I'm not mistaken."

"It could be short for Luella, Lucille, or Lucia too."

"You're right. So much for that theory."

"There is one way to find out, and that's reading the journal."

"Oh no!" Addie bolted upright and looked out into the hall at the dollhouse. "Where is it? Did we drop it on the stairs? Because there's no way I can even think about climbing any more stairs right now to look for it."

Serena heaved herself up off the bed, went into the hall and peered inside the house. "Nope, we're all good. I used it as a barrier in the parlor to keep all the figurines from falling out," she said, retrieving the diary, taking it back into the bedroom and flipping to the first page. "Since we're taking a breather, we might as well see if we can solve at least that question right now," she said, sitting cross-legged on the bed as she started reading.

"Anything about the baby, or did the trauma of David's murder make her lose it? Since there's no mention of it in the 1954 journal."

"Give me a minute. Remember, I scan for the highlights, not read the details like you . . ." Serena fell silent as her eyes skimmed the page. "Oh, but this is sad. It picks up about a month after they found David, and she's . . . not doing too well, let's say, but you can read it all later. I have to leave soon and I want to get to . . ."

"What, what did you find out?" asked Addie, propping herself up on one elbow, studying Serena's blank face.

"Here's the Lucinda mystery solved. It says that Lucinda Price was, in fact, the one mentioned before, and even names her brother George—and Ralph, Lucy's husband, Doctor Timmons—and some fellow named Vince Cornby, as being the ones Anita suspected knew more about what happened to David than they let on to the police."

"Really?"

"Yes, she says that a friend of hers saw the whole thing and Lucinda was screaming at David and threw herself at him, telling him how much she loved him and begging him not to marry your aunt. Then George got involved and accused David of taking advantage of his little sister and told David he'd pay for it. That's when the fight broke out, but then her friend fled because the lot attendant yelled that he was going to call the police."

"Hmm, I wondered about that group. Of course,

I wasn't sure who they were, but if David had to pass by their party on the beach to get back to Windgate then—"

"Oh, here we go. She did have the baby, her parents sent her to Boston for the term of her pregnancy and then . . ." Serena fell silent as she continued to read and then slammed the journal closed. Tears filled her eyes as she looked up at Addie.

"What happened? Did the baby die at birth?" asked Addie, sitting upright.

Serena shook her head.

"Then what? What happened?" Addie seized the journal from her friend's hand and flipped it open.

Serena laid her hand over the page. "Be prepared. Nothing is as you think it is."

"Why are you talking in riddles?" Addie shook her head and began reading.

April 28, 1953
Today my beautiful baby boy was born. What should have been the happiest day of my life was truly my worst, knowing his father would never know him or be able to hold him as I ache now to hold both of them.

My empty arms and heart ache for what will never be and for that little innocent child. Even now as I write this through tear-blurred eyes, the nurses wouldn't even let me hold him before they swept him away. The matron said it was the best for me to let his new parents do the bonding, and not the mother who was giving him up.

*I want him to know that giving him away was
not my choice but my father's, and that I never
had a say in any of this, including who would
adopt him. If I did, it certainly wouldn't have been
my brother and that Hattie woman he's married
to. When I protested, Father shushed me and said
since Hattie and Jack can't have children of their
own, this was a good arrangement. At least we
would know the child was well cared for. Father
also told me I was to be the aunt and nothing
more, and to never tell the child who I really was,
and then he said that we were to never speak of
this again.*

"What? I don't get it. My dad didn't have a
brother."

"Keep reading," Serena hoarsely whispered.
Addie scowled and read further.

April 29
*Father has forbidden me from returning home to
Greyborne Harbor. He said a girl named Nellie
Cummings went away last year and when she
came back the whole town guessed she'd gone away
to have a baby. He doesn't want that shame
brought on our family, so he told me to stay in
Boston.*

April 30
*I finally heard from Mama today, and it seems
I got at least one thing I wanted, because the one
time my brother came to visit me in the home for
unwed mothers, he asked me if I wanted to name*

> *the baby. I told him Emily after our great-great-*
> *grandmother if it was a girl and Michael after*
> *David's father if it was a boy . . .*

"Michael? As in my father?" Addie sensed all the blood rushing out of her head and pooling in her chest and she gasped, and gasped again, not able to catch her breath.

"Here." Serena flew to her feet. "Put your head between your knees. There, that's it. Now breathe, one . . . two . . . that's it, slow and steady."

"I can't," gasped Addie.

"Yes, you can." She rubbed Addie's back reassuringly. "Breathe slow, in . . . out . . . in . . . out . . ."

"That means . . . Anita wasn't my great-aunt, but my grandmother." Addie struggled to fill her lungs. "And that my whole life has been a lie!"

"I know, I know," said Serena softly, sitting on the bed beside Addie and taking her hand. "But look, sweetie"—she swept stray strands of hair from Addie's eyes—"you were loved and cared for and—"

"Don't you see? They all lied about *everything!*" Addie picked up the journal from where it had fallen on the bed beside her and continued reading through her tear-blurred eyes.

Her heart raced, and beads of perspiration trickled down her forehead. There it was in black and white. Anita was her grandmother, not her great-aunt. It all made sense to her now. It was all here. Why Hattie, the woman she grew up believing was her grandmother, had really forbidden Addie's father, Michael, from taking Addie to Greyborne Harbor when she was little. Also, why

Hattie never spoke of Anita throughout Addie's life, which would have been why Addie didn't know much about Anita until after she died and left Addie the house in Greyborne Harbor.

None of it had anything to do with Addie's father's relationship with Catherine Lewis, as Hattie had led her father to believe all those years ago. Hattie must have been terrified that during all his visits to Greyborne Harbor, the truth about Michael's parentage would eventually come out, and she felt threatened by that, by Anita and their growing closeness. After all, Hattie had raised Michael as *her* son.

"And—*The Velveteen Rabbit.* I *am* the granddaughter it's dedicated to. Listen to this.

> *"The last night I had with David that Halloween weekend was magical and a memory I will forever cherish. I had just told him I was expecting, and he was over the moon with the news. He vowed we should celebrate, and when we were strolling down the boardwalk at the fairgrounds where merchants were selling their wares, we spotted a stand operated by Sam Goldsmith, the old fellow who owns the used-and-rare bookstore in Salem, and since David and I both shared a love of literature, we had to stop and browse. Of course, David was like a small child at Christmas with each book he picked up. I was afraid he was going to spend the entire monthly allowance he got from his father all in one night, but then he found a copy of* The Velveteen Rabbit, *and soon forgot about the other five books he had in his hands and set them aside.*

"He told me The Velveteen Rabbit *was his favorite book when he was growing up. I told him it was mine too, and he said that was it! Then our child would have to have it. When I got back to Arnold and Maisie's after the fair, I looked at it and saw it was a first edition. It was right there and then that I vowed my child would have a collection of first editions. There is something so special about them. Knowing they are the first run of books that introduced the story to the world. It's a little like holding a piece of history in your hands . . ."*

Addie collapsed into a heap on her bed. Her chest heaved while her mind reeled with the realization that everything she thought she knew about her life had been a lie.

Chapter 22

"I wonder if my father ever knew Anita was his mother and not his aunt?" said Addie, staring up at her bedroom ceiling.

"It's hard to say," said Serena. "But you did say he'd reconnected with her after a number of years and he was here the day he was later killed on the switchback road leading to Pen Hollow, so maybe."

"Maybe that's the day she told him and he was going to see Maisie Radcliff to confirm it because he couldn't believe it, just like I can't."

"Maybe."

"But I guess we'll never know, will we?" Addie swiped the back of her hand over her wet cheeks and sniffled.

"But it makes complete sense now," said Serena. "You know, why she left everything to you. You weren't just some niece she hadn't seen since you were little and her only remaining relative. You were, are, her granddaughter."

"Yeah, so much more is making sense now."

Serena's phone pinged out a text alert.

"That's probably your mom wondering where you are."

"It's okay. I'll just tell her I'm going to be late."

"No, she has to go to the community hall. I'm fine, go and be with your family."

"Are you sure you're going to be okay if I do?"

"I'm fine."

"Come on, I can read you like one of the dozen mood rings I have."

"No, really, I just need some time to digest the fact that I'm not who I thought I was and no one in my life was either. Go, your family needs you."

"You're my family too."

"I know, but like I said, I just need some time. It's been a long, strange month, so why should today be any different."

"All right, as long as you're sure."

"I am, go hug those babies of yours and remember not all mothers get to do that . . ." Her mind recalled Anita's word about not being able to hold her baby before he was taken away from her, and she turned on her side staring at the wall.

Serena gave Addie's arm a reassuring pat, and started for the door. "On my way out I'll fill Pippi's food bowl and let her out for a minute, then you won't have to worry about that and can just stay here awhile and—"

"Thank you," whispered Addie, as she closed her eyes. Ever since the day she'd discovered there was a missing year of Anita's life, Addie had wished for nothing more than to find that journal. Now the words Hattie, her grandmother, her great-aunt, or whoever she was, used to say to Addie when she was growing up, came rushing back at her. *Be careful what you wish for.* All Addie knew right now, is she wished she hadn't found that 1953 journal and her life could go instantly back to what she knew before.

After what had been a frenzied night's sleep, to say the least, Addie rubbed her eyes and studied her surroundings. Everything around her seemed to be the same as it was yesterday, but yet everything had changed. She sat up and glanced at her phone on the bedside table, noted a missed call, and flopped back down. Somewhere in her chaotic dreams she vaguely recalled it rang, but she'd worked the ringing sound into the dream and ignored it. As she moved to throw back the duvet, Pippi nestled her little head deeper into Addie's side and licked her hand.

"Whether we want to or not, we do have to get up at some point today."

Pippi snorted and her tail thumped on the bed as she lazily wagged it. "Okay, you sleep another minute while I hit the bathroom, and then I'm pretty sure that's exactly what you'll need to do too."

Addie splashed cold water over her swollen, crying-induced fish-eyes and stared at the woman she saw reflected back at her in the mirror. She had the same eyes, same nose, same face, but she was a complete stranger. Addie shook her head, grabbed her robe, and they headed downstairs, where Pippi made a mad dash to the back door.

Coffee made, and Pippi's bowls filled. Addie stared into the cup of steaming brew she clutched in her hand. "It's been a lot to take in, hasn't it, my friend?" She glanced down at her furry little companion chomping on her kibble. "I mean, I'm not who I thought I was, but neither was anyone else in my life, and poor Anita. It must have been awful for her to have her brother and his wife raise her only child and never be able to tell him who she really was." Tears leaked from her already puffy eyes and rolled down her cheeks as she stared out the window into the backyard.

"It's clear I need to find my happy place today to sort through all this, because it just breaks my heart to think how many lives were changed back then." She looked down at Pippi, who had finished her breakfast and sat, tail wagging. "Where is the one place that always makes us happy?"

Pippi yipped, wagged her tail, darted down the hallway and returned moments later with her little bear, Baxter, clutched in her jaw. "I know that's what makes *you* happy." Addie laughed as she got up and rinsed her cup. "But where is *my* happy place? You know, like that saying goes: *You belong where your heart is.* The problem is, girl, I don't know where my heart is anymore," she said wistfully as she loaded her cup in the dishwasher. "Of course, that's it! Come on! Let's get ready to go for a car ride. Our outing today is long overdue." Addie dashed upstairs to shower and dress.

A smile played on Addie's lips when she opened the front door of Beyond the Page Books and Curios. She drew in a deep breath and was instantly transported to happier times. The aroma combinations of Martha's fresh-baked bread, along with the tang of the sea air, mixed with the delicate scent of spring flowers outside, mingled with the heady scents of old books and leather chairs wafting through the open door. These were all fragrances Addie knew she'd never tire of, and exactly what she needed and had missed these past weeks.

"Addie?" Paige said from behind the Victorian bar they used as a coffee and sales counter as she nervously glanced over Addie's shoulder to the far side of the shop. "I . . . didn't expect to see you today." She dropped the books she'd been holding in her hands and scooted around the end of the counter, her eyes filled with concern.

"I thought I should come in and welcome our newest staff member," Addie said curiously, as she eyed Paige's rapidly paling complexion. "I hope that's not a problem?"

"No, no of course not," she said, and seized Addie's arm, tugging on it. "Come on, I'll introduce you. She's just in the storeroom sorting a shipment of books," she said, hurriedly ushering a bewildered Addie down the book aisle toward the back room.

"Ah . . . if she's busy, I can meet her later." Addie was taken aback by Paige's brash reception and tightened her hold on Pippi, who was also clearly confused and squirmed in her arms.

"Nope, now's fine," said Paige, pushing Addie through the doorway. "Addie, this is Nikki Harri-

son, Nikki this is Addie. I'll be back in a minute."
Paige closed the door with a thud.

An open-mouthed Addie stared at the tall, red-
haired woman who was mirroring her reaction.

"Um, hi?" said Nikki, meekly holding out her
hand as she glanced past Addie to the door when
the frenzy of Paige's brief introduction subsided.

"Hi, nice to meet you . . ." Addie replied, shifting Pippi in her arm, shaking Nikki's hand in
greeting. "Um . . . I really don't . . ." Addie glanced
over her shoulder to the closed door. "This is Pippi.
Pippi, this is Nikki. Here," Addie said, thrusting
the little dog into Nikki's hands. "I just need to
check on something."

Addie opened the door a crack and peered out
toward the sales counter where Paige was chatting
with two customers as she rang up their sale. She
blinked, and then blinked again. It was Simon and
Laurel, and they were book shopping, of all things.

"Is there something wrong out there?" asked
Nikki, standing on her tiptoes, peeking out over
Addie's head.

Addie struggled to get her breathing in check
and shook her head as she closed the door. But
there was no mistaking the tender looks the two
exchanged as they chatted freely with each other
at the counter. This was the last thing she expected
to see today. No wonder Paige was in such a dither.
"Just some customers, nothing important."

"Really? Then why has all the color gone from
your face and why are you shaking?"

"Long story."

Nikki cracked open the door and peered out
again. "Ooh, I get it now. That's him, isn't it, and

Laurel. The woman I met last weekend is the woman you found out he's still married to at your wedding?" Nikki pinned Addie with an inquisitive look. "I'm not being nosy, I just heard about what happened, that's all, and I was trying to figure out why . . . well, everyone is suddenly acting so weird," she said, closing the door.

"By everyone, you mean Paige?"

Nikki nodded. Her earlier probing gaze had changed to one of understanding and sympathy.

"Yes, it was out of character for her. I knew something must be up, but I wasn't ready for that." Addie forced her trembling knees to carry her over to a book crate, and she dropped down, holding her head in her hands, trying to dispel the image of the *happy* couple. But she couldn't force it into the back of her mind, because all she could see was that the time Simon was spending with Laurel appeared to have rekindled something he had assured her was in the past. But was it? No, she couldn't go there. She had to believe him when he told her loved *her*, and it would all work out. Mason was his only connection with Laurel now, right?

"Do you need a minute?" asked Nikki, as she nestled Pippi against her chest.

"Just give me half a second," Addie said, holding up her hand. Phew! She drew in a few short breaths and crammed the image of them together into a box, shoving it far back in her mind. "I'm okay." She straightened up. "One heck of an introduction though, maybe we should try that again. Hi, I'm Addie Greyborne and welcome to Beyond the Page."

Nikki nodded and smiled. "Hi, I'm Nikki Harrison, Marc and Serena's cousin, and I would like to thank you for allowing me this opportunity."

"Don't thank me. You can thank the covert agent out there." Addie gestured with her head toward the door. "But seriously," Addie said, rising to her feet. "It's great to have you here. Paige filled me in on your very impressive résumé and I'm thrilled you decided to join us."

As if on cue, Pippi turned her little head and gave Nikki a lick on the cheek.

"See," Addie said, chuckling. "Even she knows a good thing when she sees it."

"She's a darling," Nikki cooed, cuddling Pippi closer, "and I take it by the dog bed out front under the counter that she's a regular fixture in the shop?"

"You'd be right about that. Some days I'm not sure who this shop really belongs to or who's in charge."

The door opened and Paige's blond head of hair poked around the door frame. "Is it safe to come in?"

Pippi yipped, her front paws scratched at the air as she tried to get to Paige.

"You can let her down." Addie let out a short laugh. "I think she's missed seeing Paige and being here every day, by the look of it."

"How's my baby been?" said Paige, crouching down and giving the little dog a belly rub. "I know, it sure hasn't been the same around here without you." She laughed as Pippi jumped up and licked her cheek.

"Okay," said Addie, her hands on her hips. "Now that this little reunion is over, do you mind telling me what just went on out there?"

"Talk about bad timing, you showing up when they were here," Paige said, rising. "They came in looking for some books for Mason. I guess he's an avid fantasy reader and Simon just put a new bookcase together for him and Laurel wanted to stock it with some—"

"I get the picture. Laurel couldn't shop for them on her own. As usual, she had to have Simon help her with it."

"The good thing was that when they were leaving, she said they should drop by the grocery store and pick up something for dinner. He said he couldn't tonight, he'd planned on surprising you with dinner because he's been neglecting you for too long and he had to do something about that."

"Really," said Addie. "He said that?"

"Yeah," added Page, then cringed, "but then Laurel laughed and said, 'You always could make me laugh, Simon, like you'd really give up the chance to see the look on Mason's face when he sees the bookcase and all these new books we just bought him. You're hysterical.'"

"What did Simon say to that?"

"He didn't reply, but he looked like he was thinking seriously about what she said."

"You're kidding," said Nikki. "That's the old guilt-trip ploy." Her hand flew to her mouth. "Sorry, that just popped out. It's none of my business and I don't know this Laurel woman, but that's the passive-aggressive tactics my ex used on me. But"—she waved her hands in a stop motion—"this is completely different and . . . Oh, never mind. I need to learn keep my mouth shut."

"That's okay. It's nothing I haven't thought about myself, that's for sure."

"You mean she's consciously manipulating him?" asked Paige.

"No. Yes. Maybe, in a way," said Nikki. "But it's clear she's found his currency."

"And that's Mason," said Addie.

"Yeah," said Paige, "and it looks like she's using that to keep Simon close to them."

"But why?" asked Addie. "I don't get it. They split up sixteen years ago and went on with their lives. Why now, and quite accidentally I might add, and due to a complete fluke, does she suddenly want him back in her life like this?"

"Maybe she doesn't?" said Nikki hopefully. "At least from what I saw when I met her and her aunt at the tea. They seemed really close, more like mother and daughter than aunt and niece. So maybe she's just struggling with that loss, and has latched on to an old friend who makes that loss easier to deal with." Nikki gave Addie a weak smile. "You can hope that's it, anyway."

"That's what I've been trying to convince myself of but . . ." said Addie, recalling the warm looks they'd just exchanged, and crossed her fingers behind her back. "It just seems weird to me, to see Simon give in to her all the time. I've never known him to do anything he didn't want to out of guilt."

"But remember," added Paige, quickly glancing at Addie. "Simon just discovered he's a father. I know he wants to do the best he can by Mason, so he will be more compliant to her wishes than he normally would. It doesn't reflect at all on how he feels toward you. He just wants to be a good father and has to learn how to do that."

"You're right. Seeing them together just made me a bit wobbly, that's all. I guess I'll find out if her guilt tactics worked when and if he shows up for dinner." She glanced from Paige to Nikki. "Well, ladies, this has been one heck of an introduction, hasn't it?"

"My aunt Janis told me there would never be a dull moment working here," said Nikki, glancing from one to the other, as they all burst out laughing.

"Now seriously," gasped Paige, holding her side trying to restrain herself. "Just before all that happened"—she waved her hand toward the front of the bookstore—"your old friend Tony called."

Addie sucked in a deep breath to stop her giggles. "Tony Radcliff?"

"Yes, he was calling to see how your honeymoon was going. I guess when you didn't answer his call last night, he figured you were still away, and he wanted the scoop on the wedding. You know, how beautiful you looked and all that."

"I guess he doesn't know what happened."

"He does now."

"You told him?"

"Sorry, I didn't think . . ."

"Don't worry, I was going to phone and tell him what happened eventually. What else did he say?"

"He said he was sorry to hear the news, but was

just going to catch a train to London. He has a new book launching this week, so he said he'd call you later." Paige wrung her hands in front of her. "Did I say anything wrong?"

"No, not at all." Addie glanced at Nikki. "Tony was an old high school friend of mine, who's an author and lives in England now."

"I gathered that, but did you say his name was Tony Radcliff? Not *the* famous author, Anthony Radcliff?"

"That's him. You've read his books?" asked Addie.

"Have I read him? I was going to do my master's thesis on gothic horror before . . . Well, before my ex changed the course of my life and we moved to Chicago." She dropped her gaze, then looked up and met Addie's. "I can't believe that you guys actually know him."

"Can you believe he was Addie's high school sweetheart?"

"You're kidding. Wow, what a small world." Nikki gazed across the storage room to a stack of books waiting to be shelved. "You know what we should do since he's launching a—"

"Have him come here as a guest author!" cried Addie excitedly.

"Exactly what I was thinking," said Nikki.

"Now you two are scaring me," said Paige. "It's like you've got the same brain."

"I know, isn't it great," said Addie, grinning as she looked from Paige to Nikki. "It's perfect timing, with his new book coming out, and if he can get here this summer, we can schedule the reading for a Tuesday evening when the cruise ship comes into port and . . . Oh, there's so much potential. I love it!" Addie clapped her hands, feeling for the first time in weeks like her old self.

Yes, this staffing arrangement was going to work out better than she'd ever hoped. Addie liked Nikki already. She *was* a perfect fit for the bookstore, and the match went far beyond a stellar résumé. Like Paige, she was Addie's kind of book person.

Chapter 23

With Addie's mood back on the same track it was on when she walked into the bookstore earlier—that is, before the Simon and Laurel show put a momentary damper on things—she hummed a popular tune, as she fastened Pippi into her car carrier. "Okay, girl, one stop to make before we head home. If Simon's going to surprise me by coming over to cook dinner, then I want to make sure he has a good selection to choose from."

At the market Addie snagged a couple of juicy-looking steaks and some fresh shrimp. She was heading for the romaine lettuce, thinking that a nice Caesar salad would pair well with those steaks, and then stopped. Did they really want garlic breath tonight? No, so she switched gears and grabbed all the fixings for a green salad, since she and Serena had depleted her stock of fresh vegetables yesterday at lunch. Chocolate fondue ingredients, definitely a must since both she and Simon could never get enough of that, it was their guilty little pleasure.

As Addie closed her fridge door, she smiled with the satisfaction of knowing he wouldn't be scrounging through her pantry again for something to make. And, on the off chance he thought ahead and brought his own dinner fixings, well then. She'd eat like a queen for the rest of the week.

Or . . . maybe, she'd invite Nikki for dinner to get to know her better. The way she spoke up today made Addie think she wasn't the same woman who had been a victim in her marriage during all those years. She was interested in knowing what made Nikki tick and how she became so resilient. Addie needed a little of that herself right about now, as she felt the crushing weight of everything she'd learned over the past few weeks, and wasn't sure how to move forward from any of it.

Addie glanced at the stove clock. No wonder her tummy had that sick, rumbly feeling. It was going on two o'clock and she hadn't had any lunch. Come to think of it, she couldn't recall eating any breakfast either. She threw together a peanut butter and banana sandwich and settled on the sofa, checking her phone for, hopefully, a missed message from Simon telling her he'd be by for dinner. Instead she found seven texts from Serena.

Are you okay?
Why aren't you answering?
I'm getting worried

That's it. I'm bringing the kids over so I can check on you.

Never mind, Elle said she saw you go into the bookstore so I guess you're okay

Call me when you get home

Are you home yet?

Addie's thumbs flew over the keypad . . .

I'm home and I'm fine. Simon is supposed to be dropping by for dinner. I'll call you later. Love you xx

She took a bite of her sandwich, savoring the nutty, sweet taste of her childhood, and then tears formed in her eyes, and she set her plate aside. Was this how it was going to be forevermore? Every one of her fond childhood memories would now be tainted by the truth that had been revealed in her aunt/*grandmother's* journal. Would anything ever feel normal again?

Her blurry gaze settled on the makeshift crime board taped to the wall. Did any of it even matter since now her whole universe had been sent spiraling out of control? If the police couldn't solve her grandfather's murder nearly seventy years ago, how could she be so arrogant to think she could solve it now? She lay back on the pillow behind her and looked at the photo albums on the coffee table and was reaching to pick one up when her phone rang.

Simon, finally! She glanced at the screen, and her eyes widened.

"Tony! Hi. Congratulations! Paige told me about your new book release."

She flipped the phone to speaker and set it on the table, eyeing her sandwich. Not only did it remind her of her now tainted childhood, but it also reminded her of happier days when she and Tony would eat their lunch out on the lawn of their old high school.

"You'll have to excuse me if I chomp in your ear, you've just caught me eating lunch," she said, taking a bite.

"Ha," he said with a laugh. "I've just finished dinner at the hotel."

"Dinner? Oh, right, there's a five-hour time difference, but I'm guessing you didn't have a peanut butter and banana sandwich?"

"Ooh, no, but that sounds sooo good. I don't think I've had one of those since—"

"High school, right? Me neither! This is the first in years and then you called, how serendipitous."

"So, my friend," he said, his voice crackling through the small speaker. "Tell me how you're really doing. Paige said you're putting on a brave face, but I know after what happened at the wedding, that face probably doesn't extend to the inside. Are you okay, really?"

"Meh . . . it's been interesting, to say the least."

"I can only imagine. Are you guys rescheduling the wedding or have you called it off?"

"We planned on rescheduling it. You know, once I got over my anger and the shock of it all, but then . . ."

Addie continued to fill Tony in on the more recent events. Valerie's murder, Simon being the nurturing Doctor Emerson he was and helping Laurel through the whole dreadful episode, and then their discovery of Mason, and how he'd moved to Greyborne Harbor too. Then Addie told him about the wedding dress in the attic and what she'd discovered about her aunt really being her grandmother, and about her grandfather's murder all those years ago.

"I did meet Anita few times," he said, "when she came to visit my grandmother Maisie. Of course, I didn't know she was a Greyborne then, but from what I can remember, she was a very intelligent and intuitive person. If she felt something was off with the investigation, then I'd tend to believe it."

"I know, I just can't figure out what it is though. Remember, seventy years ago they didn't have the capability of running DNA; although, I'm sure the police checked for fingerprints at the scene. The methods used in processing those would have been far inferior to how they are processed and matched today, besides. Any police files would probably be long gone now anyway. There'd be no way of finding out what was done, what evidence was collected, or even who they interviewed back then. The only thing I have is some notes in an old journal and a few newspaper clippings."

"You said you went to see that woman who knew your aunt. Is there anyone else still left that would have been there that night, who might have seen something?"

"There's a few of them still living, but memories are vague, given their ages and the span of time."

There was dead air . . . "Tony? Are you still there?"

"Yeah, I'm here. I was just thinking that you need some healing time to take this all in. It's too bad teleporters haven't been invented yet, and you could be here tonight for my launch party."

"I only wish I could be there."

"If I'd known before that all this had happened. I would have invited you, but all this time I was thinking you and Simon were happily married and away on a tropical island enjoying your honeymoon."

"I know, and I'm sorry I didn't let you know, but I've been . . ."

"No need to apologize. You've been through a lot in a short time. But tell you what, if you need to get away and just work through all this, that invitation I extended last year still holds. I've got tons of room in the manor, or if you'd rather, there's always the old gamekeeper's cottage. It's small, but clean and warm and cozy, and the perfect place to heal your wounds and get yourself back together."

"That sounds perfect and I'd love to come and lick my wounds. But the truth is, after the fiasco at the wedding, I ended up taking the three weeks off that I'd planned for the honeymoon and there's just no way I could leave for another few weeks. Paige just hired a new girl and I think I need to start reinvesting my time back in the bookstore."

"I get it, and I know that once all this settles in, you'll do exactly what you have to do. The girl I used to know didn't let anything stand in the way of what she wanted and she wasn't afraid to go after it. Remember what you went through when you told your grandmother, during your senior year of high school, that you wanted to go to college in New York? You didn't let her stop you, did you? And I know all this won't stop you from figuring out this mystery of your grandfather's murder either."

"But don't you see, Tony. That girl doesn't exist anymore. Everything I thought I knew about my life was a lie. From Simon not telling me he was married before, to him discovering he's a father on top of it all. To my grandmother really being my aunt and my aunt being my real grandmother, I have no idea who I am now, or where I fit in."

"Maybe that's why your grandmother was so overprotective of you all those years. She was afraid you'd find out the truth and she was trying to protect you from this exact thing happening."

"But I did, and now I don't know what to do with the information or how to move forward. Even with Simon, I'm not sure about anything anymore. It's clear he and Laurel were once close and I'm afraid that they're rekindling that, even though he says they're not. I just don't know anything."

"What does your gut tell you? It's never failed you before."

"That's the problem, my head's all haywire right now and it's overpowering anything my gut tells me. I just don't know what's real."

"I get it," he said, and then she heard him draw in a deep breath. "But you did always love to solve puzzles, so maybe it would help focusing on the one thing you do know to be real, and that's your grandfather's murder. It might help put everything else in perspective . . . Oops, sorry . . . I gotta go. My agent just tapped me on the shoulder and said we'd better head into the launch party now. I have to do my reading. Look, if it does all become too much, and you do need some time to regroup before you take it all on, don't forget my invitation. I have to go now. I'll call you later in the

week, and you can let me know if things have settled down or I should get the cottage ready."

"Thanks and enjoy your big night. I hope this
book's a bestseller too."

Addie clicked off the call and sat back. That
conversation was exactly what she needed. Her old
friend did have a way of making her feel better,
and he'd said a few things that helped her refocus
on what was really important. In addition, it was
nice to know that if all else failed, she always had
an escape pod waiting for her on the other side of
the pond.

Addie scanned the few notes she'd made on the
crime board. Tony was right. There were still a
couple of people around that she could talk to
about that night in Pen Hollow, Lucinda at the
care center, for one. Addie sensed she'd been
holding something back the other day, and of
course there were Ralph and Lucy Timmons too.

She thought about the passage she'd read in
Anita's journal where she questioned whether
Lucy, Ralph, and George knew more about David's
murder than they let on. And now after talking
with Tony, she also was questioning it.

She glanced at the mantel clock and decided
since it was nearly five that Simon should be here
soon if he was planning a surprise dinner. But tomorrow she'd drop by the senior care center and
try to speak with Lucinda again. Maybe she just
needed a gentle nudge to shake something out of
the memory tree she appeared to be closely guard-
ing. Afterward, she'd swing by the Timmonses'.
There must be something they could tell her
about that night. According to Bea, the police re-

port said they attended a beach party, which was also attended by a number of the other area youths. Perhaps they saw something or someone acting suspicious, which the police didn't follow up on at the time. It was worth a shot, albeit a long shot given their ages.

As she sat back reading the notations she'd made on the board, she realized there was no way she could even think of giving up on the case now. It was in her DNA. Hadn't Bea Harper said she was exactly like Anita and couldn't leave a puzzle unsolved?

Chapter 24

Addie raced back to the living room from feeding and letting Pippi out, grabbed her phone from where she'd forgotten it on the coffee table and checked for a missed message from Simon. It was nearly six and nothing from him yet. She groaned and dropped down on the sofa in frustration. Is this what the future held in store for them?

Was it always going to be Addie trying to trump the card that Laurel played to keep Simon a part of Mason's life? Not that Addie would ever interfere in that, but maybe Laurel didn't know Addie was encouraging him to build a relationship with his son. Although, she thought that was something Simon would have told her.

By nine p.m. she was re-evaluating everything that had occurred over the past weeks, and her mood was darkening as she replayed every moment. How, with each visit with Simon that she'd managed to snag away from Laurel and Mason, she was faced with a roller coaster of emotions ranging from ecstatic to see him to the dejection that devoured her each time they parted. He'd been the love of her life, and this recent separation confirmed that for her.

Darn it, she really needed him tonight. Even though it was bound to turn into a tear-filled evening as she revealed to him the truth about her parentage, she really needed his loving, comforting closeness. His soothing touch and especially his words of encouragement as he reassured her that her world was still the same and he accepted her for who she was.

When the minutes ticked on and there was still no word from him, Addie retrieved the half-full bottle of wine from the fridge and curled up to reread Anita's journal. Her eyes skimmed the pages and her heart broke all over again with the knowledge that Anita, like her, had lost the love of her life. They'd even shared the same name, David. Talk about a coincidence, and then Addie gasped. Had she just internalized that David was the love of *her* life? Wasn't it supposed to be Simon?

Focus, Addie, focus. I need . . . I need . . . What did she need? Closure for her? For Anita? What? But her head was spinning and she knew it had nothing to with the few sips of wine she'd had. She glanced over at *The Velveteen Rabbit* on the coffee table and her mind raced. Maybe Anita had never found closure, but Addie was here now, and that was something hopefully she could bring to the legacy of her grandmother's life.

Addie reread everything she could find about

who attended the parties at Windgate over the two years Anita was going there. She searched for any hints of who David might have had a falling-out with at any time leading up to the night of his murder. She searched for clues of what happened the night Anita told him she was pregnant and they bought the book—who they were with, who they might have spoken to after, but nothing. Just like in the Valerie case, dead end after dead end, and not one hint as to a motive for murder.

She slammed the journal closed and stared at the crime board. Tony might have faith in her puzzle-solving abilities, but without something to go on, it was an impossible task. Especially since she had no access to what evidence the police had found at the scarecrow scene.

Addie stretched out her tense shoulders and Pippi jumped up on the sofa beside her, laid her head on Addie's lap and nuzzled her hand for a pat. Then a knock at the door sent her into a frenzy. She leapt off the sofa and made a dash for the door. Addie glanced at the clock, eleven p.m. She peered out the opening in the curtains and shook her head. *Interesting time for dinner*, she scoffed, and made her way to the door.

"Hi, Addie, I hope it's not too late, but I saw the light on and took the chance."

"No, sure, come in."

Simon leaned in to give her a kiss but she turned her head.

"Did I do something wrong?"

"Wrong? No, not wrong, it's just that I had heard through the grapevine that you were going to come over tonight and cook me dinner." She sauntered into the living room and curled into her spot on the sofa.

"By the grapevine you mean Paige?" He took a seat beside her.

"Yeah, I guess she overheard you tell Laurel and so I thought . . ."

"I'm sorry if you've been waiting. Time just got away from me. We gave Mason his new bookcase and books, then he challenged me to one of his video games, and by that time Laurel had dinner ready, he begged me to stay so he could annihilate me on the battlefield after we ate." Simon chuckled and shrugged. "I guess life's just gotten really complicated lately."

"I know complicated." She took a gulp of her wine. "Yours isn't the only one that's been turned inside out and sideways recently, and I do understand about Mason. He's your son and I have no doubt that we would figure it all out with him, given the chance to do that. It's the Laurel issue I have a problem with."

"Laurel? Why would you have an issue with her? She's been grieving and I'm her only friend in town and I've been helping her through that process."

"But it's more than that, isn't it, Simon?"

"In what way?"

"I think with all the time you two have been spending together it might have reignited a spark, and you are having a hard time letting go of what you two had all those years ago, and separating it from the here and now."

"That's absurd, Addie."

"Is it?"

"I know that . . ." He reached for her hand and she pulled it away.

"No, you don't know, and that's the point."

Addie recapped what she'd discovered in Anita's journal about the baby. "So you see, yesterday my life changed dramatically and I've wanted nothing more than for you to hold me and tell me everything was going to be okay and that regardless of any of it, you still loved me and we would be okay. But now"—she glanced down to her whitening knuckles as she interlocked her fingers in her lap—"I feel like my life has been put on hold, waiting. Waiting for the annulment, waiting for Laurel's grief to lessen, waiting for you to build a relationship with your son, waiting, waiting for a sign my life can move forward again, and that's not fair to me."

"I know it's not, Addie, and I swear that when this is all over, you and I will go back to the way we were."

"Simon, since I discovered that my grandmother was really my aunt and my aunt my grandmother, I have come to the realization that nothing can ever go back to the way it was, and that includes us."

"But it doesn't change how I feel about you."

"Come on, now that you've discovered you have a son and the person who was the love of your life all those years ago is his mother, you must know things can never go back to the way they were before. Don't you see? The things we've each discovered have changed both of us down to our cores, our very belief of who we thought we were."

"I haven't changed. I still love you just as much as I always have."

"I know, and you want to believe that because it's the last shred of the old Simon you have to hang on to, but don't you see? Although Mason's been the excuse, it goes farther than that, doesn't it? I think, with you spending all this time with Laurel, something you had together all those years ago has been rekindled; but you feel guilty about it and keep denying it. But what you really need is to see it though and find out if it's as real today as it was then."

"But what about us?"

"I don't know, but to be honest, after all that's happened, I'm not sure there is an us anymore."

"Don't say that."

"Look, Simon, you have a lot to figure out and so do I. I'm not who I thought I was, my aunt wasn't who I thought she was, and my grandparents weren't really my grandparents. But most of all, you aren't the man I thought you were either."

"What do you mean? I'm still the same man you fell in love with. Addie, listen to me, I love you and want to be married to you."

"But the fact is, Simon, you are married to someone else. All this time you led me to believe that I was the first woman you'd met that you wanted to spend your life with, but I wasn't, right? And you never told me that, ever. So you see, that knowledge, combined with everything else that I've discovered about my family, has forced me to try to put my entire world back together, one piece at a time. It's only after I do that I'll know who I am really and what I want in my life." She hung her head, twisting the engagement ring around on her finger. "I've come to the conclusion that the only way we can both figure out what we need is to do that apart."

"If this is you being angry about tonight . . ."

"No." She shook her head. "It's not just about tonight, it's about all our future nights."

"Addie, I know you've been through a lot, but I think you're making a mistake."

"No, I'm not." She straightened her shoulders, removed her engagement ring and fixed her gaze on him, holding it out in the palm of her hand. "I think I should take back my house key too."

His fingers trembled as he slipped her house key off his ring. With a shaking hand he picked up her engagement ring and replaced it with the key. "Are you sure this is what you want?" he asked, his blue eyes glistening in the light of the table lamp.

"It's the way it has to be." She wrapped her fingers tightly around the key she clutched. *Breathe in through your nose and out through your mouth.* "Go, they need you," she whispered.

Addie took a deep breath as Simon nodded but turned and walked away. The crushing pain in her chest filled her lungs and she couldn't catch her breath. Then she recalled something her grandmother Hattie had said to her when Tony disappeared from her life and she was afraid she would never see him again and it broke her eighteen-year-old heart.

Loss and grief is the price we pay for love, but worth it a million times over. No matter the pain, there is always hope for a better tomorrow.

And she'd been right. If you're going to risk loving someone there is a chance that in some way you'll be hurt, but life will go on and so will you. Addie had proven that to herself when she went on without Tony, then again, when she had to learn to live without David. Surely, she could learn to live without Simon in her life too. After all, time was the healer and there was always hope for a better tomorrow.

Chapter 25

"Who's texting at this ridiculous hour?" Addie begrudgingly reached over to her bedside table. Her fingers fumbled about, searching for the phone that had the nerve to interrupt her dream. *Pfft, fleeing a burning starship in an escape pod . . . really, who has dreams like that.* Once successful, she held the device inches from her face and tried to focus her eyes on the small screen and clear her mind of the bizarre dreamscape her phone had jolted her from. *Ten a.m.?*

"Shoot!" She shook herself awake and shot straight up in bed, fixing her blurred eyes on Serena's text.

I'm dying to hear how it went with Simon last night. What did he say about your aunt not being your aunt?

Not much . . .

Suddenly her wacky dream made complete sense.

I ended it with Simon last night

. . .

. . .

Whoa, talk about life changing. Do you need me to come over?

No, surprisingly enough I feel liberated.

Are you sure? Were you sleeping, maybe you're still dreaming?

Addie edged to the side of the bed and shoved her feet into her bedroom slippers.

Nope, fully awake now and for the first time in weeks I don't feel like someone else is controlling my life.

What are you going to do now?

You mean this minute or with the rest of my life? Both I guess???

Today, I'm going to put my Agatha Christie hat on and see if I can bring some closure to Anita's story.

Okay. I guess since it's a seventy-year-old murder I don't have to worry about you getting into trouble. But I think I'd better drop by anyway just to make sure you're really okay.

I'm fine really, don't worry, it's all for the best. I've gotta go now, but I'll phone you later and tell you about it.

If you're sure, okay, xx

Addie set her phone back on the table and stared at the stream of texts. "Don't wobble now, Addie. You know it is for the best." She glanced over her shoulder at Pippi sitting patiently by the door and smiled as her dream came rushing back to her. "Our lives have turned into that spaceship, and if I hadn't done what I did last night, you know as well as I do that we would have gone down

with the ship, and I'm not ready to do that to us."
She launched herself off the bed and grabbed her
robe. Still, she couldn't help but have remorse
over the fact that last night she had closed a door
with Simon that could never be reopened again.

"Don't second-guess yourself now, girl," she berated herself, shoving those lingering thoughts
from her mind. "You know how this is going to
play out if you do, and there's no room for three
of you in any marriage that you and Simon hoped
to have. Because no matter what he thinks now, by
the way Simon and Laurel looked at each other
yesterday in the bookstore, it's clear that she's not
going away anytime soon." Addie shored herself
up and took a step toward the door.

Go where the evidence takes you. The words her father lived by all those years he was a New York City
detective played over in Addie's mind as she pulled
into a parking stall and turned off the ignition.
"Are you ready to bring some smiles to a few faces
of forgotten people?" Addie asked as she got
out of her Mini, opened the back door, clipped
Pippi's lead on her and headed into the senior
care center. She stopped at the main desk, signed
the guest book, and scanned the fireplace lounge
area.

"Miss Greyborne, how nice to see you and Pippi
again," said Mary as she came out of the small office behind the counter. "I know a few ladies who
will be thrilled to see you both."

"That's what I'm hoping. I know Janine especially enjoyed her visit with my little friend here,

and since we were passing by, I thought, why not? Because Pippi enjoyed herself too." Addie didn't dare tell Mary that Pippi was being used as a Trojan horse so she could have an excuse to talk to Lucinda again about the night David Winthrop was killed. "Are Lucinda and Janine around? Since it's nearly lunchtime, I'd hoped they be in the lounge over there, waiting to go into the dining room."

Mary's eyes darkened. "Sadly, Janine took a fall last night and she's in the hospital."

"I am sorry to hear that. I hope she'll be okay."

"We do too, and I'll let her know you and Pippi dropped by, but I know Lucinda and Bea would love to see your little friend. Maybe even a few of our other residents too. They're up in the library and your timing couldn't be more perfect because the book club meeting should be over soon. I can show you the way, if you like?" Mary came around the end of the desk and stopped. "There's Lucinda now, coming out of the elevator. Poor dear, she looks so lost without Janine."

"Let's see if we can brighten her day a little," Addie said with a wave, and tugged Pippi's leash for her to follow.

Pippi gave out a yip as soon as she saw Lucinda heading toward them and the woman's face lit up like Christmas morning.

"Hello, little one." Lucinda gripped her walker with one hand and leaned over, extending her other for Pippi to sniff. "Aren't you a sight for these old eyes today? That's it!" She laughed when Pippi rolled on her back for a tummy rub. "There you go. How's that? Now let this old lady sit down

and we can have a proper visit." She glanced at
Addie. "I don't usually use this contraption." She
gestured to the walker. "But after Janine took a
tumble last night leaving the dining room"—she
gripped the handles so tightly her knuckles
whitened—"I just don't want to end up like her.
They say she's going to need a hip replacement."
Tears filled her faded brown eyes. "The poor
dear." She shook her head and pushed her walker
to the closest seat in the lounge.

Addie sensed the news about her friend had a
serious effect on the woman's state of mind today,
as she slowly made her way over to the love seat
and gingerly maneuvered her body onto it.

"There, now I can relax." She released a heavy
breath. "Now, come here, girl. Come for a scratch."
She held out her arthritic hand and looked up at
Addie. "Will she come up on my lap?"

Addie scrutinized the woman's frail stature.
"Why don't I set her here beside you and then she
can rest her head on your knee. She likes that."

"Perfect." Lucinda grinned as Addie placed
Pippi on the sofa. She wrapped her slender arm
around the little dog, pulling her close to her side.
"Now, you are exactly what this old woman needed
today. It's been . . ." Lucinda sniffled as tears re-
formed in her eyes.

Addie took a seat in the chair across the coffee
table from Pippi and her new friend, struggling to
figure out how she was going to broach the topic
she'd come here to discuss with the woman.

"Are you Anita Greyborne's daughter?" Lucinda
asked.

"Pardon me?"

"You have her eyes—you know, your mother Anita's."

"Um . . . Anita would have been my grandmother." So much for subtly leading into the topic. "My father was her son."

"Of course." She shook her gray head. "What was I thinking? Then you must be here to visit her, will she be joining us today?"

"Ah, no . . . I'm sorry to tell you that Anita passed away a few years ago, but wait. You knew Anita was pregnant?"

"I suppose I must have?" She stared down at Pippi, gently stroking the fur on her neck. "You'll have to excuse me, my dear. Sometimes I get so confused, and to think poor Janine is lying in that hospital bed. She must be at her wits' end with it all."

Take a deep breath, Addie. "Yes, it's really too bad she took that fall."

"How is Anita holding up? You know, after that horrible thing that happened to that young man she was going to marry. What was his name?"

"David. David Winthrop."

"Yes, that's him. Very sad about what happened. I don't suppose Anita took the news very well, did she?"

"No"—Addie shook her head—"she didn't. But when I was here the other day, you told me you didn't remember what happened that night. Has it come back to you now?"

"I remember that day, yes. I didn't want to talk about it in front of Janine. It would only have upset her. She's had her own tragedies in life and . . ." Lucinda cooed and cuddled Pippi.

Keep breathing, Addie. "It's just that my aunt mentions a Lucinda in her journals and I was wondering if that was you, or Lucy Timmons."

"Not me, my dear, no. That crowd was too hoity-toity for me. You want to be speaking with Lucy Price. Back then she called herself Lucinda. I think she thought it made her sound more upper class, like them, but we all knew her as good old Lucy."

"Then she was friends with Anita and David?"

"Friends, heavens no," she said with a chuckle and shook her head. "Lucy wormed her way into that crowd when her brother George got a scholarship to Harvard. That girl thought she'd made it to the top of the ladder. Then she met that David fellow and set her cap on him." She leaned over and dropped her voice. "You know, marrying a Winthrop of Boston would have set her up pretty fine for life, and that's what she set her sights on. When Anita came on the scene and David fell head over heels for her, well, I'll tell you the fireworks started for sure." She sat back, a look of smug insight on her waxen, craggy face.

"Is that what happened that night? You know, the night David was killed. Was that what started the fight in the parking lot at the fairgrounds?"

"I don't really know. It could have been, but personally"—she leaned forward again and whispered—"I think that Ralph Timmons had something to do with starting that, if you ask me. The police never did, but I knew better."

"Ralph? Why would he have started the fight?"

"Because he knew about the baby, and I'm sure he couldn't wait to tell Lucy."

Had Addie lost this woman's focus again? Addie glanced at the clock over the fireplace. It was nearly lunchtime, and Lucinda had apparently been having a stressful morning without Janine. Perhaps her blood sugar was low. But this didn't make sense, since even Bea didn't seem to know Anita had been pregnant.

"How did Ralph find out they were expecting a baby?"

"The same way I did. We heard Anita tell David that night—you know, at the fair."

"Did they tell anyone else?"

"No, since they weren't married yet, that's not news they'd share with many."

It seemed Lucinda wasn't the only one here that got confused, because Addie was having a hard time keeping up with this conversation. "I don't understand."

"You see, my friend Peggy and I were in the jewelry stall beside the bookseller, and we could hear them talking through the canvas wall. From what we could make out, Anita had just told David about the baby and they both went all gaga about some book they found."

"Do you remember what book"

"Sorry, no."

"*The Velveteen Rabbit*, maybe?"

"That was it and yes, Ralph was there too."

"He was with you at the jewelry stall?"

"No, not with us. He was there looking at the necklaces on a tray beside the canvas wall. You see, he was real sweet on Lucy—correction, *Lucinda*." She rolled her eyes. "But I tell you his ears sure perked up when he heard what Anita and David were talking about next door." She sat back and nodded knowingly. "Yes indeed, and then he suddenly shot out of there, and ran off down the boardwalk." She leaned toward Addie, lowering her voice. "Like I tried to tell the police, I had my suspicions about what led to that fight."

"And the police wouldn't listen to you?"

"They weren't interested in hearing about some lovestruck teenager. No." She shook her head. "But I think Ralph ran off to tell Lucy that not only was David marrying Anita, but they were also going to have a baby. I'm sure he was hoping she'd finally forget about David and he'd stand a chance with her, and it seems he was right because a few years later they were married."

Addie shifted in her seat. Hearing that the police hadn't taken Lucinda seriously when she told them what she thought might have led to the argument that clearly took place only a few hours before David's death, was interesting. It made her wonder what evidence had turned up at the scene for them not to follow up closely with those involved in the parking lot altercation.

Chapter 26

"Pippi, I think we need some help with this one, so we're going to make another stop," Addie said as she parked the Mini. "Come on, girl. Let's see if Marc can work some of his police magic for us." She cradled the little dog in her arms, trotted up the sandstone steps into the main entrance of the police station, and scurried across the waiting room to the desk.

"Good afternoon, Officer Powell, I'm Addie Greyborne and I was wondering if Chief Chandler was in?"

The young officer glanced up and nodded. "Hi again, yes, I remember you, can I tell him what this is in regards to?"

"Hmm, well . . ." she said, shifting Pippi in her arm.

"That's okay, Hunter," Marc's voice called out from his office. "You can send Miss Greyborne in."

"There you go," he said with a chuckle and gestured to Marc's door.

"Thank you." Addie smiled at him and scooted around the desk and through the door off to her right.

"Addie," he said, rising to his feet, "I'm surprised to see you here. I'm hoping that means you spotted something on one of the videos?"

"No, sorry. I have a favor to ask, but I take it you still haven't come up with any leads?"

He shook his head and motioned to the chair across the desk from him. "Please, take a seat."

"Thanks," she said, settling in place with Pippi beside her. "What about the second teacup? Have you checked anyone's home for a matching set they could have substituted right under everyone's noses without detection?"

Marc let out a laugh and tapped his finger on the three-inch-high file folder on the desk in front of him. "Look, there were at least a hundred people dropping in and out that day. We'd have to check all one hundred of their homes."

"So?"

"So, to keep an operation like that on the downlow so as not to spook the killer, we'd have to hit all the houses at the same time. I don't think even the Boston police department would have the manpower for that kind of operation."

"I never thought about that."

"To make it worse, the DA has given me forty-eight hours to solve it, or at least come up with a suspect, or he's going to have to rule it as self-induced."

"But—"

He waved his hand. "I know, I agree with you. Nothing we've turned up tells me Valerie was in that state of mind. And the problem is, if it is ruled a suicide, Laurel won't get any of the insurance money, and now that she has Mason—"

"Insurance money?" Addie edged to the front of her chair. "Would she inherit a lot?"

"I don't know for certain what the insurance policy would pay out, but there's also all the properties Valerie and George owned in Pen Hollow. The house, his entire office building, and a summer home on the point."

"Isn't inheritance one of the top motives for murder?"

"Are you saying Laurel killed her aunt for the money?" He shook his head. "No way, and we ruled her out from the beginning. There was too much in all the witness statements corroborating the fact that she and her aunt were very close and had a wonderful relationship. There was no reason to consider her a suspect."

"But, Marc, since you've come up with nothing else that could be a motive for someone wanting that sweet lady dead, wouldn't it be worth considering taking a closer look at Laurel now? Remember, motive always matters. With no other leads, and until you discover which motive led to the actual murder, you can't determine which of the suspects is *the* one."

"It does seem to be the closest thing to a motive we've come across yet." He flipped on his computer and clicked on a file. "I guess it couldn't hurt to take another look. Come around this side and we can look together. Two set of eyes are better than one, because I don't know what I'm looking for now that would be any different than what we've both seen until we're cross-eyed."

"Look for anything that doesn't fit and yet might complete the puzzle somewhere else in the day, since poison requires planning."

"But," said Marc, "in this case, the poison was one of convenience and something that was in nearly every handbag in the room, and even Laurel's bathroom."

"You're right, except since we figured out the cup pattern differences and at some time during the afternoon Valerie's cup must have been switched, it also tells us this was premeditated. At least as early as someone becoming aware of what pattern was going to be used for the tea service."

"Which means whatever the motive is must be about something that happened *before* the open house, like a court case that caused financial ruin."

"Yes, and the open house is where the act occurred, so if we can spot anything that points to the who, and how, then we have the killer."

Marc clicked the mouse from one image to another. "I don't see anything that could have hinted at a falling-out between Laurel and her aunt, or Valerie and anyone else, for that matter. Everyone seems to be celebrating Mason's arrival."

"Yeah, I agree," said Addie, going back around the desk to her chair and cuddling Pippi in her lap. "It doesn't even look like Laurel poured any tea the entire afternoon for Valerie. They're seated together most of the day, but I can't see where she might have had the opportunity to doctor the tea."

"You have made a few good points though, so I'm going to keep digging. There might be something in either of Laurel or Valerie's pasts that says they weren't as close as we have been presuming."

"Promise me that if you do find anything on Laurel you'll tell Simon right away, because he could be in danger. You know, if he stumbled on anything while he was with her, who knows what she'd do."

"I'm sure you'll let him know your fears, so I won't even start with the lecture about keeping this between the two of us."

"No, I've called off the wedding and I won't be seeing him anytime soon."

"I'm really surprised and sorry to hear that. Are you okay?"

"Yes, I made the right decision. We both have to figure out how all the dropping shoes these past weeks has affected us, and we need time apart to figure out what we really want. It's all for the best."

Marc sat mute behind the desk and Addie shifted uncomfortably in her seat. The silence that settled over the room was deafening and she cuddled Pippi tighter to her side. Her mind raced. Should she say something? But what would she say to him now, or was he just processing what she'd told him?

Finally, Marc broke the unbearable silence and cleared his throat. "You said when you came in that you had a favor to ask?" he said, his voice raspy as he stared down at his fingers laced together in front of him on the desk.

"Right, we got sidetracked, didn't we?"

"We did." He looked up at her.

His eyes filled with—what? Sympathy, relief, hopefulness? She couldn't tell, but there was that tell-all tic in his cheek, when he was holding his feelings back, and she knew the news she'd shared about Simon and her had struck a chord.

Addie recalled the conversation she'd overhead between Marc and Serena last year in Pen Hollow and, in case she was seeing hopefulness in his eyes that there was a chance for her and him now, she quickly averted her gaze and focused her attention on Pippi, who had started to squirm. "I came in to ask you if you'd be able to pull a few strings with the Pen Hollow Sheriff's Department and gain access to some of their archived records."

"Does this have something to do with that wedding dress mystery you were working on?"

"Yes, but the unworn dress has been solved. I'm now working on the reason why it was never worn."

"And that's because of the fiancé being murdered before the wedding, right? Or did Serena get it wrong?"

"Does she run to you with everything I tell her?"

"No," he said and chuckled softly. "She just asked what I knew about the scarecrow murder case."

"Do you know something?"

"Not as much as you do, probably."

"Then can you help me?"

"I don't know. A seventy-year-old case is going

back a long way. I'm not sure what they'd still have in their archives."

"Even if it's an unsolved case, hey? You'd think there'd be a law or something that says they can't destroy those files, ever, until it's finally solved."

"There is, but it's a small station so who knows what they've kept all these years, but I can make some inquires. What is it you're hoping to find?" He reached for a pad and pen.

Addie proceeded to tell him about the conversations she'd had with Bea Harper, and the one today with Lucinda at the senior care home. "So, what I want to know is what evidence they collected from the murder scene and what witnesses they talked to and why they discarded some of the testimony; specifically, what Lucinda told me she shared with the sheriff back then. It might mean nothing, but it seems odd to me, so I'm thinking they found something at the scene that led them to believe it was a stranger passing through and not someone local."

"Okay. Don't get your hopes up though. Like I said, it might be a big ask after all these years, but I'll do my best," said Marc, rising and coming around the desk.

"But you're right, it probably doesn't mean anything, and I guess I've gotten so wrapped up in my aunt's life but still haven't figured out the answers I need."

"Look, I'll do everything I can to help you find justice for your grandmother."

"So, Serena told you about that too?"

Marc didn't say a word.

"Don't do that thin-lipped thing. I never mentioned it today, and there's no one else who could have told you what she and I discovered in the journals."

"She means well, but sometimes I think she thinks that having a brother who is the chief of police is a little like having a brother who is a priest or something and she needs to confess everything."

"It just makes me wonder what else she's shared with you that I've said in confidence to her."

"Nothing personal, don't worry. Like she never mentioned that you'd called off your engagement to Simon, or doesn't she know?"

"She knows."

"There you go. Your personal stuff is safe with her."

"Yeah," said Addie, nestling Pippi into her arm and rising. "But she hasn't heard the end of this . . ."

"Go easy on her. She means well, and remember, you're the closest thing she has to a sister."

"Then if there's screaming and hair pulling, we'll put it down to sibling rivalry in the police report."

Marc let out a deep laugh as they headed toward the door. "By the way, I want to thank you for giving my cousin Nikki a job at the bookstore."

"You can thank Paige for that, it was her idea."

"I know you had a hand in it too, Serena told me," he said with a soft laugh. "But I will admit I might have overstepped."

"In what way?"

"I mentioned the apartment you have above the garage, because she's desperate to get from under my parents' roof. I can't blame her. I guess Mom's treating her like a broken baby doll and it's making it hard on Nikki to find her footing and move forward in her new life. Sorry if I spoke out of turn, and I'd completely understand if you didn't want to rent it out again."

"No, actually I've been thinking about it. Bring her by one day and she can take a look and see what she thinks."

"Perfect. Thank you, Addie, and take care, please."

He clasped her hand, holding it for a little longer than she was comfortable with, and she quickly pulled hers away. "Remember what I said about Simon, just watch out for him Marc, you never know. It makes sense that Laurel would want to latch on to him though, if there's any truth to the theory about the insurance money. You know, keep your enemies close and all that. Which she might be doing with him so she can find out what developments turn up in the murder case."

"I think you're grasping at straws there, but yes, I'll keep an eye on Simon."

"Thank you." She smiled and opened the office door.

"Are you heading home now?"

"No," she said, "I thought I'd drop by to see Doctor and Mrs. Timmons first."

"You won't say anything to them about the case, will you? As I said, everyone is still a suspect until we get a firm lead, and I don't consider Laurel to be one, but you never know."

"No, don't worry. I want to express my condolences, because I think most people have forgotten them in all this, and Valerie was Lucy's sister-in-law."

"You're right. Laurel has been getting all the sympathy, but I'm sure Lucy's feeling the loss just as much, so good for you for thinking of her."

Chapter 27

Addie didn't know why she held back telling Marc she wasn't only going to offer her condolences to the Timmonses but to also try to find out more about the night David Winthrop was murdered. Perhaps she was afraid he'd accuse of her having a hidden agenda and not being as selfless as he thought she was. Even though she did have an ulterior motive for her visit, it was to bring closure to Anita and her grandfather's heartbreaking story, and that couldn't be bad, could it?

Okay, she'd admit it. Maybe it was a teeny bit self-serving, but not in the big picture, right? At least, that's what Addie tried to convince herself of as she pulled up in front of the two-story Tudor and parked. After all, Lucy was Valerie's sister-in-law, so it really wouldn't be out of place for her to drop by and offer her condolences, would it, and if the topic of David Winthrop's murder happened to come up? Well, it couldn't be helped. She crossed her fingers, hoping that moment would arise, and grabbed the box of muffins she'd picked up at Martha's Bakery when she dropped Pippi off at the bookstore for a visit.

Guilt played on her mind as she wove her way up the winding slate footpath surrounded by flower borders. She raised her hand to lift the old brass knocker and paused. As much as she hoped to discover something that might lead to solving this seventy-year-old case, she really did feel bad for Lucy and Ralph. Ever since Pippi had come into her life, both of them had made certain Addie was prepared to be a dog mommy and helped her out in so many ways when she didn't have a clue about what she was doing. Yes, offering her condolences wasn't out of place. She rapped the door knocker and took a deep breath.

The door opened a crack and Lucy's aged, pixy-ish face appeared, then her faded blue eyes lit up with recognition. "Addie! How nice to see you," Lucy said, swinging the door wide open. "What brings you by today?"

"Hi, Mrs. Timmons. I hope I'm not disturbing you, but I wanted to drop by and offer my condolences on the loss of your sister-in-law." Addie held out the box of muffins. "I know it's not much, but I wanted you to know that I'm thinking about both you and Ralph at this horrific time, and to say thank you for all you've done for Pippi and me these past few years."

Lucy took the box from Addie's hand, her eyes dampening with the tears that formed in them. "Thank you so much, dear. You have no idea how much this means to me. Come in, please. You know Valerie was my last remaining family member, ever since my brother George passed on. I think a lot of people have forgotten that. Except you." She looked up through her tear-filled eyes and held Addie's gaze. "But, given your reputation around town as a bit of a Miss Marple, or Anita Greyborne herself," she said, giving Addie a conspiratorial wink, "I can't say that I'm surprised you would know that little bit of history when so many others don't."

Addie was completely taken aback. Had Lucy known that Anita was her grandmother all this time? Maybe Addie wasn't the only one good at putting puzzle pieces together. She nodded and gently squeezed Lucy's cold, arthritic, gnarled hand and smiled. "I am sorry for your loss."

"Thank you. You've really brightened this old woman's heart today, and please come into the parlor." Lucy waved her hand toward the room off to the right of the front foyer. "You can tell me how that little cutie Pippi is making out. You know, that's what Ralph and I miss the most now that he's retired."

"What's that?" asked Addie, taking a seat on the love seat in front of the window that Lucy had gestured to.

"All of our little patients. His practice was our whole world for so long. It really is quite lonely now that we don't see people like you and Pippi anymore."

"Then I'll make sure I bring her with me the next time I come to visit."

"That would be wonderful." Lucy clapped her hands like a giddy schoolgirl. "It would do my poor Ralph the world of good too. That man is going to drive me simply crazy now that he mopes about looking for odd jobs to do. Like just this morning, he was in the office searching for something and tore the place apart. I told him, *Ralph, if you're looking for something to do with your time, how about cleaning up your mess.* Do you know what he did then?"

Addie shook her head and glanced to the open French doors into the study, where she could see piles of books and papers strewn across a desk.

"He went out into the garden to putter and left it all." Lucy tsked, and shook her gray-haired head. "But look at me rambling on. How about I fix us a nice pot of tea to go with these muffins you brought?"

"That would be lovely, yes . . ." Addie's phone pinged out a text alert and she fished it from her handbag and was about to put her phone on silent but noticed the text was from Marc. "Excuse me a minute." She looked apologetically at Lucy.

"That's fine, dear."

Addie opened the text and read . . .

You may have been right in questioning that Laurel may have had a motive. It appears that Laurel's mother and Valerie were involved in a nasty litigation suit over their parents' property. Valerie, being the eldest, won the court case. So maybe your hunch was right about Laurel having a motive for murder, since her mother died shortly after leaving Laurel with a massive medical bill to pay. I'll do some more

digging though. But who knows, maybe Valerie helped with that in the end and all was forgiven. I'll keep you posted.

"Is everything okay, dear?" said Lucy. "You look a bit peaked."

"No, I'm fine. It was just a friend telling me something that might be important, but I'm sorry. I'll put this away while we have tea." Addie sheepishly shoved her phone in her pocket.

"That's okay." Lucy waved her frail hand. "I know how attached to those things you young people are." She chuckled.

"Lucy, my dear," called Ralph, his voice echoing down the hallway.

"Oh, that man. He thinks no matter where he is in the house that we can carry on a normal conversation. The problem is he's half deaf now." She shook her head. "I'm in the parlor, dear," she called back. "We have company! Come and say hello."

"No, I couldn't find that paper in the potting shed either. I know you told me it was in the study, but I didn't see it, so I've searched the shed but it's not there either. Maybe it's here in the kitchen?"

"See what I mean?" A flush rose in her sallow cheeks as she glanced at Addie. "It seems not only is he going deaf, but his memory's gone too, and I swear he's gone as blind as bat recently on top of it. I told him this morning I found it, *after* he apparently looked and I put it back in the desk. Come here, dear," she hollered. "Addie Greyborne is here to visit us."

"Addie Greyborne? You mean Anita's granddaughter?"

"Yes, dear, come in and say hello," she said, shaking her head and tottering over to the French doors and closing them. "Ralph, did you hear me?" she shouted. "I said I was in the parlor and we have company! Now isn't the time to worry about that paper."

Addie shifted nervously in her seat. So they did know she was Anita's granddaughter and it appeared Ralph's memory wasn't as bad as Lucy made out, but here was the opening she hoped she'd find when she came here today. "Tell me, Mrs. Timmons, did you also know my grandfather?"

Lucy's face paled as she retook her seat. "And who might that be, my dear?"

"David Winthrop. I understand you and Ralph were friends with him and my aunt back in those days."

"Friends, no. We knew them, of course, but—"

"But I read in one of Anita's journals that you used to date David, or was that a mistake on Anita's part?"

"You have her journals?" Small beads of perspiration formed on Lucy's brow. She tugged a tissue from the sleeve of her sweater and dabbed at her forehead. "Then I guess you do know I did sort of date him. You know once or twice before Ralph and I . . ." She dabbed her forehead again. "Ralph, are you going to join us?" Her voice cracked as she called out.

"That's fine, dear. I'll look in the phone desk here in the kitchen. That paper must be someplace, because you know we can't take any chances."

Lucy's face turned beet red. "I don't know what

he's on about now." She leapt to her feet and scurried toward the hallway door. "Ralph, hush," she hollered. "I said now's not the time."

A loud crash echoed through the hallway. "Ralph?" Lucy gasped, stopping short in the doorway.

"You're going to be so angry," he yelled, his voice quivering. "I've made a bit of a mess in here, I'm afraid."

"I'll be back in a minute," she said sharply over her shoulder and hurried off. "Ralph, are you okay, dear? I tell you, if you've done any damage . . ." Her voice trailed off.

Addie sat back on the love seat and shook her head. The banter between this couple who had been married for nearly sixty-nine years would be comical if, on the other hand, it also wasn't sad. By the sudden rising flush in Lucy's cheeks, it was apparent to Addie that the poor woman's blood pressure was rising right along with her frustration with her husband. A few weeks ago, she might have found their exchange endearing, as it could have been a glimpse into the future for her and Simon. However, now, all she could think about was the paper Ralph was tearing the house apart to find and the stress it was visibly causing both these two poor souls.

She racked her brain trying to figure out a way she could help without seeming intrusive, since her relationship with them had always been more of a friendly, professional one that hadn't extended outside the veterinary clinic, at least until today.

Lucy's voice rising and dropping as it echoed

down the hallway caused Addie to shift nervously
in her seat. It was clear Lucy was not impressed by
what Ralph might have broken in the kitchen, and
Ralph kept telling her they had to find the paper,
but evidently didn't understand when Lucy told
him she already had and they would deal with it
later.

As Lucy's voice grew shriller, Addie had visions
of the poor woman having a heart attack or a stroke
because of her irritation with Ralph, who obviously wasn't the same man Addie had come to
know these past few years. There had to be something she could do to help this poor couple not
stroke out on her.

Then an idea struck her. Lucy had said she
found the paper Ralph seemed obsessed with; perhaps she could find it in the drawer and then place
it strategically on the top of any other papers in
there. After that she could urge Ralph to take another look in the desk. When he easily stumbled
on it, he'd feel he'd been successful in his obses-
sive goal. Then Lucy could relax and redirect his
attention away from the paper, and they all might
be able to have a nice visit yet.

Even though Addie knew what she planned on
doing was overstepping and going where she had
no business to be, this impulsive move on her part
was the only thing she could think of to help this
dear couple. Because if they continued acting the
same way they were now, the next thing she'd be
doing was calling an ambulance for one or both of
them.

She really had no idea what she was looking for
as she quietly opened the French door and stepped

inside the study. However, if any attempt she was
about to make would help this elderly couple who
were noticeably struggling with aging, she'd have
to try. After all, they had done so much for her and
Pippi over the past few years.

Lucy had mentioned the top drawer. Addie
glanced over her shoulder and opened the drawer
on the left, but it only contained various office
supplies. She quickly closed it and opened the center drawer. There was the file folder Lucy mentioned and right underneath it—yes, just as Lucy
said—was an aged, yellowing legal document.

This was hopefully the paper that had caused
the two poor old souls to continue their squab-
bling, as was clear by the raised voices Addie could
still hear drifting from the kitchen. She hoped
that once Ralph could actually find it himself and
hold it in his hands, both his and Lucy's blood
pressure would drop.

Ralph, of course, might not comply when Addie
suggested he take another look. On the other
hand, Lucy might object to him continuing the
search while they had company, but it was the only
thing Addie could think of. If her ploy was successful, it was a whole lot better than having to call an
ambulance.

She grabbed the paper and took a quick glance
to confirm her conviction she was doing the right
thing. Then a name on the page caught her attention and she paused to take a closer look.

It was a confidentiality agreement written up in
November of 1953, a document swearing all the
below signees to complete secrecy about their par-
ticipation in the events that played out during the

hanging of one David Winthrop of Boston, Massachusetts, on a scarecrow stand in local farmer John Wilcox's field on the night of Friday, October 30, 1953, which resulted in his death.

Beads of perspiration trickled down Addie's brow as she continued to read how each of the signees would face threat to life and limb if any one of them ever spoke of this matter. She glanced at the bottom signatures: George Price, Ralph Timmons, Vince Cornby, and Lucinda née Lucy Price.

Her hands trembling, Addie dug her phone out of her front pocket, snapped a picture of the document, and placed the paper back in the drawer. Aware that the raised voices in the kitchen had become silent, she peered around the door frame of the study door; coast clear, she scooted back over to the love seat. Hands trembling, she attached the photo of the document to a text.

Marc I know who killed David Winthrop, look at this. I'm at the Timmons house now, come . . .

Lucy came around the door from the hallway and entered the parlor with a tea tray. Without finishing her text, Addie quickly pressed send anyway and shoved her phone back in her pocket, pasting on what she hoped came across as a smile to greet the woman.

"I am sorry to keep you waiting, my dear," Lucy said, setting the tray on the table in front of Addie. "I finally got Ralph sorted, and he's having his tea and muffin in the kitchen. He got so worked up by that mishap he had with the sugar bowl"—she tsked—"I tried doing what our doctor told me to do and redirect him when he gets like this. But telling him that you had been reading Anita's old journals and reminding him of the old days when we were all friends just seemed to set him off again. So, I thought it best he stay in there and calm down."

Addie was at a loss as to what to do now or what to say. This woman was responsible for Anita Greyborne's heartache for all those years. She took away David and Anita's chance at happiness and raising their son together. Instead, Anita had been forced to give up her baby, and could never hold him or love him like a mother should have been able to. She'd deprived Addie of ever knowing her real grandparents. Addie was speechless until she spied the teacup Lucy was pouring her tea into.

"That . . . that is . . . is a beautiful tea set," Addie stammered, not able to take her eyes off it.

"Why, thank you." Lucy smiled and took a seat opposite Addie in a wing-backed chair. "It's fine bone china, you know, and very expensive, if I do say so. I found it at that darling little antique store down on Marine Drive about twenty years ago, and I love it just as much today as I did then. We always bring it out for our guests, so I'm glad you appreciate its quality too."

There was no mistaking the pattern, it was so similar but yet had the slight difference to the placement of the leaves around the pink and yellow floral design. Addie had to gulp to dislodge the lump burning at the back of her throat. "Isn't . . . isn't that the same set that Laurel and Valerie used at their open house?" Addie struggled to keep her voice even.

"Heavens no. That set was a rental and a cheap

knock-off, if I do say so." Lucy shivered as she raised her cup to her lips. "Something my *dearly* departed sister-in-law would never have owned herself. She was a woman of refined taste, like me, and appreciated the best in life." She took a sip, and a smile of satisfaction crossed her face. "Yes, poor Valerie, it's all so sad that things had to turn out the way they did." She glanced toward the office door that Addie in her haste to leave had left open. "Yes, it really is too bad about Valerie, but I guess the blessing in disguise is that now she won't have to sort through all George's old files and papers . . . you know, looking for any other irregularities, like Simon's divorce papers that were never filed." She took another sip, her gaze steadfast on Addie.

Addie shifted uncomfortably as a vision of the conversation Lucy and Valerie had in the kitchen the afternoon of the tea came rushing back into Addie's mind. Of course, that was it. She glanced at the study door then to the desk. It was clear in the video by their body language, and then confirmed when the conversation was later isolated from the background noise, that Lucy had been distraught. However, it wasn't as Addie guessed: because Lucy felt bad for Valerie and all the work she had ahead of her in cleaning out George's career's worth of old files. It was that he would also have had a copy of the secrecy agreement, and Lucy was terrified Valerie would stumble across it.

"Yes . . . yes, I guess that's one way to look at it," said Addie slowly, her mind racing. She glanced at Lucy and gave her an awkward smile. This woman had clearly killed twice before. One was the man she'd professed to love; the other was her sister-in-law. Just how far was this seemingly frail woman willing to go to keep those secrets? Addie wasn't sure as she glanced down at the steaming teacup on the table, but she sure wasn't going to sit around long enough to find out. She jerked and pawed at her pocket. Lucy gave her a quizzical look.

"Oops, sorry," Addie said, feigning a light laugh. "I put my phone on vibrate and forgot, it just went off and gave me a start." She pulled it out of her pocket and glanced at the blank screen. "Shoot."

"Is everything okay, dearie?"

"Uh, no." Addie shoved her phone back in her pocket and stood up. "I'm really sorry but there's an emergency at the bookstore and they need me back now."

"That's too bad and we were having such a nice visit," said Lucy, leveling her gaze on Addie as she started to rise from her chair.

"Don't get up," said Addie, starting for the living room door. "I can let myself out."

"But don't you want to drink your tea first, dear?"

Addie glanced back at the steaming cup and then at Lucy. The glint in the woman's eyes as she waited for an answer sent prickles racing across Addie shoulders. Yes, this woman had clearly killed twice before, and something told Addie she was prepared to do it again. "I can't . . . they're waiting for me. I really have to go, but thank you again. It was a very . . . interesting visit. Thanks again. Say bye to Ralph for me." Addie darted out the front door, letting it slam shut behind her.

She sucked in a series of deep breaths to slow her racing heart and then made a dash to her car to wait until Marc's police cruiser pulled up. She knew that he really wasn't going to believe any of this about the Timmonses because she was having a hard time believing it herself. She glanced down at the image of the secrecy document on her screen, but there it was in black and white, the proof that had eluded authorities for nearly seventy years. She looked up at the clear blue sky through her front windshield. "Case closed, Anita," she whispered.

Chapter 28

Addie picked up the copy of *The Velveteen Rabbit* from her nightstand and opened it to the inscription on the title page.

For my beautiful granddaughter on her first birthday . . . this book was given to me by your grandfather on the day I told him I was expecting our first, and only child. I now pass this token of his love for this story on to you.

Love, Grandmamma Anita.

Addie closed the book, swallowed hard to squelch the aching that grew in the back of her throat, and cradled the book tightly to her chest. "This was for you, both of you," she whispered. "I plan to never forget the love you shared and lost and will treasure this forever." She gently laid the book on the top of her open suitcase and zipped it closed.

"Okay, little one." She glanced over at Pippi sitting upright on the bed. Her ears perked. "I hope

I haven't forgotten anything?" Her gaze scanned the room, and once satisfied, she heaved her suitcase off the bed, extended the handle and wheeled it to the top of the stairs. When she heard a knock at the door, Pippi yelped and raced past her. "Yes, it seems our ride is here, isn't it?" She laughed as she made her way down the stairs with her luggage, and shooed Pippi back as she opened the door.

"Ready?" Marc asked, and then bent over, extending his hand in greeting to an excited Pippi. "Hey, girl. I wonder if you'd be as happy to see me if you knew what was really going on?"

"Shhh, I haven't told her yet that she's not coming," laughed Addie, maneuvering her luggage out of the door.

"Oops, sorry. But I don't think she heard me, she's too excited by all the activity this early in the day."

"You'd better hope not." Addie frowned as she turned and locked the door. "I hope I haven't forgotten anything. Tell Nikki that the list of instructions for Pippi is on the counter, all the food she'll need for the next two weeks is in the pantry, the emergency number for the vet—"

"Whoa, calm down," Marc said, chuckling as he took her suitcase. "I was at Mom's last night when you phoned Nikki and gave her an hour's worth of instructions then. I'm pretty sure you covered everything and I'm fairly sure that when we drop Pippi off at the bookstore, you'll cover it all again."

"You're right, and it's not like I'm falling off the edge of the world. I'm only going to England for two weeks, and they have phone service, right?"

Addie's eyes widened. Her voice rose to a fevered pitch. "They do have cell phone service there, don't they?"

Marc shook his head as he placed her bags in the back of his Jeep Cherokee. "Yes, Addie, you're not going into the depths of the Amazon rainforest. Rest assured they have cell phone service there."

"Okay, okay, I'll calm down now," she said, clipping Pippi's travel carrier into the back seat. "It's just that I've never left her before and she barely knows your cousin, and—"

"I promise, Serena and I will keep an eye on them. Stop worrying, go and enjoy your visit with Kalea, and all those antique bookstores you and your old friend Tony plan on scoping out," he said with a laugh as he got in the driver's side and clipped his seat belt. "Now take a deep breath, it's going to all be fine here."

She hopped in and nodded. "You're right. It will be." She glanced over at him and really saw him for the first time that morning and thought how good it was to see him out of his police issue and in good old jeans and a T-shirt. "And thank you for taking the time on your day off to drive me to the airport. I could have driven myself and used the Park and Fly lot though."

"And pay for your car to sit there for the two weeks? Don't be silly."

"Considering the difficult week you had with the Timmonses, you definitely earned your days off, and I just want you to know that I'm grateful you're spending one of them doing a favor for me."

"Addie, if it hadn't been for you, we would never have solved Valerie's murder case. Remember, we had no suspects or motives and without you, the case files might have gone downstairs and been locked away with the cold cases, just like David Winthrop's murder did all those years ago. The DA's office owes you a debt of gratitude, not to mention what I personally owe you with this. So, it's me who is grateful." He glanced sideways at her as he wound the Jeep down the hill toward the bookstore. "Why are you smiling?"

"I'm not smiling."

"Yes, you are." He stopped at the bottom of the hill and looked directly at her. "I can see that twitch in the corners of your mouth."

"It's just kind of ironic, isn't it?"

"What is? You mean about a ninety-year-old couple being arrested for two murders?"

"Not that, that's sad. I mean to think that what started as a joke to scare David into leaving Anita for Lucy, ended up in his death and would take seventy years to be solved, and by his granddaughter no less."

"Look, David's death might have been accidental at the time, but four people also never came forward after their drunken prank to just scare him by hoisting him up on a scarecrow stand went horribly wrong, and then kept it a secret all those years. But there was nothing accidental about Lucy poisoning Valerie. From what Lucy finally confessed it was premeditated. As soon as those unfiled annulment papers of Simon's and Laurel's showed up at the wedding, and then later when Valerie told Lucy she had to start going through all George's old files to see if anything else had been missed before she could dispose of them, Lucy knew that she couldn't let that happen. She was afraid Valerie would find the copy of George's secrecy agreement. So, my hat's off to you, Sherlock! It was exactly as you thought it was when you feigned an urgent problem at the bookstore and dashed out of there to wait for me out in front of their house, which, by the way. Proved to be a life-saving move on your part because when we tested the tea she was serving you, it contained—"

"Eye drops, right?"

"Right, they're cheap and easy to come by and hard to trace."

"A poison of convenience."

"Yup. It seems when you mentioned that you had been reading Anita's journals, which Lucy never knew Anita kept, she panicked. She had no idea how much Anita might have known or had heard from others over the years about what happened the night David was killed, and then might have written about it in her diaries. Then when you asked her if she knew David, and had figured out that he was your grandfather, she was afraid you had figured out the rest of it too, or was close to it. So, she prefilled your cup with a little something extra before she poured in the tea." He looked over at her and grinned. "It seems she was well aware of your reputation for solving a murder or two in the past but didn't want you to solve these ones."

"A murder or *two*?" She glanced sideways at him and let out a soft chuckle. "But, wow, who'd have thought that sweet old lady was really a serial killer in disguise."

"What I find ironic is that after all the times I've

told you to stay out of my investigations, the one time that you do, and focus on your own little wedding dress mystery, then quite by accident, it ends up solving two murders."

"Yeah. It's funny how things work out sometimes, isn't it?"

"All I know is, if it wasn't for you spotting those slight differences in the china patterns in the videos, and encroaching on the Timmonses for tea that day, I'd still be racking my brain to figure out at least one of the two murders."

"Three, if she'd been successful in killing me, too."

"You're right, and by her using the same poison on you, it would have helped me solve at least Valerie's murder." He shot her a teasing side glance.

"I for one am thankful that it didn't take my demise to solve Valerie's case."

"I'll second that," he said, and smiled as he pulled over to the curb in front of Beyond the Page.

"What I don't understand," Addie said, "is why would they write a secrecy agreement in the first place? I mean to confess like that in writing. Why would they risk leaving a paper trail?"

"I asked Lucy and Ralph the same question."

"What did they say?"

"Lucy said it was because they were all heading down a professional career path. George law, Ralph veterinary medicine, and Vince Cornby was on the road to a career in politics, thanks to his father. He was a state senator. She said it was written as insurance so that even if one of them ever messed up and said something about that night, even by accident, then that person couldn't point the finger at the rest of them and try to leave themselves blameless."

"So they'd all go down, not just one of them."

"Yes, and here we are seventy years later and the two of them that are still alive are all being charged with murder."

"If they'd only known then that all these years later that contract would be their downfall." Addie shook her head and glanced over at the bookstore. "Okay, I'll get this over with and we can be on our way."

"Do you want me to come in with you?"

"No, I won't be long. I'll just give Nikki last-minute instructions—"

"Addie!"

"Okay. I'll just drop Pippi off, say my goodbyes, and be back in a flash."

"That's better." He chuckled and turned off the ignition as Addie unclipped Pippi's carrier and headed into the shop.

The door opened, and she drew in a deep breath. These were exactly the same aromas of old leather and vanilla-scented pages of antique books that she hoped to fill her memory banks with when she explored all those quaint little bookstores in Hay-on-Wye—that adorable book town on the Welsh-English border she'd always wanted to visit. A place Tony promised to take her while she was there on her holiday.

"There's my girl," chirped Paige from behind the counter, meeting Addie at the door and reaching for a squirming Pippi. "How's my baby," she cooed as Pippi greeted her with doggie licks and kisses on the cheek.

Addie placed the car carrier behind the counter and scanned the front of the bookstore. "Where's Nikki? I have some last-minute instructions for her."

"She's just in the back," Paige said, setting Pippi down on the floor.

"Addie! Hi," said Nikki, wheeling the book cart out of the back room.

Pippi yipped and sprinted off toward her, rolling on her back for a tummy rub. "And how are you today, little missy? Ready for some fun with me for the next two weeks?" Pippi licked her hand, and her tongue hung to the side of her mouth as though she were smiling. Nikki stood up and grinned at Addie. "This is going to be fun. I can't wait to get to know this little girl better. Isn't that right, girl? We're going to be such good friends, and to think after mommy comes home, you'll be able to come right next door and visit me anytime you want."

"Yeah, this is going to work out perfectly, isn't it?" said Addie. "While I'm away, you'll be able to move your stuff into the garage apartment, and then when I come back, you'll be all settled in and we'll take it from there."

"I can't tell you how much I appreciate all you've done for me; the job, the apartment, and now the chance to spend some time with Pippi. I had no idea when I fled Chicago that my life could ever be this full of good things again."

"It's our pleasure to have you as part of the team, and my pleasure to have you as a houseguest and new neighbor. Speaking of which, I've set up the yellow room for you to stay in until I get back.

You can't miss it. It's at the top of the stairs and on the left." Addie fished around in her travel tote. "And . . . before I forget, here's my travel itinerary. You know, just in case any problems arise, you can contact me. And I left a copy of all the instructions for Pippi's food and daily habits on the island counter and—"

"Addie," Paige said with a soft laugh. "I think you've been over all this a hundred times with both of us in the last week. Now don't you have a plane to catch?" She took Addie by the shoulders, turned her around and steered her toward the door. "Don't worry, you'll be back sooner than you know and, in the meantime, there's a whole village of people here looking out for Pippi."

"You'll call me if anything happens at the bookstore I should know about, won't you?"

"Of course we will," said Paige, giving Addie a gentle shove out the door. "Now, go, and have some fun. You deserve it."

"But, but . . ." Addie looked back forlornly at the closed door.

"Addie?" called Simon, walking toward her from the doorway of Martha's Bakery. "You look upset, is everything okay?"

"I didn't say goodbye to Pippi."

"What do you mean, say goodbye to her?"

"I'm going away"—she gestured to Marc's Jeep—"and I didn't get a chance to say—"

"Wait." He looked confused. "You're going away, where?"

"I'm going to England for a few weeks."

"To see Tony?"

"Yeah, we plan on getting together, and to

spend some time with my cousin, Kalea. She's still there. She's staying over for a while longer to set up the European distribution office for her dress stores."

"I'm confused. Are you running back to Tony or Marc?" He glanced over at Marc's Jeep.

"I'm not running *to* anyone. We're all just friends."

"This is kind of spur-of-the-moment, isn't it?"

"Maybe," Addie said, "but what's happened over the past weeks hasn't just changed your life. I had a life-changing experience too. Since I found out I'm not who I thought I was, I decided I needed to get away for a while and figure out this new me. Never mind, I don't need to explain this to you, do I? You've had a few life-changing surprises yourself lately. Let's just say, I need to take time to figure out everything that I've learned recently and how to move forward. It's all been a lot to take in."

"It has at that, and I want you to know that Laurel and I are grateful for all you did in helping to solve Valerie's murder case."

Laurel and I? "Right, glad it helped bring both of you some closure. And speaking of closure, how's the annulment process going?" She glanced past Simon to Laurel, standing by the bakery door. "Or, have you decided to put that on hold?"

Simon glanced over his shoulder. "I'll be there in a minute," he called to her and smiled. "Sorry," he said, looking at Addie. "It's just that Mason's over there in the truck, waiting. We're taking him to the New England Pirate Museum in Salem, but I saw you and . . . Uh, yeah, about the annulment," he said, awkwardly raking his hand through his dark hair. "What you and I hoped would be completed quickly has taken a bit of a turn. It seems since a child was the product of the marriage, it cancels the prospects of a straightforward annulment now. The only way to move forward in dissolving the marriage is to file for a divorce, which also complicates and could threaten Laurel's application to legally adopt Mason and not just foster him. So"—he shrugged—"we're still working out the details, but it's going to take time to figure out the best way to proceed."

Addie glanced over at Laurel again. "It's okay, it really is. I get it."

"Look, Addie, I've wanted to talk to you for weeks, but you shut me out and now you're flying off with Marc?"

"No. He's just driving me to the airport. But look, I have to go and it seems you have a family outing planned, so go, enjoy your day and take care, Simon."

"Maybe we can talk when you get back?"

"Sure, but go now. Laurel's waiting for you. Do what you have to and I'll go and do the same thing."

Addie took a deep breath, turned, strutted away with her head held high, and slid into the passenger seat.

"I saw you talking to Simon. Are you okay?"

She nodded and with trembling fingers fastened her seat belt.

"Are you having second thoughts now about calling off the wedding?"

Addie glanced in the side mirror at Simon still standing at the curbside. The vacant look in his usually sparkling blue eyes was like a hand clenching at her heart. She drew in an unsteady breath, and then over his shoulder, she spotted Laurel, who had now been joined by Mason, as they both waited for Simon by the bakery door. She pulled herself upright and stared out the window straight ahead. "No . . . no second thoughts."

"Then next stop, the airport," Marc said, pulling out into traffic.

"Yes, to the airport," she murmured without taking another glance back.

As Marc's Jeep Cherokee hummed along toward the interstate to Boston, Addie rested her head against the cool side window, and closed her eyes. A hollow sensation in her chest took hold, and her eyes fluttered open. She glanced in the side mirror at Greyborne Harbor gradually disappearing from sight behind her and the void inside her grew, as had the distance between the girl she used to be and the woman she was now.

Addie struggled to remember a time in her life before her whole universe shifted sideways and turned upside down, ultimately sending her to live in the little seaside town she called home. In this moment, she yearned for those times in her life before her world started spinning out of control. A time before her David was murdered, before her father was killed, before Marc and Simon, and before the discovery of her true relationship to Anita and a grandfather she'd never know except through Anita's journals. Then in a flash of random images bursting like lightning bolts in her mind, she recalled that simpler, carefree life.

She smiled to herself and snuggled with satisfaction back into her seat. Comforted by the thought that the first thing she was going to do when she went to visit Tony was to make them peanut butter and banana sandwiches. Then, just like the good old days, they'd eat them out on the lawn and talk about their dreams for the future . . . her future, what would it hold?

As Greyborne Harbor disappeared behind her on the horizon, she knew that this trip to England was exactly what she needed right now. With the prospects of what might lie ahead of her, butterflies exploded in her chest, replacing the empty void. Because as her grandmother Hattie used to say to her, *There is always hope for a better tomorrow,* and her better tomorrow was going to start right now.